Wicked
SCANDAL
USA TODAY BESTSELLING AUTHOR
RACHEL LEIGH

Cover designs by Lori Jackson

Photographer: Miguel Anxo

Model: Sergio Carvajal

Editing: Fairest Reviews Editing Service

Proofreading: Rumi Khan

www.rachelleighauthor.com

For those who know the fruit is forbidden, but eat it anyway. Enjoy.

"The heart wants what it wants, or else it does not care."
-Emily Dickinson

PLEASE READ

I'm so excited for you to read Wicked Scandal. Wilder and Catherine's love story is emotional, heavy, and full of romance. On their quest to find their HEA, they face many obstacles. With that said, if you have any trigger warnings, you should know that this story has dark elements, such as physical abuse, domestic violence, and murder. Your mental health matters, so please be mindful while reading.

I hope you enjoy Wicked Scandal. I welcome you to share your spoiler-free thoughts in my Facebook Reader's Group, Rachel Leigh's Ramblers. If you share on social media at all, a tag would be appreciated so I can thank you!

xo Rachel

PLAYLIST
CLICK HERE TO LISTEN
https://bit.ly/wicked-scandal-spotify

Enchanted / Taylor Swift
I Wanna Be Yours / Arctic Monkeys
Happier Than Ever / Billie Eilish
Face Down /The Red Jumpsuit Apparatus
Look After You / The Fray
Beautiful Things / Benson Boone
Don't Blame Me / Taylor Swift
Yellow /Coldplay
Hanging By A Moment / Lifehouse
Dare You To Move / Switchfoot
Drops of Jupiter / Train
Trouble / Coldplay
Tonight / Seether
Hide / Creed
Fix You /Coldplay
You and Me / Lifehouse
Can't Let You Go / Matchbox 20

CHECK OUT THE: PINTEREST BOARD
https://pin.it/4fQx3yVPq

PROLOGUE

Breaking News: Willow Creek's Mayor Jenkins Dead at Age 39.

Troy Jenkins, mayor of Willow Creek, was found deceased late last night from an apparent gunshot wound. Police crews were called to his home on Merry Lane at 10:13 p.m. after an anonymous call tipped off law enforcement. Investigators are working to determine if foul play is a factor in the mayor's death.

This news comes as a shock, not only to the residents he served, but also to those who worked closely with him.

"Willow Creek will not be the same without him," says life-long resident, Bob Denver.

Mayor Jenkins's former assistant, Beth Hill, also expressed her disbelief. "I have no words. It's such a shock," she told reporters. "Mayor Jenkins was such a generous and kind man. He'll be deeply missed."

Jenkins is one of two mayoral candidates in the 2024 election, set to be held November 8th. His opponent, Grant Cromwell, was not available for comment at this time; however, his campaign manager, Jillian Hancock, has informed reporters that he is prepared to step in as mayor of this beloved town.

Details to follow as they become available.

Catherine
Seven Months Earlier
October 19, 2023

My head snaps to the side, pain cutting across my face as my husband lashes out at me. He is usually more careful, more in control. He hardly ever hits me on the face, but apparently tonight I really pissed him off.

I already know what started this one. I was late. I got caught up with a student, helping him finish an essay he's been working on. Even though Troy said he'd be working late tonight, I should have paid closer attention to the time. Nonetheless, he showed up in my classroom and pulled me away like a disobedient child. I'm not sure how I'll ever face Wilder, my student, again. It was humiliating.

I take full responsibility, though. I should have known better. I'm just glad he waited until we got home to do anything about it. Had he hurt me at the school, I would never have been able to hide it. And I have become a professional at hiding.

Some days I don't know what makes Troy rage. Was dinner too cold? Was the house not clean enough? It's hard to put a finger on what sets him off. Though, I've learned the dos and don'ts with him over the years.

It's not always like this. With the election year coming up, Troy is stressed. I'm not making excuses for his behavior, but the upcoming months before his campaign can be taxing for him.

This will mark our third election year together, and I know there is a light at the end of this very dark tunnel. I just hope I make it out alive because each term he gets worse. He never used to put his hands on me. It was always just a lot of yelling, but one day I yelled back and he snapped. For a while, though, I believed I deserved it.

But eight years and two terms later, I have realized that Troy's anger has nothing to do with me and everything to do with him.

Troy's hand shoots up in a fit of anger, his features twisted with rage. I instinctively flinch and lower my head, shrinking away from the blow of his open palm.

"You're worthless, Catherine!" His blistering voice echoes off the walls of our bedroom just before he sends a sharp smack to the back of my head. "I don't even know why I keep you around anymore."

My ears ring and I stumble backward until my back collides with the closet door. I reach behind me, searching for the handle as hot tears of anger stream down my face. Sadness, terror, and agony no longer consume me. I haven't felt those things in years.

Now, I only burn with an inexplicable fury. I've contained the rage that has been building inside me as I do what is demanded of me day in, day out. But I fear I'll explode at any given moment and do something I'll immediately regret. Or maybe I won't regret it at all.

Pulling the door open, I step forward, jaw clenched as I glower back at him.

"Oh," he laughs menacingly. "Are you going to hide now?" The cocksure grin on his face unnerves me.

Lips pressed tightly, I exhale through my flared nostrils. "I don't hide. I simply walk away."

"You hide. And the reason you hide is because you're a coward. A worthless fucking coward." He shakes his head disappointedly. "Come on, Catherine. Fight back. Hit me. Tell me I'm wrong."

Temptation claws at my insides. I'd love more than anything to punch him square in the face.

Troy steps into my space, his hot breath fanning my face as he laughs again. "You're too much of a chicken shit, aren't you? You thought you could stay back and help your little student, all the while letting me suffer at home alone. I should have put him in his place when I came to retrieve you. You are *mine*, Catherine."

My hand shoots forward, fingers splayed wide as my palm connects with his cheek. I couldn't help it. The thought of him hurting Wilder, or any of my students, makes the fury in my veins boil over.

Troy takes a step back, a hand going to his face where my palm left a red mark. I can't allow him to think about it, though. If he realizes I reacted out of fear for someone else and not myself, he will have another thing to threaten me with, and soon, he would no longer be just my problem. I can't let that happen.

My hands fly to my cheeks. "I'm sorry. I'm so sorry, Troy." I reach for him, hoping to defuse the situation before it escalates. I watch his face, searching desperately for his temperament. He rolls his neck, teeth grinding. "Troy," I whisper. "I didn't mean to…" I rub his arm, but he jerks it away.

Without warning, he yanks a handful of my hair and slams me against the wall. My skull jars with the impact, and I taste blood in my mouth as my cheek connects with the hard surface.

I cry out, barely recognizing the sound because it wasn't intentional. I fight so hard not to show Troy the fear he's instilled in me because it gives him power. I'm not usually one to take his beatings lying down, but lately, he's gotten worse, and I feel the need to cower just to protect myself.

It's too much—the pain, the heartbreak, the unknown.

I can't do this anymore.

"I can't do this anymore," I say the words in my head, not even realizing I've said them out loud until Troy lets go of me, his face contorted in confusion.

"If that's really how you feel, Catherine, then let me know when you're ready to leave and your dirty little secret will be front-page news."

Drawing my fingers around my lips, I glance down at them, noticing the blood dripping into my palm. It doesn't even faze me. Bloodshed has become a common occurrence in this house.

I rub my fingertips together, spreading the sticky, warm

blood between them. "You're bluffing," I hiss, unable to even look at the bastard I call my husband.

"Try me." He laughs menacingly. "You'll be a goner before you even get to the state border." I catch a glimpse of him turning around, walking toward the bedroom door, my heart racing in anticipation of him leaving. But he pauses with his hand hovering over the doorknob, and I gulp. "We both know you're not going anywhere, Catherine. Now go clean up the mess you made in the kitchen, and while you're at it, throw away the chili you made. It tastes like shit."

I prepared chili this morning in the slow cooker, knowing I wouldn't have enough time since I was helping Wilder. I even made sure the kitchen was spotless. I washed the dishes, wiped down the counters, took out the trash, and even swept the floor three times. All that so this asshole could have a meal when he got home from work. Heaven forbid he makes himself something to eat.

If anyone's worthless, it's him. As the current mayor of Willow Creek, Troy is worshiped by many, but I know the real man behind the mask.

He's cold and calculated. A narcissist in the worst form. He steals from the poor and keeps the rich richer. He preys on the weak and bargains for your soul. At least, that's what he did to me. I can only hope one day I'm strong enough to bring this son of a bitch down. Only then will I truly be free from the cage he's put me in.

As soon as his footsteps fade down the hallway, I tiptoe toward the door. Making sure to avoid the squeaky floorboards, I peek out into the empty hallway. With a sigh of relief, I gently lift up on the door handle to keep the hinges from making any noise as I close it.

After grabbing my cell phone off my dresser, I make my way back to my large walk-in closet and go inside. With the door closed, I drag the chain link lock I put on it a couple weeks ago, just in case I ever needed to bide my time to call the police. Not that I'm sure I would. Troy has made it clear what will happen if I ever try to leave him—my life will be over.

He isn't joking when he says I'll be arrested before I could leave him. Troy saved me from my darkest secret.

Some days, it sounds like a blessing. Other days, I know it's a curse.

When Troy was first elected as mayor of the town, he gained the respect of everyone here. Within a matter of months, I watched the man I thought I loved transform into a beast I didn't recognize.

Now here I am—crawling on my knees to the back wall in my closet to the only space I feel safe in my own home. I move behind a long row of evening gowns, settling in on the stack of blankets I've put down. Picking up a bottle of water I left back here last time, I twist the top off and take a swig, swishing it around in my mouth to erase the taste of blood on my tongue.

Peeling up a loose slab of carpet against the wall, I expose the floorboard where I cut a small square, creating a hiding space for necessities. I reach inside to pull out the metal box and I flip the clasp.

Inside is a pocketknife, a handgun I purchased last year—loaded and ready—a prepaid cell phone, instant ice packs, and a first aid kit. I take out one of the ice packs and shake to activate it.

Bringing the cool surface to my cheek, I flinch on impact. My eyes close and I relish the coolness against my battered face. The last thing I need is to show up to class with another bruise. I've done a fairly good job at hiding most of them, but after what Wilder witnessed tonight, I cannot allow for rumors to spread. If anyone ever tried to piece my life together and expose my husband, I'm not sure I would survive the fallout.

I have invested heavily in the right makeup to counter the bruises under any light. Troy is usually careful with where he hurts me when an event is coming up, but he has messed up a few times and left marks where people could see.

It's the reason I invest in long gowns with long sleeves that cover most of my neck. Troy claims it's because I'm modest. I, however, want to laugh at that. I would love to leave the house in the summer in anything but a turtleneck and pants, but he likes to make that damn near impossible, and I have to continue to cover myself so that none of my students notice.

Fortunately, I see these kids nine months out of their lives then they move on and I'm just a teacher in their pasts. One who probably didn't even make a difference but certainly tried. No matter what shape I'm in, I always show up. Even if I hate that my career was chosen for me, I still try to give it my all because these kids deserve it.

I grab my phone on the floor beside me and bend my legs, bringing my knees to my chest as I open my SnapTok app. Seeing the smiles on other people's faces is a nice distraction and a reminder that there is life out there waiting for me.

There's one person in particular I enjoy watching. He's my student, but it's innocent. Nothing more than one person admiring another's work. He also doesn't know it's me because my profile is private, and I never make my own content. Even though we've chatted on the app, I've kept my responses to a minimum without giving him any inclination of who I am.

Wilder has become quite the social media star with two hundred thousand followers. His videos are usually short and comical. Just random things he does that makes other people laugh. I can always count on smiling when I see him on my phone screen.

At the start of the school year, he expressed his need for help on an essay he was writing, and I offered to give him a hand with it. That's when he told me about his passion for creating content and showed me his account. The next day, I created mine. I've been watching him ever since.

I tap his profile pic from the video and I go to his account so I can watch it again. As suspected, I'm taken away from my shitty life where I have to hide in my closet and put ice on the wounds my husband creates.

There's a sort of peace I've found in social media. One I never thought was possible. Somehow, watching these other people live makes me feel like maybe one day I can find a way to do the same.

I catch myself smiling as I scroll through the last few days' worth of videos, even though I've already watched them all a dozen times. There's something about Wilder's smile and zest for life that gives me hope. He's nothing like his twin brother, Rome, who's always raising hell at school. Wilder is different. He's different from all of my students.

He's a football star but doesn't flaunt it. The girls all watch him with adoring eyes, but his face is always in a book or on his phone creating new content. He speaks like he wants to be taken seriously and raises his hand to answer most questions in my class. Something about him is just…different.

The more we worked together on his essay, the less Wilder felt like my student. Some days I felt like I had a new friend.

Troy never lets me have friends; he says he is the only one I should be focused on. But for a brief time with Wilder, things felt different. I felt different. For a moment, I had hope that my life was turning around for the better.

Except Troy crushed that hope tonight. I can't help Wilder any longer. I fear what Troy might do to him. Even if it hurts, I have to put my walls back up and keep my distance. At least, in the real world, as Catherine Jenkins, I do.

CatEyes can be anyone she wants to be and talk to whomever she wants.

I type out a comment on his latest video, curious to see what his response is. Wilder always responds to his comments and he always says the sweetest things, even if he doesn't know who's on the other end of the words.

CatEyes: Good one! Can't wait to see what you come up with next.

For the next few minutes, I escape the life I know. I'm metaphorically out of this house, away from *him*, and in a place of happiness.

Until I'm pulled back to reality.

"Dammit." I hear Troy holler. "Get your ass out here, Catherine. I spilled my fucking drink."

Just like that, I'm back in the closet, back in this house, and still married to that monstrous man.

Crawling out of my safe space, I put my phone back on my dresser, knowing it's never safe on my person. I leave the closet —then the room—my heart thudding in my throat.

Slow, measured steps lead me down the polished wood hallway of our picture-perfect Victorian home. The walls are adorned with photos of mine and Troy's wedding, along with vibrant paintings. To the world, we're in a happy marriage, madly in love. Yet, instead of these walls echoing with laughter and happiness, all that lingers is a somber, heavy silence.

When I reach the kitchen, I see Troy rubbing his shirt down with a kitchen towel. "What the hell took you so long?" he grumbles.

Head down, I approach the puddle of sweet tea at his feet. I was never a timid woman, but I have found that if I raise my eyes to Troy's, he finds a way to make it a challenge. So, I do my best to be the obedient meek, adoring wife he needs until I can find a way to get out of here. "I'm sorry," I say in a hushed tone. "I was just cleaning up."

Troy tosses the towel in his hand to the puddle. "Good. Now you can clean this mess up, too. Had you not stacked the dishes so goddamn high, they wouldn't have fallen over and spilled my drink." There are no dishes on the counter so I have no idea what he could even be talking about. But it doesn't matter. He knows and that's it.

Gritting my teeth, I drop to my knees like a servant. Just as I grab the towel, Troy puts the sole of his shoe on my head, pushing until my face is lying in the cold puddle. My face and head hurt from the other injuries he caused tonight. The sweet taste of sugar seeps onto my tongue, my body trembling as my breaths grow tight.

"Troy, please," I beg kindly when all I really want to do is reach up and grab him by the balls and make him be the one to have to beg for mercy. "Just let me clean this up so we can go to bed."

Forcing pressure, my face grinds against the tiled floor. "You're calling in tomorrow. I need you here. I want the entire house cleaned and a nice home-cooked meal on the table when I get home from work. We're having company."

"No," I blurt out with my lips squished together like a fish. "I can't miss work, Troy. You promised you'd never interfere with my job."

Pushing a little harder, he leans down. "What can I say? Politicians lie and so do husbands. But you wouldn't lie to me, would you, Catherine?"

I swallow hard, feeling a hard lump lodged in my throat. "No," I answer him, because if I don't, I know he'll step harder on my head, and while I would be okay with dying right now, I'd prefer not to go down like this.

My heart hurts fiercely. My soul is wounded. My body battered. I'm not sure what I did to deserve a life like this, but I hope one day it all makes sense.

Tears stream down my face as a sob escapes. I can't hold out any longer. I cry for the woman inside of me who knows this isn't right but has no idea how to stop it. I cry for others Troy has abused with his power. But most of all, I cry because as much as I want to live, I also want to die.

Life has never been fair to me. My parents didn't care that I existed and kept me in boarding schools year-round so they never had to deal with me. The last time I saw them was the day I graduated and they showed up just to pay the final bill and tell me they wouldn't be paying for my college.

That led to desperation, and a willingness to do anything in order to create a life for myself. I got into college and that was where I made the biggest mistake of my life.

I will never forget the sound of those three gunshots.

Suddenly, the pressure from my face is relieved and Troy crouches down beside me. He looks concerned, worried even. "Are you crying, Catherine?"

I raise my head slightly off the floor, knowing if I make quick movements, he'll be triggered. Troy doesn't like when he doesn't have all my attention when he's giving me his.

"Honey." He places his hand on my sticky, wet cheek as I lick the sweet tea from my lips. "I'm so sorry."

Here we go. Use. Abuse. Gaslight. Now the apologies.

As if he could erase everything he did with those words. Words he doesn't mean.

I'm all too familiar with how Troy behaves. For the longest time, I fell into the trap. Troy made me believe I deserved his brutality. I was putty in his hand. He played with me—molded me. It wasn't until a couple years ago that I realized this isn't love. It never was, and it never will be.

Troy grabs my head and cradles it against his chest. His fingers stroke through my matted, damp hair. "I didn't mean it, honey. I had a hard day at work today."

"I'm sorry you had a bad day." The lie slips off my tongue like sweet honey. It's best this way. Honesty might actually kill me.

"I know you are, Catherine. And that's why I know tomorrow, you'll do as I've asked. This is important to me, therefore it should be important to you, too."

He lets go of my head and I raise it off his chest, feeling so disgusted with myself for even sitting here on this floor with sweet tea stained on my skin and his slimy hands holding me. "Okay." I nod slowly. "I'll get a substitute tomorrow."

A smile spreads across his wicked face. "I'm the luckiest man alive, Catherine. I don't know what I'd do without you. I didn't mean what I said earlier." His fingers stroke my cheek tenderly.

"I'll always protect your secret because I love you. And I know how grateful you are that I saved you from a life of misery all those years ago."

He looks at me, awaiting praise for his good deed. "I am." I gulp. "So grateful. Thank you for…thank you for saving me."

"That's my good wife." He pats my head like I'm a fucking lap dog. "Why don't you mop these floors and meet me in the shower. I could use a nice release after the stress you bestowed on me tonight."

Of course it's my fault. It always is. And now I have no choice but to go pretend to enjoy having sex with this bastard.

Troy kisses the top of my head as he stands. Once he's on his feet, he pulls open the drawer above my head and tosses another towel at me. "Don't take too long. You know I don't enjoy waiting."

The second he's gone, I curse under my breath. "One day you will pay, Troy Jenkins. If it's the last thing I do, *you will pay.*"

CHAPTER 1

WILDER

May 8, 2024
Present Day

"It's with extreme pleasure and elation that I announce my candidacy as mayor of Willow Creek." Dad takes a step back from the podium, basking in the excitement coming from the residents gathered beneath the stage. I watch from the side with my family as he begins to read the speech I helped him write.

When he announces the big changes he wants to make, I clap my hands, along with my siblings, though my thoughts are anywhere but here.

"Not only do I have the support of my loving wife, but also the support of my sons, Wilder, Rome, Callan, and Sayer. As well as my stepdaughters, Elodie, Brogan, and Lake. With them, and all of you by my side, we can do this." His voice booms as he shouts, bringing the crowd to life. "Let's make Willow Creek the best damn town around."

The cluster of residents burst into a frenzy of cheers and chants. Celia, my stepmom, pats my dad on the back. Her support and love for my dad's endeavor doesn't go unnoticed.

With my hand in my pocket, I pull my phone out slightly

with my SnapTok account on display. I look at the comments of a video I posted this morning, a grin tugging at my mouth. It was a silly video—just me mouthing the words to a viral sound about living with your parents. The comments are unreal, though. Two hundred of them so far. But one in particular stands out to me.

Lifting my eyes to my dad as he continues speaking, I nod subtly as if I'm agreeing with everything he says, when in reality, I'm not even paying attention.

The hot spring sun is beating down on me while sweat dribbles down my back beneath my long-sleeved white button-up shirt. We've been standing here for twenty minutes, doing absolutely nothing while my dad talks. I know I shouldn't be reading my comments right now, but this speech is boring as fuck. Not to mention, I have read and heard it at least fifty times by now.

Staring at the three dotted hearts in the comment of the girl whose profile caught my eye, I find myself smiling.

I don't know who she is, other than her profile name is CatEyes. After chatting with her a bit, I found out she lives in Willow Creek, and she doesn't make her own content. Her profile picture is an image of a black dragonfly tattoo with the words "still I rise." I'm not sure if it's hers, or if it's just a picture, but it's catchy.

She's been persistent on keeping her identity a secret, so I've respected her privacy. But I've really enjoyed our conversations. She seems very mature and a bit mysterious, which I dig.

Rome, my twin my brother, nudges me. "Put your phone away," he grits out, as if he has any sort of authority over me.

I sigh, the sound barely audible as I give my phone one last look. Just as I tap the like button on her comment, Rome nudges me again, this time harder, and somehow the volume on my phone goes all the way up, playing the sound on the video.

"It's cool but you have to keep it down. My roommates are still sleeping." It's not my voice, but it's the sound I used on my video that's playing out loud. "You mean your parents?"

I fumble with my phone in my pocket, pushing my hand hard against it, trying to silence the sound, but it's not working.

Dad pins me with a scathing glare and I gulp as I pull my phone out, holding my finger on the volume button until the sound disappears completely. "Sorry," I mouth the word as my cheeks fill with heat.

"Should have listened to me," Rome whispers with a low chuckle.

My chin drops to my chest and I shake my head, unable to look at anyone now. I can't believe this shit just happened.

Even if my dad is holding it together right now, there's no doubt I'm gonna get hell for this one. He's made it very clear how important this is to him and he wants it to be equally as important to us.

Dad places his hands on either side of the podium and leans forward to continue. "As a lifelong resident of Willow Creek, this town is my home. I plan to use the skills I've garnered, as well as the relationships I've built, to achieve prosperity for every single one of us."

The applause resumes and when I steal a glance at my dad, I notice his eyes are sparkling with pride. The crinkles around his mouth deepen as a broad smile stretches across his face. I really need to take this more seriously for him—we all do.

With this new venture for my dad comes great responsibility for our family. I get it. I'm not a complete idiot. I just hope this fuckup didn't change my dad's mind about me jumping right into my position at his company as his financial writer this fall.

College was never part of my plan. I've never been ashamed or embarrassed to admit that and my dad has never pushed me in that direction. My patience is lacking and I really want to jump right into the workforce after I graduate. After my mom passed away a couple years ago, I didn't think I'd ever see my dad this happy again.

Yet, here he is. Basking in bliss from the electric energy of almost all of Willow Creek with his family surrounding him. He deserves this, and I hope like hell he buries the current mayor, Troy Jenkins, in this election.

"A word, Wilder." Dad's voice is stern as he curls his fingers from the bottom step in the basement back at the house. He turns around, giving me his back as he walks upstairs, knowing I'll follow him.

Rome chuckles, his eyes locked on the video he's playing on the television in front of the couch. He leans forward, tapping his fingers on the controller with his elbows on his knees.

"None of this is funny," I assure him. "This mayor shit means a lot to Dad. Had you not…"

"Whoa, whoa, whoa. Don't turn the blame on me. I tried to warn you, but you just had to keep on checking that stupid app." It's just like my brother to claim no responsibility for the chaos he causes while also discounting the thing I care about. He has this ability to float through life as if he rules the world around him, making me feel about two inches tall next to him.

"It's not stupid. It's a lifestyle, and now a job. It's my escape from college." I have tried to get him to understand, I've tried to explain it to everyone in my family. But no one gets it. No one understands how much social media is an escape for me, just as much as it can be for my followers. It makes life feel less over-whelming. Almost like I actually have control even when I know I don't.

Rome shrugs on the couch, spreading his arms as if he couldn't give a fuck. "Thought working for Dad was your escape from college? Not that you need it. Your grades are better than mine and I'm going to UCLA."

"Football got you into UCLA." Rome side-eyes me with a snarl. "I'm not saying you're not smart. You've got the brains, but football paved the path for your future. As for me, working for Dad is my plan to keep *him* satisfied. My real passion is creating content. I don't need college for that."

"Wilder!" Dad's voice booms down the stairs. "Now!"

With a heavy sigh, I walk shamefully upstairs, prepared to take whatever he gives me. Fortunately, Dad doesn't yell at us often, so I don't think I'll be on the receiving end of rage and threats. He does, however, have a tendency to make us think really long and hard about our behavior and how it will affect us in the future. Especially when we've fucked up.

I find him in the kitchen, swirling a small crystal glass of scotch on ice. As soon as he sees me, he sets it down on the granite center island in the kitchen, eyebrows raised.

"Look, Dad," I begin, hoping to explain myself before he reminds me of what I've done. "I know what I did was stupid. I just—"

"Just what, Wilder? Decided my candidacy speech was a good time to make one of those little videos of yours?" His voice is calm, but his expression is loud as fuck.

"I wasn't making a video," I say quietly, feeling like I made more than just one stupid mistake. "I was watching one."

"Oh," he pipes up, grabbing his glass. He brings it to his mouth, smiling coyly over the rim. "You were just watching a video in front of hundreds of people while I spoke to them. Everything's fine then. Carry on with your day, son." The sarcasm in his tone is apparent and it literally makes me feel two feet tall.

Shrugging my shoulders, I bow my head shamefully. "I messed up." I pinch the bridge of my nose and take a deep breath. "I'm sorry, Dad."

There's a stillness in the room that's unnerving. A drawn-out silence that has me desperate to get out of here. Just when I think my dad might excuse me and we can move on from what happened, he gestures toward the barstool. "Have a seat, Wilder."

I should've known he'd use this situation as a teaching moment. *Everything* is a teaching moment with my dad.

I sit down and instead of him joining me on one of the stools, he leans into the center island, elbows pressed to the countertop as he grips his drink, the ice clanking against the crystal as he swirls it.

"I can't stress how important it is to me that all of us put our best foot forward. Not just right now, but always. It is my job to raise respectful children, and most days, I feel I have succeeded, but it's moments like this that I am reminded that I am still your father and there is still work to be done." He takes a sip of his scotch before dragging his tongue across his bottom lip.

"I know this isn't going to be easy for any of us, and I take full responsibility for that. It's a rare situation to be under public scrutiny. Nonetheless, here we are." He points the glass at me. "You've always been a model of exemplary behavior for your siblings and others around you. Please continue to do so, son. I know this dream of mine is altering your life and I don't want to ask too much of you. But, what I do ask is that you at least hold yourself to a high standard."

I nod in agreement. He's right. I know I messed up today and I know I can do better. "Yeah, Dad. I get it. I know how important this is to you."

"I'm grateful I have your support." His eyebrows rise. "But what happened at the campaign announcement won't happen again. I expect you to have self-control. I know you love making those videos…"

Here we go. Dad doesn't get it. He doesn't give me too much shit. But he *just* doesn't get it.

"…maybe one day you will realize there are just more important things in life than SnapTok."

This time when I nod in response, it's not in agreement, but more to be able to get the fuck out of here. It's pointless to try defending my passion for creating content to him. SnapTok is more than just something I do in my free time. I enjoy doing it. I get to make people laugh—brighten their day while giving them an escape from their lives for a little bit. It's also a means of money now. I'm not making much, but it's more than most people my age.

Dad drinks down the rest of the liquid in his glass, leaving nothing but an inch of ice as he sets it down on the countertop. "You've got two more weeks left of school then graduation, and only two months before you'll be taking the helm in your new position at CB."

CB is the abbreviation for Cromwell Banks. My dad owns many of them across the United States, with the head office in Westerlund Falls, which is only twenty minutes from Willow Creek.

"I know this, Dad. And I'll be ready. I'm taking a couple fast-tracked courses in business and digital marketing in preparation for starting my job at CB this fall. I'm also applying for a part-time job until then." He smiles over the rim of his glass. It's these moments where he is proud of me that I feel like I can connect with him. Like a sponge that's been in the desert, I want to soak up his pride.

I'm pretty damn excited to start my new job as the company's financial writer. Not only will I be writing marketing commentary for newspapers, I'll also be handling all the social media marketing and content creation.

It's funny to me how my father discounts my "little videos" when he has an entire branch of his office that basically does what I do for marketing. He just can't see it that way, though.

I won't be starting until September when the current financial writer retires, but I'm not complaining. It gives me a couple months to enjoy my life as a graduate before diving right into a career. However, Dad made it clear that too much time off depletes motivation, so he and Celia insisted that Rome, Elodie, and I get summer jobs to remain active and focused.

Dad nods in agreement, and I'm thankful he's still on board

with the plan. "Have you thought about where you'd like to work this summer?"

"Actually," I drag out the word, my hand going to the back of my neck. "I was sort of hoping I could do something at CB. Data entry, mail room, anything that helps me to build rapport within the company before I take on a larger role." I look up at my father with hopeful eyes.

"What if I told you I have a better job available for you and your siblings in the meantime?"

My eyes widen, showing my surprise. "Really?" I didn't think it would be that easy. My father has always been adamant that we have to work for our positions in his company; they will not be freely handed to us.

"Jillian, my new campaign manager, and I were very impressed with your final touches on my speech." His mouth tugs up in a grin while excitement ripples through me. The thought of not having to fill out another damn application for a low-paying job as a dishwasher or floor sweeper has me anxious to hear his offer. "Rome and Elodie agreed to work on mailers, and some door-to-door campaigning. As for you, how would you like to help me with my speeches, starting immediately?"

I arch my brows, surprised he'd even consider having me help with such an important task. "You want me to help with your speeches?"

As much as I want to help, I'd much rather take on a job with less pressure. Speeches are the forefront of his campaign. I have no skill set when it comes to political mumbo jumbo. I whipped up his speech for today on a whim and personally critiqued it for hours before handing it over. It was stressful and not anything I enjoyed doing.

"I believe in you, Wilder. I think this would be great for both of us. Obviously, I'll write out the details and touch on the matters I feel are important for discussion. But I'd like you to be the one who fine-tunes them. You've always had a way with words and today's speech was proof of that."

I roll my neck, working out the kinks and stress that has accumulated since this conversation started. "Wow." I gulp. "I wasn't expecting this."

Dad tosses his hands out, his enthusiasm trumping mine tenfold. "What do you say? The pay is good."

Reminding myself, again, that this is important to him and I want to show my support in any way possible, I randomly blurt out, "Sure. Why not?" Immediately regretting it because I have no doubt I'm going to disappoint him. This isn't my forte. I'm not a speech writer.

Gleefully, Dad pats my shoulder. "That's my boy. I have no doubt your words will take us to the top in the election."

I nod, forcing a smile on my face. "Yep. To the top we go." The sarcasm in my tone is apparent, but he doesn't take notice as he pours himself another shot. "I better get to bed. Finals are coming soon and I need a clear head."

Dad raises his glass in cheers, still beaming. "Always thinking ahead, son. I'm proud of you." He takes a sip before continuing. "I'll have Jillian email you some key points I'd like to touch on in the article being published Thursday in the *Willow Creek Gazette*."

"*This* Thursday?" I gasp. "That's four days away. You're giving me too much credit, Dad. I don't think—"

"Nonsense," he interrupts. "You're the one who's not giving yourself enough credit. Together, we can do this."

His faith in me has always been astounding. To the point it doesn't seem real. And it's not just me, it's all of his children. Dad cheers us on and encourages us to seek out our dreams no matter how impossible they may seem. He's not one of those parents who forces you to do what he wants to do. I know if I really didn't want to do this for him, he'd understand—no hard feelings.

The way he looked at me when he offered me this job wasn't something I could turn down. At the end of the day, he's right. This could be great for both of us.

"I guess it's settled then." I shoot a thumb over my shoulder. "I should get some sleep. Night, Dad."

He holds up his glass in cheers to me again and I smile before walking up to my room. Everything lately feels like it's happening so fast. High school will be over soon. My friends and Rome and my stepsister Elodie will head off to college, then I'll start working and eventually move out of my father's house.

As much as I'm ready for these changes, I can't help but feel like it's a lot to handle.

As I lie down on my bed, staring at the ceiling, I feel an immense amount of pressure. I fear my dad is putting far too much faith in me. I helped him one time and now he wants me to work on his speeches for the entire election. Aren't there professionals who do this shit?

The only way I can do this satisfactorily is with help.

A random thought pops in my head.

I think I know who can help me.

A few months ago, Mrs. Jenkins, our American literature teacher, helped me with an essay. Dad might not like it, considering she's married to our current mayor who he's also running against. But, I'd be doing this for him. That's assuming she'd even help me, given the circumstances.

Mrs. Jenkins is well versed in literature and grammar. She's the type of person Dad should want working on his speeches, not me.

I have so much respect for him as a father, a businessman, and as a human altogether. If I'm going to do this, I want to do it right.

There are a few other people I could ask, but Mrs. Jenkins and I work together so well and I actually learn from her. A lot of our other teachers try, but they don't have the same spark she does. When I walk into her class, I feel like she wants me to walk out a smarter person, and she gives me every tool I could need to make it happen.

That's probably why my essay got me into the business

classes I wanted to take early. They are technically classes for juniors in college. But Mrs. Jenkins helped me prove I was capable with my essay.

I find myself smiling as I think back to us working together. We had a lot of fun and laughs during that time. After a while, she didn't even feel like my teacher anymore. She became someone I just wanted to spend more time with.

It was also during that time that I formed an opinion of our current mayor, her husband.

One night Mrs. Jenkins and I were working late at the school when Mayor Jenkins showed up unexpectedly. Fuming, as if he had just caught her doing something illegal, he demanded to speak to her in the hall. I could tell he had embarrassed her as she whispered that she'd be right back. I could hear him plain as day out there. His voice was loud and authoritative as if he was speaking to a rebellious juvenile, not his wife.

He told her she needed to get home immediately and that she should know better. *Know what better?* I couldn't understand why he was so pissed, but I chalked it up to marital issues that were none of my business. Regardless, I didn't like the way he talked to her.

A minute later, Mrs. Jenkins came back into the room, rushing to put everything away. I could see the humiliation on her face as she hung her head low and avoided eye contact with me.

I tried to make things easy on her and helped clean up the coffees I brought us before packing my bag quickly. She didn't even look at me as she gathered her things and tried to apologize. I said it was no big deal and walked out, but not before looking back at the man I thought was the composed leader of our town. It was shocking to see him so out of sorts. His hair was tousled, as if he had been pulling on the strands, and his shirt was only halfway buttoned and crooked.

Something tells me he's not the man everyone thinks he is. But I didn't say anything as I watched him all but shove her into his car and slam the door so hard it rattled. I just let her go because I feared that saying anything would only make the situation worse.

I got an unsettling feeling that night. When she wasn't in class the next day, that feeling only grew. By the time school ended, my stomach felt like it was in knots, so I used our email portal to reach out and check on her. She assured me everything was fine and she just had a bit of a head cold.

The next time I saw her, she pretended as if nothing had happened. I still get this uneasy feeling today when I think about that evening, and my opinion of the current mayor has only worsened since then.

As for my opinion of her, she's too good for him. I don't even have to know him to know that. Mrs. Jenkins is class and beauty—she's timid and kind.

I turn on my side in bed and a smile stretches across my face just thinking about getting to work with her again, one-on-one. Maybe this speech writing thing won't be so bad, after all.

CHAPTER 2
CATHERINE

"If everyone could find their seats, we'll get started." I stand up from my chair behind my desk and smooth my hands down my burnt orange turtleneck dress. It's not fitting for the weather, considering it's supposed to hit seventy degrees today, but it's raining so I won't have to be outdoors.

My eyes skim the crowd of students who are now seated, all but one. "Rome." I clear my throat, eyebrows raised as he continues to chat among his classmates. "That means you, too."

Rome scoffs before kissing his girlfriend, who is also his step-sister, on top of the head. It's a weird situation but also none of my business. To each their own.

Rome drops down beside Wilder, stretching back in his seat with his hands folded behind his head. "Happy?"

Shaking my head at him, I make my disappointment in his sarcastic attitude known, but I also don't make a fuss about it. I'm really not in the mood to argue with the guy who everyone defends, even when he's nothing but a bully.

I look at Rome's brother, Wilder, wondering how these two are even related, let alone twins who shared a womb. Their personalities, and even looks, are complete opposites. Rome has lighter hair and blue eyes, while Wilder has dark hair and light brown eyes. Rome is outspoken and slightly obnoxious, whereas Wilder is mature and kindhearted.

Wilder catches my gaze and a rush of heat shoots through me as if I've been caught doing something I shouldn't. In reality, I'm just thinking too much. I'm always thinking too much. My mind never stops thinking.

I blink my eyes away from him, knowing in just two more weeks the seniors will be done with this class and I'll never see ninety percent of them again.

That's not true, actually. I'll be seeing Wilder, Rome, and Elodie frequently since last night their dad made his official announcement that he's running against my husband in the mayoral election. Six months of campaign work, debates, fundraisers, advertisements, meetings. All of which Troy expects me to attend because it's my duty as his wife.

Troy has served Willow Creek for two consecutive four-year terms and he thinks he has this in the bag. I personally think he should be scared. Grant Cromwell will not go down without a fight. He's a successful businessman who's been on the city council for as long as I can remember.

Needless to say, the rest of this year is going to be brutal with the upcoming election. I've already prepared myself to be on the receiving end of my husband's wrath. Though, once it's over, and Troy wins, he'll be an entirely different person. One that, at times, I think I could love again. Until he's not that person anymore and I'm reminded why I hate him so much.

If he doesn't win, I can't imagine how he'll react. He's never *not* won. I shiver at the thought of what that nightmare might look like for me.

I push away thoughts of my misery and focus on the here and now. This is where I love to be. Teaching students about literature and exercising the imagination. It might not have been the path I would have chosen for myself had the choice been mine, but I make the best out of what I have been given. I can make a difference here. At this school, students look up to me. I am needed in a way that doesn't feel demoralizing.

As I look out over the classroom full of students, I can't help but remind myself that getting to be here and out of that damn house is a blessing.

"Continuing our discussion on symbolism." I tap on the open tab on my laptop, displaying the screen on the whiteboard. "Who can give us an example of symbolism?"

I look around the room, observing the lack of participation from what I call "my senioritis class."

Fortunately, there are a couple students here that are still eager to learn. Elodie raises her hand immediately, much like she does with any question I ask. "Yes, Elodie."

"A great example of symbolism is the heart being a symbol for love." She blushes as she looks at her boyfriend, Rome. He stretches his arm out and puts it around her shoulders as he sinks comfortably into his chair.

I wonder what that feels like—to have someone adore you like that. To catch them watching you in amazement as if you just hung the moon. That rush of excitement when you see them after being apart for any amount of time. The sound of their voice speaking to your heart while butterflies flutter through your stomach.

I long for that and it's a deep fear that I'll never have it again. When Troy saved me, I felt that. The way he tried to shield me from the world so I no longer had to fight so damn hard. It wasn't until I realized he only did it for his own selfish gain. Find the damsel and save her, but keep enough evidence that you can destroy her in case she ever wants to run away.

It's a tale as old as time. But no one tells you that the prince who rescued the princess was really another dragon in disguise. He saved me just to lock me in a different tower.

"Is that…wrong?" Elodie asks, pulling my attention back to the subject at hand.

"I'm sorry. Yes. That's a great example. Thank you, Elodie."

I click the touch pad on my laptop, going to the next page. "The example Elodie gave us is a general symbol. It's obvious and clear. But oftentimes in literature, the symbols are more subtle. Who can tell me what this form of symbolism is called and give an example from the book we just finished, *To Kill a Mockingbird?*"

My gaze wanders in search of any hand that is not Elodie's, even as she's waving it in the air, stretching toward the ceiling.

I catch a pair of eyes staring back at me as if he doesn't want to answer, but also pities me for standing here talking to myself because no one is listening except him and Elodie. Wilder lifts his hand and I point, smiling back at him. "Yes, Wilder. Thank you."

He straightens in his seat, his eyes locked on mine. "The mockingbird, of course. It's a specific symbol."

"That's right. Do you care to explain how the mockingbird represents specific symbolism?"

Wilder deepens his gaze on mine as if he's searching for the answer in my eyes. "The mockingbird is a symbol of innocence," he says. "Specifically the innocence of the characters. To kill a mockingbird is to kill innocence." When I smile, he relaxes in his chair, pleased with his response.

"Thank you, Wilder." I tap the touch pad again, moving to the next screen.

We continue our discussion and time seems to move too quickly. The next thing I know, the bell is ringing and students are packing up their things so fast I almost forget to mention the exam.

"Our test on symbolism in conjunction with our reading will be on Friday. Be sure to study, and reread if needed," I practically yell as they rush to the door.

Everyone scatters, some fleeing before I even finish. Others linger as they gather their belongings.

I'm preparing my notes for the next class when Wilder approaches my desk. I see him before he even stops, but I continue to click on my laptop so I can get things ready before students start piling in again.

"Did you need something?" I ask. I glance up at him, not wanting to feel like he towers over me the same way Troy always tries to. Except, when his dark gaze connects with mine, fear isn't what rushes through me. Instead, it's a feeling of comfort.

"Umm. Yeah, actually, I do. I need to ask a favor."

My eyebrows pinch as I try to think of what he could be about to ask. "A favor?"

His hand shoots up to scratch the back of his head, much like his brother does when he's nervous. It's the only mannerism they really mirror in each other. But Wilder is different. With Rome, it looks like he is trying to flex his muscles to distract people. With Wilder, it's as if he is just genuinely nervous. His fingers tangle in his ruffled hair and I find myself smiling. His apprehension is odd for someone so confident and smart. "So you probably heard my dad is running for mayor…"

I slam my laptop closed, the snap echoing through the room. I'm not sure why I did it, but I did. I suppose the word "mayor" just took me by surprise. Anything that involves Troy makes my guard go up instantly.

Wilder's posture stiffens at my sudden outburst. "Everything okay?" he asks, alert and wide-eyed.

Keeping my cool, I force a smile on my face. "Yes, everything's fine. And that's wonderful news about your dad."

"It is?" he asks, surprised at my response. "With your husband being the current mayor and all, I guess I just thought…"

His words trail off, but he doesn't need to finish. I know it's an unlikely situation. Wilder is my student and his father and my husband are now opponents, what I consider, a fierce competition. I say fierce because I know Troy, and he is not going to make this an easy feat for Grant Cromwell.

"It is wonderful news," I tell him again. "The position is open to all residents of Willow Creek. I think your dad is a worthy contender. Look, Wilder." I stand up, moving from behind my desk because I'm feeling restless—uncomfortable, even.

These elections always heighten my nerves and even discussing it with Wilder has me on edge. If Troy knew I was talking with anyone about it, let alone his opponent's son, I can't imagine how he'd react. He might try to take away my position here, and I can't let that happen. I need this place; it's my only escape.

A wide smile spreads across his face, his shoulders visibly loosening as he exhales. "You don't know how happy I am to hear that."

"I'm glad," I tell him. "This doesn't have to be awkward. May the best man win." I tilt my head slightly to the left, crossing my arms over my chest as my nails dig into the fabric of my sweater dress. I need to be composed right now or he will know something is wrong. He always knows. And I hate having to lie to him every time he asks if I'm okay.

"You mentioned needing a favor. Does this have anything to do with the reading material this week?"

"Actually, it doesn't have anything to do with class. You see, my dad asked me if I'd help out with his campaign. Speeches, news articles, that sort of thing. In fact, I already got an email this morning from his campaign manager, Jillian." He snaps his fingers. "You probably know Jillian, right?"

I nod. "I know who Jillian is. She worked with Troy, err, Mayor Jenkins his first year." I shake my head, not wanting to divulge any more information about Troy and his job. I draw back my shoulders, chin up. "She'll do great work for your dad."

"I'm happy to hear that. Anyways, Jillian has already sent me over some notes for an article being published *this* Thursday that my father wants me to write." He chuckles as he continues, "Me. Can you believe it? I'm not even out of high school, yet my dad wants me to handle something this big. Crazy, right?"

"That's amazing, Wilder," I tell him excitedly. "I have no doubt you'll do impressive things in this position. You've always had a knack for entertaining the public eye."

I speak the truth. What Wilder is taking on is a big task, but I know he'll do incredible work for his dad. Though, I can tell by the look on his face, he doesn't feel the same way.

He sighs heavily. "That's what my dad said, but I can't help but feel like I'm gonna screw this up for him."

I press my lips into a flat smile. I feel so conflicted. On one hand, I don't want to talk about any of this with him. On the other, it's so nice to be talking with him. "You're an intelligent young man who is eloquent with his words. Give yourself more credit."

He chuckles airily. "Also what my dad said. Anyways, I was sort of hoping maybe you could help me out with this article being printed Thursday. I don't know the first thing about politics and—"

I can feel the sweat start to bead on my forehead as he begins to ask the question I know will end up getting me killed if I agree. My heart rate speeds up and my vision gets blurry.

I can't breathe, I can't see…I… "I can't," I blurt out, moving quickly behind my desk to shuffle through papers as I try to calm my nerves. My hands are trembling as the panic attempts to consume me, but I refuse to give in. I can't fall apart in front of a student, not this one especially. "I'm sorry. You'll have to ask someone else." My voice nearly cracks, but I hold it together.

"But you were so helpful with that essay last fall and I know you'd—"

My voice rises unintentionally. "I said no!"

The air stills. Tension hangs heavy in the room to the point I have to loosen my turtleneck because I feel like I can't catch my breath.

A few seconds of silence pass and I finally look at him. He's perplexed—at a loss for words. *That makes two of us.*

I don't know what's gotten into me these last couple days,

but it seems every day something catches me off guard and I react impulsively. I've always done such a good job at holding myself together, but lately, I feel like pieces of myself are scattering.

"I'm so sorry, Wilder," I say with sympathy in my tone, trying desperately not to let him hear how afraid I am. "I didn't mean to react so harshly. It's a conflict of interest. You understand, right?"

"Yeah." He nods, lips pressed tightly. "Yeah. I get it. It was dumb of me to even ask." He gives me a low wave and a crescent-moon smile. "See ya tomorrow, Mrs. Jenkins."

I watch as he walks away, shoulders slumped in defeat. I wish like hell I could help him. I care about Wilder. I care about all my students. There's just no way I can do what he's asked. Troy would blow a gasket if he knew I was helping his opponent with his speeches.

Then again, what he doesn't know won't kill him. Not that I would care if it did.

No. I can't, and I won't. It's too risky.

CHAPTER 3
WILDER

PUSHING my feet on the floor in my bedroom, I propel my desk chair backward. My head falls back, the cool leather of the cushion feeling nice against my skin. I shouldn't have even asked Mrs. Jenkins for help. Of course it's a conflict of interest, and of course she'd say no.

The thing is, I'm not confident enough to do this on my own. I know this probably comes as a shock to people, but there are very few things I am confident in. Even posting on social media is hard for me. I tend to focus too much on how people might react instead of just releasing the content and letting them decide.

I want more than anything to prove to my dad that I can handle the tasks he throws at me—at CB and for his campaign. I don't wanna let him down, but this is hard. It's heavy shit knowing what I put in this document will be read by every voting resident of Willow Creek.

I suppose there are other teachers who could help me. I was just hoping she'd be the one. I think a lot about the time we spent working on that essay. How we got closer, became friends, even. Up until that last night when her husband showed up and acted like a fucking psycho. She was embarrassed, naturally so, and I've been just another face in her class ever since.

Moving back toward my desk, I open my search engine on my desktop and type in our school's web address.

After scrolling through the staff directory, I decide to email Mr. Chen, my old government teacher. He and I got along well and he was always good at looking at both sides of history, not just one. I liked that. It made me feel like I had to actually learn something in order to decide which side I agreed with instead of being fed bias.

I get stuck on what to put as the subject but finally decide on something I think will get his attention. If I want to be taken seriously, I need to come across as such.

To: Mr. Chen

Subject: Request to Discuss an Important Matter

Hello Mr. Chen,

I am not sure you remember me from our class last semester but I was inspired by your teaching methods and would like to discuss something with you if you have the time.

Recently my father announced he would be running for mayor. This came as a shock to me, however, not as much of a shock as when he requested my assistance with his campaign. In short, he would like me to be his speech writer as well as assist in writing news articles.

Having been inspired by you to really look into politics and form my own opinions, I thought maybe you could help me. If you're interested I would love to meet with you. I know this would take place over the summer and I would be willing to take any sort of help even if it was via email.

Thank you for your consideration.

Respectfully,

Wilder Cromwell

I ponder for a minute, rereading it a few times, all the while reviving my suspicion that my words are not eloquent.

After staring at the screen for fifteen minutes and running the email through an editing software to make sure I didn't make any dumb mistakes, I hit send and roll my chair backward.

I can't help the disappointment that sits in my gut as I stare at the unopened email from Jillian. For some reason I was dead set on Mrs. Jenkins helping me and now that the plan has changed, I feel less motivated.

Fuck it. I'll just try to attempt this shit on my own.

I move forward in my seat and open the email to read the cliff notes for the article.

Should be easy enough. Mention his background as a member of the city council, the history of Cromwell Banks, a few words from him that Jillian added, his upcoming appearance on *Channel 6 News* next week, and the election date.

I've got this.

I start with the headline: Grant Cromwell Declares Candidacy in Willow Creek's Mayoral Election.

That's good. I'm pretty proud of myself for coming up with that all on my own.

Then…I fucking freeze.

My fingers hover over the keys, but I can't seem to get out a single goddamn word.

Why is this so hard for me? It's a news article for my dad. It's not like I'm the one running for office. It's not like I have anything to lose.

Five minutes later, I've got one sentence when a response from Mr. Chen pops up at the bottom of my screen.

My eyes skim through it quickly, picking out the words "I'm sorry" and "upcoming wedding."

I completely forgot Mr. Chen is getting married this summer to the middle school art teacher. I can't fault him for shooting down my request. He's got a lot going on.

I slump in my seat in defeat as I rub a hand over my face. That's two rejections for help today and I'm getting nervous. Maybe I should just tell my dad I'm not equipped for this. I don't even think it's the work, but the fear of letting him down by submitting something that isn't up to par for this type of position. I'm not a professional and I know zilch about what a mayor even does.

Taking a break for a minute, in hopes the creative juices start flowing, I open my SnapTok account, noticing about a hundred new notifications. One in particular stands out. I tap the message and read, an instant smile gracing my face.

> CatEyes: Your last video had me rolling LOL. It might tell my age, but I used to be a huge Bon Jovi fan.

Interesting. So, she's older than me. I'm not sure why, but I'm even more intrigued now.

The video was a good one, though. Me rolling down the street on a skateboard in a 90s outfit while mouthing the words to "Always".

I shoot her a quick message back.

> WildMisfit: I'm glad I could make you smile. What else makes you smile?

Her response is immediate, which surprises me because she usually takes a few hours to read my messages.

> CatEyes: Books. I love to read. It's a nice escape.

> WildMisfit: What books do you like?

> CatEyes: Mostly historical romance, but I'll read just about anything as long as there is a happy ending. How about you? What makes you smile?

> WildMisfit: Everything. I'm a simple guy who enjoys the simple things in life.

> CatEyes: I love that. But I also call bullshit.

I laugh out loud at her message. What's funny is that she isn't wrong.

> WildMisfit: You just might be right. Can't say I'm smiling much right now. I'm starting a new project for my dad and I'm second-guessing myself. I'll probably just throw in the towel and tell him I can't do it.

> CatEyes: Don't give up so fast. You never know if you don't try. I believe in you.

Even if she is just a stranger, knowing she believes in me gives me hope.

> WildMisfit: I better get back to it. Thanks for the boost of confidence. It means a lot.

> CatEyes: Always.

Twenty minutes later, I've got a mess of a draft, but I think I have a plan.

My phone buzzes on my desk. Quickly I close my laptop and snatch my phone to read a text message from my brother.

> Rome: Heading to Big John's for pizza. Meet us there.

I don't even type a response, I just get up and grab my car keys to head out because I'm starving.

When I get to Big John's, I immediately spot my crew crowded around a large corner booth—Rome, Elodie, Aiden, Luke, and his fuck buddy Olivia.

The waitress, Sam, who's a senior at Willow Creek, walks toward them, balancing two large pizzas, one in each hand. Before she can even set them down, hands start flying toward them, grabbing slices.

As I approach, Sam spins around, bumping right into me.

When she looks up, the shock on her face quickly fades and a smile spreads. "I'm so sorry, Wilder. I didn't see you there." She runs her hand down my side, giving my bicep a gentle squeeze.

I step around her and slide into the booth. "No worries."

Recently, a rumor has made rounds that Sam has a thing for me. She's hung out with our group a few times, but she's fucked pretty much every upperclassman at Willow Creek. I try to be friendly with her, but I don't reciprocate any touches because I don't want to lead her on. The truth is, I'm not interested, but I don't want to be that guy that hurts a girl's feelings by being a jerk. Unlike my brother and his friends.

Sam lingers quietly for a second, her hands clasped in front of her, and she sways back and forth with her bottom lip tucked between her teeth. "Can I get you anything to drink?"

"Diet cola," I tell her with a pressed smile as I shift my attention to the pizza.

"Just in time," I sing as I grab a grease-filled piece, topped with only pepperoni and cheese. Folding it in half, I bite off the triangular end and turn my head slowly to see Sam still standing there.

"How's it taste?" she asks. It's sort of cringy the way she's watching me like she wants to take a bite out of me.

With a full mouth, I say, "Really damn good."

"Bet it would be better if he had his cola to wash it down with," Rome blurts out. "Just saying."

"Dude," I huff at him with a snarl while Elodie swats his shoulder.

"Be nice," Elodie scoffs. Fortunately, there's one other person at this table with a sense of decency.

I'm not into Sam, but I'm not an asshole like Rome and Luke. Neither of them has a filter and nine times out of ten, I wanna slap the fuck out of them when they speak to anyone who's not part of our group.

"Actually," Sam says, her tone proving she doesn't give a shit about Rome's jab at her, "I was sort of hoping to ask you something."

Her eyes are on me and I can feel my cheeks flush with heat because whatever she's about to ask me, I'd rather her not do right here in front of my asshole friends. No matter what her question is, Rome and Luke will find a way to make a joke out of it and I really don't wanna embarrass her.

Dropping my pizza down on an empty paper plate, I slide out of the booth and get to my feet. I brush my hands together, wiping away the flour from the crust. With a nod of my head, I gesture for Sam to follow me, away from *them*.

As I'm weaving through the tables toward the back wall, I stop walking when I spot Mrs. Jenkins. She's still wearing the same turtleneck dress she had on in class. I find it odd that she's been dressing so modest lately. It's damn near summer and she's wearing a turtleneck with long sleeves and leggings.

Seated at a high-top round table, her husband sits across from her. He's eating a sub while she pokes at a salad. There's something off with her—a sadness I've seen a few times before. Those times I chalked it up to stress, or just a typical bad day. We all have them. But this doesn't feel the same.

Her eyes are downcast as she continues to poke at her salad, yet she doesn't take a bite. Her other arm holds tightly to her stomach and it has me wondering if she's pregnant and maybe the salad is making her nauseous.

That doesn't explain the anguish in her eyes, though. She doesn't even lift her head to look at Mayor Jenkins while he sits straight with his shoulders drawn back as his eyes roam the restaurant. I bet he's searching for people to try and sway. Anyone who will listen to him talk himself up. He's such a fucking douchebag.

"Wilder," Sam says sharply.

My eyes snap to hers. "What?"

She chuckles. "Are we going to talk right here in the middle of the restaurant?"

"Sorry. I got distracted." I keep walking to the back of the restaurant, and once we're away from the crowded area, I press my back to the wall. "What's up?"

She rolls her lips together, grinning from ear to ear. "Will you…go to prom with me?"

My eyebrows shoot to my forehead. *Fuck. Fuck. Fuck.* That was blunt. Nothing like laying it right out there.

I draw my fingers around my mouth, trying to think of a quick response that won't have her running away in tears. "Prom, huh?"

"I know it's short notice with prom being in just a couple weeks, and I know you don't have a date." She puts her hand on my forearm, her tone shifting to a more tender tone. "Not because you couldn't get one, but I heard you didn't want one this year and…well, I thought maybe I could change your mind."

She's right. I don't have a date, and it's because I don't want one. I'm not into any girls at our school and it doesn't feel right to go with one just because of the pressure to have a date for these things. I'd rather go with a group of friends who I actually want to hang out with.

"Damn, Sam," I grumble. "I really wasn't expecting this. And I'm sorry, but…"

Her hand drops, disappointment painting her features. "I get it. No need to apologize." I watch as she walks away with her chin held high and a smile on her face that says she isn't fazed. I hope she truly feels that way inside. The last thing I want to do is hurt her, or any girl for that matter.

I must say, I have a lot of respect for Sam for even asking me. She's the only girl who has. I'm not sure why, but for some reason the girls at Willow Creek High have always looked at Rome and I like we're unattainable. It's comical how they behave as if being chosen by one of us is the equivalent of winning a gold medal that makes them special.

I don't get it. I'm just me. It's no secret I don't date. Like ever.

I've never had an official girlfriend. I hang out with girls just because they are in our group or I think of them as a friend. I may have fucked a few, but I've never expressed interest in anything more than a one-night and I made sure the girls were okay with that before doing anything.

High school girls lack depth and substance most of the time. Half of them flaunt themselves with their insecurities on full display, while others are dramatic and come off as easy and immature. I don't dig that and I have no interest in playing their games.

I want someone mature. Someone who challenges me to be the best version of myself. I want a girl that forces me to prove I'm worthy of her time and attention.

I sweep the restaurant, noticing everyone at my table has their heads turned, waiting to hear the gossip. *What did Sam ask him? Why is he still standing there? Did he reject her?*

I look away, my eyes landing on Mrs. Jenkins, who's now sitting alone. Her head is still down and it doesn't look like she's eaten a single bite of her salad. Both arms are now wrapped tightly around her waist. *Shit.* I hope she's okay.

Suddenly, she lifts her head, turning it slightly to meet my gaze. Her eyes glisten in the corners as if she's on the verge of tears and I'm not sure why, but my instincts tell me to go check on her.

Moving around the tables, I keep my eyes on her. She straightens her back, her shoulders tensing. "Hey, Mrs. Jenkins," I say with a subtle wave. "Everything okay?"

Her thumb sweeps under her eye and she smiles back at me, but I can tell it's fake. Something is definitely wrong.

Averting her gaze, she picks up her fork and continues to poke her salad. "Hi, Wilder. Everything is great. How are you?"

"Doing well. Just having a bite to eat before I go home and try to work on this article."

"About that," she begins, setting her fork down again. *Why the hell won't she eat?* It's so odd. "I'm sorry, again, Wilder. I really wish I could help you."

"We can talk about that later," I tell her with a tip of my head toward her food. "Is everything okay with your salad? I'm friends with the waitress, I can ask her to get you another."

There's that fake smile again. "No, no. The salad is great."

"You sure? Because it doesn't look like you've taken a single bite."

She crinkles her nose as she rubs her stomach. "I'm not feeling great today. Probably a bug of sort. Germs spread quickly in schools."

"Right," I drag the word, not buying her excuse. Ever since that day her husband burst into her classroom acting like an animal, I've had my suspicions that her life isn't as pleasant as she wants everyone to believe it is.

Now that I think about it, I've never even seen Mrs. Jenkins engage with other teachers. I haven't seen her out with friends. She's only ever with her husband. Of all her years in Willow Creek, you'd think she'd socialize more, especially given her husband's pull in this town. "Look," I continue, "I know I'm just your student, but if you ever need someone to talk to I'm available. I'm actually a pretty good listener."

She smiles. "That's really sweet, Wilder. Thank you."

The sound of a gruff throat clearing comes from behind me just before I see Mayor Jenkins round my left side. "Can we help you, young man?" he asks as he eyes his wife with a seriousness that's unsettling.

But I watch her, too. I watch her eyes downcast again, her posture slumping as if she's about to be scolded.

She speaks but doesn't lift her head. "Wilder was just asking about the assignment I gave out in class."

She's lying. Why the hell is she lying about something so miniscule to her own husband? She could have just told him I came over to make sure she was okay, or to say hi.

"Did you get what you needed?" Mayor Jenkins asks, tone forthright.

"I did," I tell him before turning my attention back to her. "Thank you, again, Mrs. Jenkins. I'll be sure to get the assignment done tonight."

She forces another damn smile and says, "See you in class tomorrow, Wilder."

I walk away, glancing frequently over my shoulder when I see her husband lean down and whisper something in her ear. She nods repeatedly, timidly even.

I don't trust that guy, and I don't like him either.

Once I'm back at the table, I get grilled by the group about Sam, along with a few jokes about Mrs. Jenkins. Since the start of her class, everyone fucks with me, thinking I have a thing for her. It got so much worse when I started spending time with her on that essay, and I won't lie, maybe I did sprout some ridiculous feelings. But our time together ended abruptly and she's kept our interactions short ever since.

My responses to the group are short with simple yes and no answers. Even as they keep going with their antics about Mrs. Jenkins and Sam.

For some reason, I just can't stop watching her. There's this agonizing feeling in the pit of my stomach that tells me she's in danger. It's crazy, though. She and Mayor Jenkins have been married for years so if there was something going on in their marriage, why would she stick around? Why not just leave the asshole?

The first time I saw Mrs. Jenkins, she caught my eye. There's something about her that has me wanting to know more. I never even knew who she was until this school year. I've seen her around, but she always moves quickly through the halls and doesn't interact much outside of her classroom. I just always assumed she was an introvert who kept her head down. Which is odd for someone so beautiful and smart.

A sudden burst of pain in my shoulder has me snapping my

eyes to Rome. "What the hell!" I seethe, rubbing the spot he just punched.

"Snap the fuck out of it." He laughs. "You're practically drooling over our teacher."

Sam returns with my drink, eyes wide as she listens in on our conversation. "You're drooling over Mrs. Jenkins?" she asks as she turns her head to steal a glance for herself.

"No!" I huff. "Sorry, Sam. My brother's just an idiot."

"I wouldn't blame ya," Sam says. "She's hot as hell. But she's out of your league." Her hand rests on my shoulder and she leans close, whispering, "I think you need to get over her and think about my offer for prom."

Nibbling on her bottom lip, she waggles her brows as she walks away.

"She's right, ya know," Rome says, opening his big mouth again. "Mrs. Jenkins is out of your league. Just fuck your feelings for her into Sam."

"Shut up," I growl, blinking my eyes around the room, landing on Mrs. Jenkins. "I'm just concerned about her."

"Concerned?" Luke chuckles. "About what? The color of her panties?"

My eyes roll as I pick up my half-eaten pizza slice, ignoring his crude remark.

I've got a mouthful when Elodie asks, "Why are you concerned about her? Is something wrong?" There's sincerity in her tone, which I appreciate because I sure as hell don't get that from Rome or Luke.

"I don't know," I tell her. "I'm sure it's nothing. She's just been extra quiet lately."

"She's always quiet," Luke butts in and I notice him staring at her now, too. In fact, everyone is. I never should have opened my mouth. Now she's gonna notice we're all watching her. "She's like this goddess full of mystery and secrets."

"I bet she's a murderer on the run or some government spy," Rome says, and I immediately shake my head at my idiot brother. "Probably rigs the election for her husband, too." He shrugs his shoulders when I glower at him. "Just saying. The quiet ones hold the darkest secrets."

I sigh heavily. "She doesn't rig the election. Her husband was the only candidate both terms he served. This is the first year he even has an opponent."

Luke sets his empty glass down, eyebrows raised. "So you agree she's probably just a murderer then?"

"I gotta get out of here." I swing my legs out of the booth and get up. "You all are too much for me."

"Come on," Rome sings. "We're just fucking with you. Sit down." He pats the seat but I shake my head. Elodie is watching Mrs. Jenkins as well and I'm kind of glad I brought it to her attention. Elodie is smart and maybe if Mrs. Jenkins won't open up to me, there is a chance she could open up to her.

"I got schoolwork," I lie, not wanting to go into detail about my new job for Dad's campaign.

Reaching into my back pocket, I pull out my wallet and retrieve a crisp ten-dollar bill. "See y'all later." I toss down the money and make my way toward the door.

As I'm leaving, so are Mrs. Jenkins and her husband.

She looks at me, our eyes lock, and I swear for a moment she is pleading with me to help her.

Am I delusional? I must be.

"Have a good evening, Wilder," she says softly with a pressed smile as Mayor Jenkins holds the door open.

Well, at least he did that. He can't be that much of an asshole.

"You, too," I tell her as I walk out behind them.

I'm definitely overthinking this whole thing. One time he showed some aggression toward her and I've been running with it ever since. They're married. Married people have ups and downs.

Keeping my distance, I carefully watch as they walk down the sidewalk. Mayor Jenkins grabs her hand and something about the way he's holding it, as if he refuses to let go, irks me.

Part of me thinks I'm being irrational until he walks around the side of the car and shoves her in her side, making her cry out. I want to go over and say something, but I quickly notice no one else is around. Neither of them can see me from where I am beside my car. But I don't miss the evil glint in his eye as he speaks to her, still clutching her arm in his grip until he tosses it to the side.

I watch as she cradles it to her chest, pain in her features.

I know what I see, and I can't be the only one to ever witness this. He just acted abusive toward her in a public area, which means this isn't the first time. Not with the way he walks around the car and adjusts his tie as if this is a normal day for him.

No, other people have to have seen this. They might be cowards, unwilling to stand up to the mayor, though. However, I'm not like that. In fact, I might be the only person who is willing to do something about it because Mayor Jenkins doesn't intimidate me the way he does everyone else in this town.

As they drive off, I catch a glimpse of her face. Terror and pain are all I see as the car pulls out of the lot.

She needs help, and I might be the only one who can save her.

CHAPTER 4
CATHERINE

"ONE MORNING I just woke up and a thought popped in my head…"

My head snaps up from my computer at the sound of the voice in the doorway. There, I find Wilder, balancing an open laptop in his palm as he walks toward me, reading something.

He continues, "I think I might make a good mayor. Yeah. Maybe I'll try it out."

I can't help the chuckle that escapes me as he prowls closer, that all too confident expression on his face as he jokes around. "What are you doing, Wilder?"

I already know what he's doing. *He's not giving up.*

He keeps reading aloud, his eyes darting to mine every few words. "With that said, I want to let you all know I'd like to be the new mayor of Willow Creek."

He slaps the laptop closed, his head tilted slightly to the left. "Are you really going to allow me to destroy my dad's reputation with this mess?"

I sigh, shaking my head. "Wilder, I can't help you." Mornings are always nice because I know Troy would never interrupt my day. This is my real safe space, a quiet classroom with the birds chirping outside. Normally having people in here early would feel like a violation, but it's strange that I actually want Wilder to be here.

Wider fakes a pout, and it's hard not to fall for his charm. "I came to school early just to talk to you. Doesn't that prove how important this is to me?"

More than anything, I want to do this for him. But the soreness in my wrist and the ache in my stomach serves as a reminder not to test my limits. I care about Wilder—probably more than I should.

I know it's because I've been chatting with him more lately on SnapTok. It was never supposed to go as far as it has—to the point where we're checking in with each other daily. But for some reason, I can't stop. Wilder makes me feel important. Of all the girls who follow his account, he talks to *me*.

There's just something about him and the way he flirts with the camera. I've memorized the dimples on each side of his cheeks when he smiles. The way he blinks rapidly when he's feeling nervous, which is rare because Wilder was born to be in the public eye.

He sets the closed laptop down on a stack of papers on my desk and presses his hands to either side of it. "I need you, Mrs. Jenkins."

My mouth drops open before I force my lips back together. A rush of adrenaline coursing through me. "You need *me*?"

Wilder leans closer, his face only inches from mine. I can feel the warmth of his minty breath on my cheek and it sends shivers down my spine. "Desperately."

If he only knew I need him, too. His videos give me the escape I crave from the life I hate. But he'll never know. He can't learn that he is the only thing that holds me together on days I think about just ending it all for good. It's inappropriate and so unlike me to be fixated on a younger man like this.

I make a vow to delete the app tonight. Hopefully that will end this strange fixation.

I'm finding it so hard to say no to him. I can see the desperation in his eyes. He really does need me, and it's my duty as his *teacher* to offer a helping hand.

Or at least that's what I tell myself.

"Okay," I say softly, lost in his gaze as I suppress the haunting thoughts of any potential consequences. "Just this once."

A smile grows on his face. "I knew I could count on you."

"We've got twenty minutes before class begins. I'll do what I can." I open his laptop and begin reading. There is no way I can allow this to require an after-school session; it has to be now.

"Twenty minutes is perfect." Spinning around, he grabs a chair and with a flick of his wrist, he sets it down beside me.

He's so close. Too close. Every couple seconds, I find myself looking at the door, as if I'm expecting Troy to burst in like he did the last time we were sitting here together. He's at work, though. There's no way he'd come here at this time of day. I tell myself that, but here I am glancing between the words on the screen and out the windows, scanning for his car.

When Wilder leans in to watch me, I feel less worry and more comfort. It's strange, but I feel like Wilder would never let anything happen to me. Not if he could stop it.

I push away that thought and focus on the document. It's hard not to notice the worried look on Wilder's face. He wants to do a good job on this article, and I can respect that.

His fingers drum against his knee nervously. "Can you tell me your thoughts? This silence might actually kill me."

I read through this dumpster fire of a very rough draft, and when I'm done, I slap my hand to my forehead. "Seriously, Wilder?" I heave. "I know you can do better than this."

The corner of his mouth tugs up. "With you I can. On my own, I'm doomed."

Although I disagree with Wilder because I fully believe he can do this, it's nice to hear him say he needs me. I tried to help Troy with something like this once and he insulted me before he could even read it. Said I was just a teacher and he has professionals who know what they're doing to work on his press releases.

"I don't get it," I tell him, turning his way. "You're one of the smartest students in the senior class. Why is this so hard for you?"

His joyous expression quickly fades. He shrugs, going from the confident top jock everyone else sees, to someone vulnerable. "I guess it's the pressure of it all. A fear of failure." He sighs, shaking his head as if he is disappointed in himself.

While this is a rougher draft than I imagined, it's not the worst I have seen.

"You're much too hard on yourself." I pat his hand and he smiles.

Quickly drawing my hand away, I give him a knowing look. "And I know darn well you purposely made this terrible so I'd help you. Am I right?"

"Okay." He smirks. "I'll admit, it's not my best work."

He clenches his fists and I'm shocked when the action doesn't make me flinch. With him I can see it's not in anger, just frustration with himself. "Look, I'm not lying when I say I freeze up every time I try to write anything of substance. If it were for myself, it would be a breeze, but doing this for someone else's future is hard as fu—" He immediately corrects himself. "Heck."

I nod, understanding exactly what he means. The pressure to impress others can easily be all-consuming. In doing so, we put on a mask of perfection, hiding our true selves. The world is full of people who are too afraid to reveal their vulnerabilities and imperfections, so we sacrifice ourselves and our own happiness just to get validation from others.

While I may be thinking of something much bigger than an election, campaign, or news articles, it's the same wall we're putting up. One that we fear is full of judgment on the other side.

"Your intro is good." I move the laptop between us so we can both see it clearly. Pointing to the next line on the screen, I say,

"Delete this and add more emphasis to his plans for the beautification of the town's parks."

I watch intently as he taps at the keys, piecing together the key points in his notes with filler words that paint a much bigger picture of his dad's plans. Plans that I'm actually excited for, given he wins the election.

"Here would be a great place to put the information on his hope for the preservation of the town's historic homes," I say, pointing to the following paragraph. "The hardest thing about writing from information someone else gives you is the temptation to write as if you were making a grocery list. You're too focused on making sure all the information is there, instead of focusing on making it flow."

He nods his head in agreement, so I continue, "When it feels like that's what you want to do, stop and look at each thing individually, then add three sentences to each bullet point to help further explain. This will also help when writing speeches."

He immediately gets out his notepad from his backpack and starts writing down what I am telling him. This is why I love to teach Wilder. He values the information I bring to the table.

"Now that you have talked about how he wants to improve the look of the town, I think here would be a good place to expand on how he wants to help further other sports that are not just football."

He sighs. "I feel weird writing this because all I know is football, though. How can I introduce other sports I don't know that much about?" His brows are pinched as he stares at the screen. It's so cute I pause and forget to answer his question for a moment.

"You still with me, Mrs. J?" A casual smirk plays on his lips.

I blush and roll my lips. "Of course, I was just thinking." I pause for another second to compose myself because I am not sure what is happening to my brain right now.

"All right, so think of it this way. You might not know much about other sports, but what would the boosting of other sports do for the people of this town?"

He sits back in his chair, hand resting on his chin as he ponders my question. I can actually see the light bulb come on in his head when he grins back at me.

"It would bring in more scouts, which means more money. They will need places to stay and food to eat, thus bringing in more funds and helping improve the town's image. Plus, if these kids get scouted to major teams, it will also bring tourism here."

I beam at him. "Exactly! Now, write that down."

He gets to work immediately, his fingers flying over the keys like this is what he was made for. I always believed he could do it, but I think now he is starting to believe in himself too.

Once he's finished, he sinks back in the chair, watching me anxiously as I pull the laptop close to read. This is good. Actually, it's really good.

My hands go up in excitement, a widespread smile on my face. "This is great, Wilder. I knew you had it in you."

A shy smile touches his lips. "Really?"

"Absolutely," I assure him with a pat on his shoulder.

He reaches up, placing his hand over mine, and I curse the electricity that runs through me. It's wrong and I hate the way his touch makes me feel. For just a moment, it's as if time stands still and the only thing I see are his light brown eyes shining back at me. "I couldn't have done it without you, Mrs. Jenkins."

I pull my hand away, averting my gaze as my face starts to feel like it's on fire. "Of course you could have. You had it in you the entire time. You just needed a boost of confidence."

Wilder has so many amazing qualities he doesn't acknowlededge; yet, he's by far the hardest on himself out of any of my students.

I refocus on the article and fix a couple grammatical errors, then push the laptop back in front of him so he can read through it one more time. His lips move as he mouths the words and I find myself entranced.

The next thing I know, he's turning in his chair to face me. "You're amazing, Mrs. J. I don't even know what to say, except thank you."

The sincerity in his tone sends a rush of warmth through me. It's such an amazing feeling when someone expresses their appreciation for you. It's one of the reasons I love my job so much.

I raise my shoulders, caging in my neck because what I'm about to say next is wrong, yet crucial. "Say you won't tell my husband."

"It'll be our little secret." He winks and a swarm of butterflies flutter through my stomach.

Wilder stands up and pushes the top of his laptop closed. "Thank you again," he says before leaning down and wrapping his arms around me. "This means more to me than you know."

I gulp, hesitantly embracing his hug. "You're welcome."

My eyes close and I savor this moment, relishing the safety of his strong arms. I inhale the scent of his woodsy cologne as the heat of his body infiltrates mine. It's overwhelming, yet everything I needed in this moment.

My heart hammers against his chest. This is a feeling I've craved for as long as I can remember.

But it's wrong. I shouldn't feel these things for another guy, and certainly not for my student, who is eleven years younger than me.

The door to the classroom creaks open and Wilder steps back, letting me go. I take a deep breath, putting on my mask of perfection as I stand up, ready to greet students. My stomach flips from the pain of last night's assault, and the confusing emotions running through me, and my hand covers it instantly.

Wilders eyes follow my movement and I swear I see a flash of anger. Before I can register it, he looks away and I focus on the student in the doorway.

"Good morning," I say to Elodie as Wilder picks up his

laptop from my desk. She squints, giving Wilder an odd look as if she just interrupted something.

She had to have known that was a simple hug. Nothing more, nothing less. Does she suspect it was something more? Was it? Does she know Wilder makes me feel things inside that I haven't felt in ages? Is it written on my face that I'm crushing on my student?

Oh my gosh, Catherine, pull yourself together right this instant.

I wonder if Wilder told her he was asking me for help with the article. Maybe she knows it's a conflict of interest and that's why she seems so puzzled. I try to breathe and ignore the churning in my gut.

Wilder flashes me another smile before finding his seat. All the while, Elodie is following behind him whispering something, only causing my paranoia to grow.

My cheeks fill with heat, pulse racing. That's it. I *have* to delete that app and get him out of my head.

CHAPTER 5
WILDER

MAYBE I SHOULDN'T HAVE PUT SO much pressure on her to help me. She's been a ball of nerves all class. I swear I have never seen her so flustered. When everyone had taken their seats and class began, it was as if she couldn't get her train of thought. The way her gaze darts around the room and she keeps shuffling papers on her desk just proves she is feeling antsy and tense. But what bothers me most is her eyes seem to land on everyone except me.

She already seems stressed out enough and I'm hoping I didn't just make things worse. I should have asked her if everything was okay. I also should have asked why she's dressed like a blizzard is heading our way in another long-sleeved turtleneck —this time with a puffy vest over it—and a pair of black dress pants, but I didn't want to come across like I knew too much. Not yet at least.

Had it not been for her behavior lately, I wouldn't even suspect anything is wrong based on her clothing choice, but things aren't adding up. Especially after what I saw last night.

Last night I laid in bed thinking about Mrs. Jenkins and how she's been acting the last few months. I drew up many different scenarios, but in the end, I came to the conclusion that her husband has been physically abusing her for a while now. I could be way off, but my gut tells me I'm spot on.

She's going to try and push me away, I know it. But I have to gain her trust because it breaks my heart to think that she might be in any sort of danger.

Mrs. Jenkins continues to talk about symbolism, but I don't pay much attention to anything but her body language. Like a detective, I search for clues. Any sign that I'm right. Yet, the more I watch her, I desperately hope I'm wrong. It hurts to even think about anyone harming such a beautiful, kind person. She's a gem and I hope like hell her husband knows that.

Once class is dismissed, I hang back, not caring if I'm late for biology. This is more important.

"Was there something I can help you with, Wilder?" she asks as she taps into her phone, still avoiding eye contact with me while she stands at the front of the room.

I slide out from my chair and move to the door with my laptop tucked under my arm. Instead of walking out, I close it, grabbing her full attention.

She raises a brow, gripping her phone. "What are you doing?"

I walk toward her with slow steps so I don't freak her out. The last thing I want is for her to think I'm coming on to her. "Is everything okay, Mrs. Jenkins. Call me crazy, but I'm sort of worried about you." My eyes drift to her stomach that she clutched when she stood up, and the wrist I watched her cradle to her chest last night.

An airy laugh slips through her lips as she forces a smile on her face. I know it's forced because her eyes lack the sparkle they hold when her happiness is genuine. "If this is about what happened a few months ago, I can assure you, everything is fine. Just like I assured you then."

I step closer, and she steps back. "You need to get to your next class, Wilder." This is a planning period for her, so I know no one is about to walk in.

Another step forward, and she takes another step backward. "What are you doing?" This time her voice is just a whisper as she strains her neck up to try to appear strong. But I see the worry, the fear.

But what's worse is when I see that all my worries were justi-fied. At the very tip of her turtleneck is a subtle bruise. It's barely visible, but it's there. Pain slices through me as if I were just hit in the stomach, but I don't let her see. This isn't about me.

Her chest rises and falls rapidly, her eyes beginning to dampen with moisture. Why do I feel like she's begging me to ask her? To save her?

More than anything, I want to pull down the fabric and expose the mark while begging her to tell me the truth. She crosses her arms over her chest and her sleeve rides up, exposing another bruise on her wrist. This one is more subtle. In fact, I probably wouldn't have noticed it if I didn't know just what happened last night.

I swallow hard, wanting to say something else, but instead I say, "I wanted to thank you again for your help."

She turns her head slightly but doesn't look at me. "You're welcome. Now get going. I'd hate for you to be late for your next class."

With a heavy heart, I walk to the door but pause with my fingers wrapped around the handle. "Mrs. Jenkins," I say softly. I don't know if I can walk away right now.

I'm used to being the nice guy, that's who I am. But right now I want to say fuck it to giving her space. The need to pull her into my arms no matter how much she fights it is strong. I want to press her body against that damn whiteboard and I want her to confide in me every secret she has ever had to keep.

Our eyes meet with a fierce intensity. It's as if a magnetic force is pulling us together. It's nothing I've ever felt before. I take a step toward her and when she doesn't step back, I eat up the distance between us.

Her back touches the whiteboard with hardly an inch of

space separating our bodies. She smells like lavender and I'm surprised to find my mouth watering. Looking her up and down, I watch her throat bob as she swallows nervously. "Wilder?"

She says my name like it's a prayer, and I want nothing more than to be the savior she prays to. But I need to prove she can trust me, that I'm not like that asshole who already took advantage of the gift right in front of him.

Carefully, I tip her chin so she has to look into my eyes. "You think no one sees you, Mrs. Jenkins." I lift a smile as tears glisten in her beautiful blue eyes. "But I do. And I think you're worth seeing."

I've been drawn to Mrs. Jenkins for a while now, but whatever is happening inside me is a whole new level of emotion. She stumbles to the left, reaching out to steady herself on the edge of her desk, confirmation that she feels this undeniable connection between us. *How can she not?*

Giving her space, I head to the door, but not before giving her one last look that I hope conveys everything neither of us is ready to say.

Earlier I told Mrs. Jenkins I need her. I didn't realize the depths of those words until now because she might not know it yet, but she needs me too.

CHAPTER 6
CATHERINE

"DELETE AND DONE." I tap the button on my screen, erasing the SnapTok app. I should have done this yesterday after I helped Wilder with his dad's article. But temptation got the best of me and I stayed up all night in the closet, watching every one of his videos, one last time. That's when I realized, I'm crazy. I mean, who stays up all night watching their student's social media? If anyone knew how often I'm viewing his account, they'd think I had a thing for him. When I started to think so myself, I knew it was time. Now it's done.

I set my phone down on the center console in my car, so I can drive, almost wishing I'd waited a few days to delete the app off my phone. Troy is going out of town for the next four nights and I'm going to need something to do to keep myself busy. Even if I'm never watching Wilder's account ever again, there are many others I enjoyed. I've actually fallen down the rabbit hole of watching farm animals more times than I care to admit.

Regardless, I'll have to find something to do to occupy my time. Chances are, Troy will arm every camera in, and around, our house, so going out isn't an option unless I want to be hammered with text messages and phone calls asking where I'm at and who I'm with.

After all this time, you'd think my own husband would trust me. I've never given him any reason not to. Sometimes I wonder if it's just because of his own insecurities, or his own guilt.

Honestly, I don't care what Troy does. I prefer he just stays the hell away from me. And for the next four nights, he will.

A sense of peace settles inside me knowing he'll be out of my hair soon. Now I just have to get through this lunch with him. It's all for show. Troy wants the community to see us out, together and happy. I'm forced to put on a smile and pretend life is dandy. That my husband doesn't smack me around behind closed doors and that the reason I own so many turtlenecks really has nothing to do with the way he seems to get off on strangling me.

A few days ago, it wasn't so easy to pretend. We went to Big John's for pizza and before we left, I couldn't find my wedding ring. I took it off before scrubbing a stubborn bloodstain out of my favorite pair of white jeans, and I forgot where I put it.

To say Troy was livid is an understatement. The fact that I even took it off in the first place had him raging. He completely lost it and accused me of taking off my ring so I could fuck another man. Not just any man, though—Mr. Chen, one of the history teachers at our school.

The insanity in that statement alone had me dumbfounded!

Mr. Chen is getting married soon. Where Troy came up with that is beyond me. Sometimes I think he just sits in his office and creates scenarios in his mind that he actually believes. Mr. Chen has never even made a pass at me, or vice versa. We hardly even talk. Actually, I don't talk to anyone just so I can avoid Troy losing his shit. Yet, it still happens.

As we approached the front door to leave for dinner, out of nowhere, Troy thrust his knee into my stomach. The unexpected blow knocked the wind out of me and I collapsed to the floor, gasping for air.

Of course, then he apologized and pulled my damn ring out of his pocket. Apparently he found it on the kitchen counter when he got home. I have no doubt he had it the entire time he was screaming at me.

It doesn't matter, though. At least not for the next four nights because I'll be free of him. Just to be a bitch because I can, I might not wear my ring the entire time he's gone.

Now to get through this next hour.

The town is pretty quiet this time of day. Students are in school, adults are adulting. So I make it to the city hall in less than five minutes. Not that it's a far drive, but certain hours are busier than others downtown.

I maneuver my car into a parallel parking spot in front of city hall. Before getting out, I give myself a quick glance in the rearview mirror. My makeup is intact, my hair is tame and neat, and my wedding ring is on. Hopefully he doesn't give me hell for my casual outfit. I'd hate to *embarrass* him in front of his colleagues for not looking like the perfect Stepford wife.

I take a deep breath, preparing myself for whatever mood he might be in today. It's not often I see him during work hours, so there's no telling how he's going to act at lunch. It could be good because he is at work and has to put on a fake smile. However, I know better than to feel safe here. Troy has his own private office with a nearly soundproof door. This place is no safer than my own home.

As soon as I open the car door, a gust of wind jerks it from my grasp. Reaching out and grabbing the frame, I hold to it tightly as I step out. I don't even need to close the door because the wind slams it with a thud. Looking up, I notice the dark clouds rolling in. The threat of a storm looms and I'm oddly excited for it.

Maybe I'll start a fire in the fireplace this evening and read a book with takeout food. The possibilities are endless. I'm giddy inside just thinking about it.

Moving quickly, I go through the front entrance, the smell of fresh-cut paper and political garbage immediately flooding my senses.

As soon as I enter city hall, I'm immediately greeted by Beth, Troy's assistant. "Hi, Catherine."

She looks adorably professional in a crisp white blouse and it's impossible not to notice the growing bulge of her stomach. If I had to guess, she's expecting. But I won't guess, nor ask because of the possibility I'm wrong.

"Good afternoon, Beth. It's so nice to see you," I say kindly.

Flashing a toothy grin, she sets down her tall tumbler. "You as well," she chirps. "I had no idea you were coming in today. Don't you have a class to teach?"

"I took an hour of personal time today. Troy wanted to take me out for lunch before he leaves for Chicago."

She claps her hands to her chest, awestruck. "How thoughtful! Such a selfless man he is." I can't tell if she's being sarcastic or serious, but I vote for the latter. Everyone loves Troy. They think he's this heroic man sent to save our town from doom. Everyone but *me*.

Holding up a finger, she says, "Give me just a moment. I'll shoot Troy a message and let him know you're here. I believe he's on an important phone call with the chief of police."

It's odd hearing her call him Troy. Almost everyone refers to him as Mr. Jenkins, or Mayor Jenkins, because that's what he prefers. He's a true pompous asshole. But he works closely with Beth, so I am sure they are closer than most.

"Thank you, Beth." I fold my hands in front of me, prepared to wait awhile. When Troy gets on the phone, he will talk as long as the person on the other end will listen—mostly about himself and his *good* deeds.

Beth stands up behind the desk, and I catch another glimpse of her stomach. There is no doubt she is very pregnant. It's been a couple months since I've seen her, but I definitely didn't notice she was expecting then.

"Almost six months," she says with a smile, noticing my stare at her stomach.

I breathe a sigh of relief, thankful she is pregnant because I would have looked like a fool just staring if there wasn't a baby there.

"Congratulations," I tell her excitedly. "Is this your first?"

She nods. "It is. It was quite a shock, but I'm getting more excited as time passes. He started kicking a couple weeks ago and I immediately felt this instant bond."

"He?" The idea of a little boy bouncing around brings me so much joy for her.

"Yes." She rubs her adorable bump. "We're having a baby boy."

"I'm so happy for you, Beth. Please let me know when your baby shower is, I'd love to send a gift." I can just imagine a cute little sweater vest with khaki pants. I'm excited just thinking about walking around the baby section to get things for her. She puts up with Troy's shit and has for four years, she deserves all the gifts.

"Nonsense." She sweeps her hand through the air. "You have to be there. I'll be sure to mail out an invitation."

"That's so kind of you. I'll keep an eye out for it." My chest burns slightly thinking about Beth going on maternity leave. Troy does not handle change well, so it is good to know this is coming up so I can prepare. Maybe I can cook him his favorite meal and buy a new dress he might like to help keep him calm.

I put a hand on my stomach, then quickly drop it and make sure Beth didn't notice. I'd give anything to be a mother one day.

Unfortunately, a baby is not in my cards because I make sure it isn't. Troy and I tried for a while before things got bad. Then two years ago, while Troy was at work, I went to a fertility specialist. Turns out, I can have babies. The doctor said the problem was likely with Troy's sperm.

At the risk of him being wrong, I immediately went to my gynecologist and got birth control implanted. My husband thinks I'm infertile, and he loves nothing more than to throw in my face how broken my body is. He's even gone as far as telling me God made me infertile because I don't deserve a baby. That hurt more than his fists ever could, even if I knew it wasn't true.

Troy's office door opens and I'm immediately met with the biggest, cheekiest smile. "There she is," he gushes with wide open arms. Closing the space between us, he wraps his arms around me and I'm forced to hug him back. "I'm so glad you could get away from work, honey." He kisses my cheek softly.

If only this were real. This charm and adoration. It's not, though. It's as fake as the smile on my face. This is not our life. This is a show for anyone Troy thinks is watching. Which is hilarious because Beth is the only person here and I have a feeling she knows our life isn't so perfect.

I wish it were real. I wish Troy wasn't a monster and he loved me as much as I once thought he did. I even wish I loved him, too. Maybe this is just a phase he needs to get through and then he'll go back to being the man who would dance with me in the living room after a long day.

Troy steps out of the hug and grabs my hand. "Shall we, my love?"

I notice Beth walking quickly past us down the hall as she gags, her hand over her mouth. Those pregnancy hormones are probably a bitch.

"It was nice seeing you, Beth." I speak loudly so she can hear me as she jogs.

Looking over Troy's shoulder, I watch her wave her hand in the air before she enters the bathroom.

"My car is out back," Troy says with a nod of his head. I follow him down the short hall, and when I pass the bathrooms, I hear Beth crying.

My gut tells me to check on her, but I don't want to upset Troy by making him wait. I have no idea what could be making her feel so emotional. Maybe seeing Troy be so sweet to me made her think of her partner and she must miss them.

I debate on asking Troy if we should invite them to dinner, but he would probably just get angry and say it's not a secretary's place to eat with her boss. He likes to remind me often that women should work in education or serve as secretaries until they become mothers. He knows better than to say that on stage, but behind closed doors, he brags about how ninety-three percent of the workers in this town are men. As it should be, according to him.

When he found out that Wilder's new stepmother was going to be the new district attorney, he hit me so hard her name felt branded on my skin. He blamed me for having to work in the same building as the woman, as if I had anything to do with the decision to bring her in.

We make it to the bottom of the back stairs when I realize he has been quiet for too long. The air goes rigidly cold around me, as if my body can sense the storm brewing in him before he lashes out.

With a venomous snarl under his breath, Troy shoves the back door open and glares at me. "Could you be any more fake?"

I gasp, stopping in my tracks as he palms the door, holding it open. "Excuse me?"

"It was nice seeing you, Beth," he mocks me. "Come on, Catherine. For once could you act like you're not better than everyone else?"

"Wow," I drag the word, completely dumbstruck. "You are… unbelievable." I walk past him, knowing damn well he's not going to make a scene out here on the sidewalk in *his* town.

Rain falls lightly, and a roar of thunder booms in the distance, so I move quickly toward Troy's car. In a matter of seconds, he's at my side, grabbing my upper arm and squeezing the hell out of it as he drags me to the passenger door. He's seething as he pulls the door open and tosses me inside.

Before I can even get my legs all the way in, he slams the door closed. Fortunately, I kick my foot out just in time to stop it from crushing my shin. While he's rounding the car to the driver's side, I pull it closed.

Thank I'd love nothing more than to scream at him. Punch him, insult him, bite his fucking arm off. I want to do anything to hurt him as much as he hurts me, but nothing I do to him will ever touch the pain I feel inside.

Troy slams his door shut. After a quick glance around, his fingers dart out and wrap around my throat. "How dare you try and walk away from me like that." Spit flies at me from his mouth as he seethes mere inches from my face. "Do you have any idea how humiliating it is when my wife throws a tantrum in the parking lot of *my* city hall?" His words drip with malice as he tightens his grip.

I gulp, feeling my throat bob against his palm. "I'm sorry," I choke out, my eyes nearly popping out of their sockets while I suck in as much air as I can in his vise grip. I still want to hurt him, but I know that if I dig my nails into his hand, he will keep squeezing until I pass out. I'm not sure what he will do after that, but I cannot risk him postponing this work trip for his "sick" wife.

So, like an obedient wife, I stay still. He glares at me, his jaw clenching and unclenching as darkness creeps around my vision. After a long, forced breath, his eyes start to change.

With a forceful shove, he pushes my head away and retreats to the driver's seat of his car. As he starts the engine, I pull my turtleneck down slightly and graze my fingers over my already tender skin.

I don't allow myself to think much of it; instead, I just stare out the window while he continues to huff and puff, every few moments tossing out an insult or two. This is his calming down phase, I know it well.

I'm at the point where I'm no longer fazed. Nothing Troy does surprises me, and I no longer live in a state of fear and panic because this is the norm for me. But as I look out the window, pain shooting down my throat to the point where I am unsure if I will be able to eat anything, I think about ending him —even prison would be better than this.

Sure, there might be fighting, but there is no way it could be as often as the fights that occur in my own home. I could probably sleep in my own bed and not in a locked closet with my knees pulled to my chest.

No more turtlenecks that make me feel itchy inside and out. No more long dresses. No more pretending.

Then I sigh because I have thought this same thing before and I'm not sure I'd have the guts to do it.

It's a quick ten-minute drive to Moonwalk Cafe, and in that ten minutes, Troy has calmed himself down.

He gets out of the car, and I remain seated with my door closed because if I dare open it myself in front of onlookers, he'll lose his ever-loving mind.

Like the gentleman he pretends to be, he buttons his suit jacket, then pulls the passenger door open for me. Reaching inside the car, he takes my hand, helping me to my feet.

We both put on our proverbial masks and head inside the cafe as the happily married couple everyone believes us to be.

"Good afternoon, James," Troy beams at the host. Unlike myself, he knows everyone in this town by name, and they know him, too.

Could you be any more fake? For once could you act like you're not better than everyone else?

I don't say it, but I would love to repeat the words he said to me only minutes ago. The thoughts I have. Oh, the things I wish I could say to this man. If he only knew how deep my hatred for him runs.

"It's great to see you, Mayor Jenkins," James gushes as he grabs two menus and napkin-rolled utensils. "And you, too, Mrs. Jenkins."

I smile politely as we follow behind him to our table. I've learned to keep my mouth shut and to only speak when necessary. Something as little as "it's great to see you, too" could hit a nerve with Troy and in that same breath, I'll be accused of flirting with another man in front of my loving husband.

Troy's thumb grazes over the skin of my knuckles, a clue that he's over his fit and we might actually have an enjoyable lunch together. It helps the tight ball of anxiety in my stomach ease. Living in constant fight or flight is exhausting, to say the least.

We stop at a high-top round table beside the window, and Troy pulls out my chair for me. I smooth my hands down my pants and take a seat before he sits down in the chair across from me.

After ordering our drinks—ice water for me, and an iced-tea for Troy, he reaches his hands across the table and lifts a brow.

I take that as my cue to hold his hands. Naturally, we are picture-perfect once again.

"You look beautiful today," he says softly. I'm pleasantly surprised at not only his words, but the sincerity in them. I thought for sure I'd get slack for dressing so casually. He also spoke low, not for show. He is likely feeling bad for hurting me in the car and trying to make up for it.

I respond with a simple, "Thank you." I do not want to trigger him again. I just want to get this meal over with so I can get away from him.

The server returns with our drinks—a beautiful blonde lady, middle-aged, with a low-cut tee shirt. She's got bright pink lipstick and a big wad of gum smacks annoyingly between her teeth. "If it isn't my favorite customer." She winks at Troy and I just roll my eyes to look out the window.

"And if it isn't my favorite waitress. How has everything been, Hillary?"

I'm not sure if he knows her name by heart, or if it's because she's wearing a name tag, but the conversation between them irks me. Only because the phoniness of it makes me want to vomit. Hillary is being kind because he's the mayor and she wants a fat tip. Troy is being kind because he wants her vote. And that's as deep as their kindness for each other actually goes.

Without even looking at the menu, Troy orders for us both. Two ham and cheese paninis and a side salad with ranch. I can't even remember the last time I ordered off the menu and got what *I* wanted to eat.

Troy says it's common courtesy for husbands to order for their wives while getting the same meal. He argues that it shows compatibility. Whereas I think it's bullshit and I want to scream at him that this isn't 1950.

I keep my lips sealed, though, because it's a battle I don't want to fight, and one I won't win either.

Instead, I opt for a more positive conversation. "How has the campaign planning been going?" I ask, lending him the opportunity to talk about himself.

"Marvelous. Couldn't be better. You know, I thought it would be stressful having an opponent this term, but it turns out, it's enlightening. It will be all the more satisfying when I win."

"Absolutely," I agree with him. "You're a brilliant mayor, Troy. I have no doubt you'll come out on top." *Lie.* Troy has done nothing for this town but make the rich richer and the poor poorer. Then he takes those said poor people and forces them to move to the neighboring town where violence and gangs cause many issues.

He calls it "cleaning up the city" whereas everyone else calls it prejudice.

"*We*," he corrects me. "*We* will come out on top. I couldn't do this without your support, Catherine. I know I don't say it enough, but I'm extremely grateful for you."

His words touch a spot in my heart that I rarely feel. A lonely corner that begs for adoration and praise. This is the man I fell in love with years ago. This is the man who saved me.

"That means a lot to me," I tell him truthfully. It's moments like these that I mourn the loss of the man I once loved. It hurts so much and it leaves me with so many questions that have me second-guessing my feelings and our marriage.

Maybe Troy really does love me and he's just overly stressed with work. He wasn't abusive until after we moved here. Maybe something happened that he isn't ready to talk about. Maybe something changed him.

I can help him. I can change him. I can love him.

Maybe it really is my fault and I deserve to feel his wrath on occasion because it puts me in my place. Troy grounds me.

I can do better. I can be better. I can be worthy of his love.

He squeezes my hands, his eyes looking tenderly into mine. "I love you, Catherine. So much."

"I love you, too," I whisper, and in this moment, right now, I think maybe I do love him.

He releases my hands and unravels his silverware. "I know you do."

The waitress returns with our food, placing our dishes directly in front of us.

"Thank you, Hillary," Troy says as he fluffs a napkin and rests it on his lap. "This looks delicious, doesn't it, Catherine?"

He eyes me, and I clear my throat. "Most definitely. Thank you so much," I tell her as I mirror Troy and rest my napkin in my lap.

Troy watches as Hillary walks away, his eyes on her ass. Once she's out of sight, he returns his attention to me. It makes me want to call him out, but he is trying, so I want to try, too. Anything to make this lunch peaceful and not a total shitshow.

He takes a bite of his salad and I do the same. I used to save the salad for last in my meals. There is something about ending the meal with a belly full of veggies that made me feel good. However, Troy helpfully informed me that that's not proper, so I just do what I can to mimic him in hopes that he will stay calm.

When Troy looks up at me, he smiles. Victory in his gaze. It's candid and I can't help but smile back.

"I had a call with Dean Hathaway, the police chief today," he says, the change of topic throwing me off a bit, but I go with it.

"Oh?" I say, waiting for him to elaborate.

I remember Beth mentioning he was on a call with the police chief when I arrived at the city hall.

"Let's just say, my win is the bag. Dean is faxing over some info on one of those bratty Cromwell kids and let's just say, boy do I have some dirt on him. Not to mention, the adored *district attorney*." He makes a face and my brows pinch slightly.

Oh no. I remember hearing about some trouble Rome got himself into, but I'm not sure what he could mean about the district attorney. Everyone loves Celia Cromwell and she is practically a saint.

Troy continues, "Once I threaten to expose his son and his wife, I guarantee Grant will be dropping out of the race."

"That good, huh?" I ask, digging for more information. As much as I want Troy to win and save me from having to deal with who he becomes over a loss, I also don't want Wilder's family thrown under the bus if it can be helped.

"Good?" His tone shoots up. "It's great. Celia Cromwell, Grant's wife, is the district attorney and she worked the case that had her stepson's charges thrown out. Now if that isn't a conflict of interest, I'm not sure what is."

This is bad. This is very bad for Grant, Celia, and Rome. I can't allow Troy to do this. I'm not sure how conflicting it is, but blackmail is not the way to win an election. At least, not in my eyes. I'm not sure how other politicians deal with this sort of stuff, but it's wrong.

I grit my teeth, holding back everything I want to say. This is such a Troy thing to do. He'd love nothing more than to paint the Cromwells as horrible people when he's done so much worse. If the residents of Willow Creek knew what a monster he is, they'd never give him their votes.

"Are you sure this is how you want to win?" I ask, forgoing what I really want to say. "You said yourself, beating Grant will be all the more satisfying when you win. Don't you prefer to win with votes?"

He quirks a brow. "Are you questioning my abilities? Because it sure as hell sounds like you are."

I keep my head down, hoping if I can express my concern maybe he won't do this. "I'm just saying, I think you should—"

His fist hits the table, enough to startle me but not quite enough to attract attention. Troy glances around when my panicked gaze meets his, and the second he realizes no one is looking at us, he grabs his knife and grips it tight. "Don't pretend you know a damn thing about what it takes to win an election. You know nothing about what I do, Catherine, so keep your ignorant thoughts to yourself."

I nod in response and continue to eat with my head down because if I look at him right now, I just might lose my fucking mind. His breathing is heavy, that knife held out almost like a threat. He wouldn't do anything in front of witnesses. At least, that's what I try to tell myself as I force another bite down my throat.

CHAPTER 7
CATHERINE

HE'S GONE.

Troy is gone for the next four nights.

I'm literally bursting at the seams with excitement. Even my students take notice. Brady Newton made a comment about how I look exceptionally happy this afternoon. A minute later, Julia Denver said I was glowing. I have to agree with both of them, not only am I happy and glowing, I want to dance and sing and shout.

This is how I want to feel every day. The simple freedom to make my own choices and have my independence back. Even if it's brief, it makes me wish for more.

I step in front of the class, looking out at all my students. "If everyone could sit down, we'll get started."

They scramble to find their seats, and once they do, I make an announcement. "I'm feeling extra generous today, so instead of continuing with our lesson plan, I'm allowing quiet free time."

Instant chatter begins, so I raise my hands then lower them. "I'm not finished." Once they settle again, I continue. "I highly suggest you study as much as you can for the practice exam tomorrow. If you have homework from other classes to catch up on, you can do so for the next hour. Or, you can talk *quietly* amongst yourselves. If the class gets too out of hand, I'll be happy to continue our discussion on literary criticism."

Chitchat rings around the room again, but for the most part, they keep their voices to a minimum.

Taking a seat at my desk, I open my laptop and log into our online portal to check assignments that were submitted from an earlier class.

As I'm clicking through them, I lend an ear to some gossip from a trio of girls.

"I can't believe you actually asked Wilder Cromwell to prom," one of them says with a mixture of shock and admiration. "What did he say?"

I glance over my laptop, anxious to hear Sam's response. Word around the school is, Wilder isn't going with anyone to prom. He even made a video about flying solo with his friends.

"He said, maybe," Sam tells them. "Which basically means yes."

Instant jealousy strikes. I don't know why, and I don't like it, but it's there. How is it that I'm happy for Wilder, but not at the same time? I can't make sense of my own thoughts.

Good for him, though. Wilder deserves to live out these experiences. He's already too mature for his age. It will do him some good to let his guard down and enjoy a night out with a date to prom.

But Sam, really? I would never speak my thoughts to a single soul, but he's too good for her. Hell, he's too good for any girl in this school. Sam has bragged about having sex with many guys on the football team; I even heard about her sleeping with a few of them at the same time. I'm not judging, I just think Wilder is too mature for her.

Sam's friends gush over her response, squealing and hugging her. "Oh my God! You are officially the luckiest girl alive."

I have to agree with her friends, though. Sam's pretty lucky. Wilder is a great guy. So great that I find myself envious of this eighteen-year-old girl. It's ridiculous. Of course, he would go to prom with someone his age.

It shouldn't bother me like this. I shouldn't care. And when I see them slow dancing together at prom, it won't bother me one bit because these are monumental moments in their lives that each one of them should experience.

It's an event I'll be experiencing as well since I signed up to be a chaperone. I haven't even mentioned it to Troy yet, but one of our deals was that he will not interfere with my job. Even though he doesn't hold true to his word nine out of ten times.

"This is crazy!" Sam's best friend, Abby, exclaims. "Did you see the video he posted today? Do you think…"

"No fricken way," Sam says. "It couldn't be about me."

Nyla clicks her tongue against the roof of her mouth. "Girll-ll," she drags out the word in exasperation. "If he said maybe to prom, it has to be about you. I mean, who else would it be about?"

Dammit. I picked a terrible time to delete that app. I listen intently, hoping to get a clue as to what he said or did on his video to make them think it was about Sam.

Is he crushing on her? Of course he is. Sam's beauty is undeniable. She draws the attention of all the guys at Willow Creek High. Rumors have swirled around the school about her, some not so great, but they could just be whispers of jealousy from other girls.

Jealousy of my own is biting at my stomach right now. So much so that I reach out and grab my phone. Before I can talk myself out of it, I redownload the app.

Bouncing my knees under the desk, I wait impatiently for the loading circle to disappear. Anticipation gnaws at me, and I don't even recognize who I am anymore. Wilder is eleven years younger than me. *Eleven years!*

I can't even begin to entertain the idea of *us*.

But, no one will know I watch him in secret, or that we chat outside of school hours. No one will ever know because I will never tell a soul. Not even Wilder.

As soon as the download is complete, I open it up and log into my account.

Before I even start his recent video, I open my chat and see three unread ones from Wilder.

> WildMisfit: Can I ask you a question?

> WildMisfit: Never mind. I don't want to pry. Curiosity is just eating at me.

> WildMisfit: Screw it. I'll ask anyway. Do you go to Willow Creek High? Lately, I find myself looking for you, but I don't know who I'm looking for.

It ends there, awaiting my response. I chew on one of my nails, debating a response. Why is he looking for me? Especially if he's interested in Sam. I shouldn't want him looking. He needs to stay in his world and I need to stay in mine.

So I type out an answer.

> CatEyes: You're not prying. And yes, I do go to Willow Creek High. I see you every day. But you shouldn't be looking for me.

I hit send, hoping I didn't go too far with this one. I'm not being dishonest. I do go to Willow Creek High—just not as a student.

I'm surprised when his response is immediate, especially since he's in another class right now. If I remember right, he's in computer science and it is his least favorite. Is it creepy that I know his schedule? *Probably.*

I sigh as I wait in anticipation for his message.

> WildMisfit: So when do I get to officially meet you?

I smile at my phone, wishing I could tell him we've met while he fully ignores my advice not to look for me. As much as I want to tell him I know more about him than I should, and he knows me too, I also know I need to be the one to draw the line here.

So, I play it safe. I need to get him off my trail, not closer to it.

> CatEyes: What makes you think we haven't already met?

> WildMisfit: I see how it is. You're toying with me now.

> CatEyes: Maybe I am ;)

One thing I know about kids like Wilder, it's they get bored when responses aren't immediate. If I can keep it vague maybe he will become less interested. And maybe I will lose this pull to him in the process.

> WildMisfit: Ok. I'll play along. Can I at least get a hint? Do we have any classes together?

I bite my lip because now he sees this as a game, which was not my intention. Now I'm stuck, because I don't want to lie to him.

> CatEyes: We have one class together.

> WildMisfit: You're a senior?

> CatEyes: That's more than one hint. But I'll bite. I'm older than you, if that tells you anything.

This is getting dangerous. What is it about him that has me forgetting my head every time we talk? No matter how much I want to kill the conversation, I can't help but keep it going.

> WildMisfit: Older, huh? I'm intrigued. Any plans once you leave this hellhole?

As if I can ever leave…

> CatEyes: I have big dreams when I get out of here. Doesn't mean they'll come true, though. How about you? What do you aspire to be when you "grow up"?

I put grow up in quotes because I don't picture him as a kid. He is more mature than my husband the vast majority of the time.

> WildMisfit: Doesn't matter what I do. For me, it's all about being happy. Happiness is the driving force behind anything I do, both now and after graduation.

That's an odd answer. Is Wilder not happy here?

> CatEyes: And what is it that makes you happy?

> WildMisfit: Right now? Talking to you.

I blush at his answer, unable to contain my smile. He is my escape from my life here, and maybe I am his too. But I won't fall for his charming ways so easily. After all, I can see right through it.

> CatEyes: Smoooooth!

> WildMisfit: I'm trying.

I laugh out loud, give the room a quick sweep to see if anyone noticed, then return to typing when no one seems to care.

CatEyes: I like talking to you. Not much makes me smile these days, but you do.

I don't know why I'm being so open and honest with him, but it feels right.

WildMisfit: There is so much in life worth smiling about. Care to tell me what has you down?

There's a pang in my chest—an uncertainty if I'm ready to tell anyone about my misfortunes in life. But, I know I can trust Wilder, even if he doesn't know who it is that's putting their trust in him. I guess that makes it easier to be honest with him, in some sense.

CatEyes: My home life is…let's say, rough. Some things happened in my past that make it hard to leave.

WildMisfit: You can't let your past be an anchor. Life is too short.

CatEyes: If only it were that easy.

He has no idea what hangs over my head, the sins I committed that keep me here and chained to a monster. What's worse is, I could never tell him. He would look at me differently if he knew what I did. Everyone would.

WildMisfit: Who says it can't be?

CatEyes: Honestly, only you. But you're only getting a small glimpse into my life. If you knew about my sordid past, or what I endure daily, you'd run. I promise you that.

The ugly truth hurts. If Wilder had any idea what he was

getting mixed up in, he wouldn't just run, he would never speak to me again.

> WildMisfit: Give me a chance. You might be pleasantly surprised.

> CatEyes: You surprise me every day just by being you.

> WildMisfit: In that case, I think it's time I return the favor. Let me be surprised. Are you ready to tell me who you are?

A giggle escapes me and I look out at the class, making sure no one noticed before returning to our chat.

> CatEyes: I'm warming up to the idea.

Lie. He can't find out and I won't tell him. He already knows too much. If he figured out it's me, I have no doubt he would be able to put all of the clues together and see who I really am. I just can't be a monster in his eyes.

> WildMisfit: Guess I need to up my game. What is it that makes you smile?

> CatEyes: Right now? Talking to you.

> WildMisfit: Look at you being smooth ;)

> CatEyes: I'm trying.

I mirror his words, hoping I can help bring him as much joy as he brings me. Even if it can only be like this through messages.

WildMisfit: Well, I'm currently walking around the classroom like a creep, peering over shoulders to see if you're in here. I've officially ruled out this class. That leaves only five other options. One way or another, I'll find you.

CatEyes: In that case, I wish you luck.

WildMisfit: Thanks. I think I need it. Plans this weekend? Luke Aaron's party, perhaps?

CatEyes: I wasn't invited.

I feel like I just got a cold bucket of water dumped over my head. He is going to a party this weekend with high schoolers. *Jesus, Catherine, why are you still talking to him?*

WildMisfit: Consider this your official invitation. Will I see you there?

CatEyes: Parties aren't really my thing. I'm not allowed to go out much.

WildMisfit: Strict parents?

If he only knew.

CatEyes: Something like that.

WildMisfit: You don't know it, but you pretty much just cut my list in half. I'm getting closer to finding out who you are.

CatEyes: Maybe you shouldn't try so hard. You might not like what you find.

Suddenly, the bell rings, startling me. I immediately slam my phone down, face down. Students rush out of the room and I raise my voice, slicing through the chatter and shuffle of feet. "P-practice exams tomorrow. Get some studying in tonight."

It's pointless, no one is listening anyway.

Once the room is empty, I pick my phone up to read the last message from Wilder.

An instant smile cracks my lips. I know I'll never expose who CatEyes really is, but that doesn't mean I can't enjoy the way talking to Wilder makes me feel.

"Mrs. J," I hear Wilder holler from behind me in the parking lot. I know it's him because I'd know his voice anywhere.

I spin around and see him jogging toward me, wearing a sweat-drenched white tee shirt with the sleeves cut off and a pair of gym shorts. Nervously, I adjust the stack of folders I'm carry-ing. "Hey, Wilder." I smile as he closes the space between us.

"Sorry to hold you up, but I wanted to share the news." The excitement on his face is uncanny. His hands fly up, his grin stretching from ear to ear. "My father loved the article."

"Wilder. That's amazing." Instinctively, I throw one of my arms around him while the other smashes the folders against his body. He embraces me in a hug and it feels calming, like I can finally breathe. Even as I inhale the smell of sweat, I can't help but think this is one of the best hugs I have had in a while. There's a safeness in his arms that has me holding on even when I know I should let go.

"I couldn't have done it without you." His voice is a whisper in my ear, a yearning deep inside it. I can't help but want to reach out and reciprocate. I feel his fingers run through my hair and I shiver before immediately letting go and taking a step back, careful to put the folders in my hand in front of me, almost like a shield. I need distance to think around him.

He looks down at the space between us, something shifting

in his demeanor. And when he looks up, surprise has white-washed his excitement.

"Wilder? Is everything okay?"

Time seems to slow down as he stands there staring at me as if he just had an epiphany of sorts. I can't put my finger on it, but something is different.

"Umm…" His fingers draw around his mouth. "Yeah. Every-thing's fine." His smile returns, even bigger than it was seconds ago. "Actually, everything is perfect."

"Good." I run my hand down his arm because I can't help but touch him. "I'm really happy for you. You deserve all the praise you're getting from your father."

His honey brown eyes pierce mine. The tension between us growing heavy. And when I watch his gaze dip to my mouth, I gulp.

Everything I'm feeling inside is wrong on so many levels. My heart shouldn't be pounding like this for him. My hands shouldn't sweat. I shouldn't want to cry and let go of all of the pain inside me. He's my student, and that has to be all he is.

"Mrs. J?" Wilder says softly and I can't tell if it's a question, or if he has something more to say. His eyes meet mine and I try like hell to show him I can't do this. No matter how much I want to, I can't.

When his hand reaches out and his fingers wrap gently around my wrist, I'm certain I'm going to break. But not in the way that will cause me physical pain like Troy brings, I am going to be torn in half by the two sides of my heart that are warring over this being right and wrong.

As his fingers graze my skin, causing a rush of electricity to shoot through me, every nerve ending feels like it's been lit on fire. I gasp, my lips falling open while Wilder pins me with his gaze, intention and determination swirling in the depths.

My chest rises and falls rapidly as we stare longingly at each other. I watch him carefully, the way he's reacting proof that he feels the exact same way I do.

"Wilder," I whisper, knowing I should follow it up with "I should go," but I don't. Instead I stay rooted in place, letting the weight of his name hang between us like a heavy rain cloud ready to burst.

He steps closer, his eyes darting from my mouth to my eyes, and back again.

Moving his hand to my cheek, he strokes his thumb in gentle circles. "What are you doing to me, Mrs. J?"

His question brings me back to reality.

What the hell am I doing?

Wilder is my student.

I'm in a position of authority here. He's eleven years younger than me and hasn't even graduated high school yet.

I jump back, so quickly that I know he senses my anguish. I can feel my heart splitting as I put distance between us. It is so painful that tears fill my eyes.

"Go home, Wilder." My voice trembles as I shake my head. "This moment never happened. It *never* happened. Do you understand?"

His brows pinch and that smile from earlier fades as he comes to terms with what I'm saying. "I understand," he says quietly, but I feel a "but" hanging in the air.

I turn around quickly, my heart in my throat as I fight the urge to look back at him. I can't. I won't.

"Mr. J," he calls out as I open my door. I glance back at him, keeping the door between us.

"Yes, Wilder?"

"Pretending it never happened doesn't change that it did." His voice hits me like a tidal wave and I find myself practically running from it before I allow temptation to draw me back to him.

I get in my car and toss the folders in the passenger seat as my heart threatens to pound out of my chest. They go flying, sending papers all over.

Cursing under my breath, I lift my eyes to the windshield,

only to find Wilder still standing where I left him. His shoulders are slumped in defeat and the scorned look on his face sends an ache to my chest.

If only we'd met at another time, in another place—then maybe. But reality grips us too tightly and the here and now is not meant for us.

CHAPTER 8

WILDER

THE DAY my mom passed away, she requested time alone with each of us boys. I laid beside her on the bed, holding her hand while we laughed and shared memories together. Then when it was time for me to go, she said something I'll never forget. She told me, "Take chances, Wilder, because the one that could change your life might only happen once."

It's her. She's CatEyes. At least, I think she is. After I told her the good news, I looked down momentarily. Her pants were raised up just slightly, but enough for me to see the tattoo on her ankle. A beautiful black dragonfly with the words "still I rise."

I'm not sure how I didn't realize it sooner. Granted, it was only recently that I began talking to CatEyes almost every day.

There was always this feeling in my gut that she wasn't a student. I just never could have imagined that she was right under my nose this entire time.

My instinct was right—Mrs. Jenkins is in trouble. She mentioned that her home life is rough and that her past stops her from leaving. I have to find out what she meant by that. If she's in danger, I have to help her.

She said I might not like what I find when I unveil her identity, but boy was she wrong. Now that I know who she is, everything makes more sense. That pull I feel toward her every time we are in the same room. The way my eyes always seem to find hers. I think I would be devastated if it were anyone else. We have a bond that no one will ever understand. For the first time ever, I think I believe in fate. She may be my teacher, but we both know she has become so much more. These feelings started back when she was helping me with my essay, and they have only grown since. I should have known it was her the day I received a new follower after our chat about social media.

I pay for ads to boost my account, so it is typical that I get a lot of followers at once. However, when I am not running one, my followers stick out more. And I wasn't advertising that day.

I don't know what it was that made me message her the second I saw that dragonfly tattoo, but even then it was like the universe wouldn't allow me to ignore this person.

Mrs. J was helping me find a way to be more authentic when I wrote my letter. I needed to make the administration feel for my situation and not just prove my capability as a student. She asked me how I felt about social media since I spent so much time on there, then she listened as I went into a twenty-minute deep dive of why SnapTok is so important to me.

She never judged me or said that my dreams were pointless or shallow. Instead, Mrs. J looked at me with this smile on her face as if she envied the joy I could find in such a simple task. Then, a few hours later, I had a new follower that I could not help but talk to.

I would force myself to go a day between messages some-times so that she didn't think I was obsessed with her. But I thought about her every day. Except for the moments when I was in class with Mrs. J. That was the only time I didn't find myself fixated and searching for this person. Which should have been another clue.

I get in my car and follow Mrs. J home. She must be flustered because I don't think she notices me at all.

I overheard my dad talking about how Troy Jenkins is

leaving town for a few days to attend the US Conference for Mayors. I know that this is beyond inappropriate, but I just need to see her so I can piece together all these emotions running through me.

I need to settle my nerves and hear her tell me that she's not in any immediate danger and then come up with a plan from there. I'm not a wait-and-see kind of person. That's why I'm going now, only minutes after she tried to tell me what happened in the parking lot didn't happen.

I understood what she meant. She's a teacher. If we were seen by anyone, she could lose her job. Not to mention the scandal it would cause for my father. He asked us all to keep our heads low, so I need to be careful about this.

I feel something for Mr. J, but if I know she will be safe these last few weeks or so of school, I might be able to stay away until I graduate and this is no longer a conflict of interest.

Well, at least it takes away one conflict. She is still married, after all. I need to figure out what her husband is holding over her. She said her home life wasn't the best, so there has to be a reason she stays.

When I pull up to her house, I watch as the garage door slowly closes with her car inside. I pull up behind it and kill the engine, getting out immediately. Since the garage is already closed, and there isn't a side door, I go to the front.

Without hesitation, I ring the doorbell. But I'm surprised when a man's voice comes over the camera facing me.

"Can I help you, young man?"

Fuck. I'm certain he's out of town, probably out of the state by now. He must have gotten an alert on his phone when I pressed the button. That's the only explanation.

Think fast, Wilder.

"Hi, Mayor Jenkins. I umm…I'm so sorry to drop by like this but I desperately need Mrs. Jenkins's help with an assignment from class. We have a test tomorrow and in our study group we realized we forgot to ask about a vital part of symbolism in the text. We don't want to risk our grades and scholarships so I volunteered to come ask in person."

Please believe me. Please believe me.

Static comes through the speaker, followed by the sound of the door opening slowly. I'm met with wide, cautious eyes and I flash her back the same look.

Before I can say anything, Mrs. Jenkins hurries away, leaving the door open as her husband speaks again, and I do my best to pretend that I don't see her there. "This is our private home, Wilder. If you need to speak to my wife, you can do so during school hours. This is highly inappropriate. Leave now before I alert the authorities and have you arrested for trespassing. How do you think your father would feel about that?"

This is the first time he's ever called me by my name. Seems he's starting to pay attention, which is probably a bad thing.

Mrs. Jenkins comes back holding up a small piece of paper while nodding her head to the right. "Under the camera," she mouths the words, but I understand what she's saying.

I reach under the camera where my arm is out of Mayor Jenkins's sight, and I take the note from her.

"Yes, sir," I tell Mr. Jenkins while facing the camera. "You're right. I'll ask her tomorrow before the test."

I blow out a breath as the static cuts off, then tuck the note into my pocket quickly while rushing back to my car.

There is so much I wanted to say to that man, but I need to stay calm until I figure out exactly what is happening.

Drive your car to the guesthouse next door. It's a
separate driveway. No cameras there.

Red flags are flying. Mayor Jenkins is definitely holding something over her head. Something that keeps her under his control. I could see it in her eyes when she opened the door and heard his voice.

This might be worse than I thought. I merely came to check

on her—talk to her. But if my suspicions are right, the last thing I want to do is get her in any trouble.

As I pull my car out of the driveway, I look up at the house, noticing all the cameras attached. I understand being cautious as a political figure, but the amount of cameras installed on this house is a little over the top. So far I've spotted four…five…and now six, all on one side. Is he trying to keep people out, or keep one in, in particular inside?

Taking a sharp turn onto the dirt driveway beside their main house, my hands start to sweat with anxiety. This is a bad idea, but I need to know the truth.

The guesthouse sits back on a small amount of property surrounded by apple blossom trees and an abundance of greenery. Mayor Jenkins used to rent it out in the summers but haven't for the last couple years. As far as I know, nobody lives here.

I'm actually surprised he doesn't have this place wired as well. For such an overprotective man, he sure is dropping the ball here.

I bring my car to a spot directly in front of the house where the driveway ends. It's much smaller than I imagined. Almost like one of those tiny houses people are buying these days.

Instead of getting out at the risk of screwing this up, I wait for Mrs. J. She says there are no cameras here, but after what I just witnessed at the front of the house, I'm not willing to take any chances.

About five minutes later, I see her walking briskly down a trail that connects the two properties. The way she keeps stealing glances over her shoulder reminds me of a teenager sneaking out, not a grown-ass woman who is in charge of her own decisions. Her arms are crossed tightly over the chest of a beige knit turtleneck that she's paired with a pair of gray sweatpants.

It's a strange combination and she wasn't wearing that turtleneck before she opened the door. But I couldn't pay too much attention with her husband watching. Something tells me she chose this outfit with the intent on hiding something from me, which makes me just want to tear it off her and demand to know all her secrets.

Gripping the steering wheel tight, I take a deep breath. *Don't do this Wilder, you're the nice guy.*

Once she's close, I swing my door open and practically jump out. "Is everything okay?" I ask her, genuinely concerned about her nervous state.

She stares at me looking scared and confused. Every cell in my body is telling me to go to her and comfort her, but I'm not sure she would accept that right now.

"Why did you come here, Wilder?" Her voice gives nothing away. I can't tell what she's thinking at all and it drives me insane. She's hiding from me. As if I have the capability of hurting her the same way I suspect her husband does.

"I had to see you," I tell her truthfully. "I know it was dumb but I...I just had to and now I'm glad I did because you look like you could use a friend."

Her hands drop from her chest. "We're not friends, Wilder. I'm your *teacher.*"

Wow. Way to knock me off my fucking horse.

If she only knew what I know—that she is CatEyes—she might be singing a different tune. Her act has to be a show. Either that, or the guilt she's feeling for building a friendship with one of her students is overpowering her desire to talk to me in person. I can't tell her I know yet. I worry she'll run away and shut me out. For now, I need to build her trust.

This word friend keeps coming up, and I think we both know it's total bullshit. She doesn't need a friend; she needs to escape her abusive husband. And I don't want to be her friend. I want to be her savior.

"I'm sorry," she blurts out, defeat marring her features before she looks to the ground, like she often does with her husband. "I don't mean to sound harsh, but for your own good, please don't come back here."

I walk around my car and use my fingers to lift her chin. I

hate when she tries to pull away, but I let her. "Your husband doesn't scare me, if that's what you're worried about."

"Well," she drawls, fixing her eyes on my car. "He should. Troy does not take kindly to people coming on his property. Especially when he's not home."

Instead of moving her head, this time I step into her line of sight, my chest nearly touching hers. "Then why'd you send me over here?" I ask gently as she finally looks at me. "Why not just tell me to go home on that note."

"Because…" She takes a step back, as if she's nervous being this close to me. "Because I was worried you wouldn't go home and it would make things worse."

I quirk a brow. "How can things get worse? Are things bad?" She doesn't know just how much I have seen, but I want to see if she will just tell me herself.

"Why are you doing that?" She shakes her head, her bottom lip trembling in a way that has rage boiling inside me. Not at her, but at the man who made her so afraid.

"Doing what?" I ask, trying to stay calm.

"Acting as if I'm some damsel in distress." She throws her arms out, but I see the tremble in them. "I'm fine, Wilder." By the way her voice shakes and her shoulders slump in on herself, I know it's not true. I can't tell if she wants me to see that or not, but I already know, so this time I push.

"Are you?"

"Yes!" she shouts, throwing her hands in the air again. "Do I not look fine?"

I grab her shoulders and really look at her. The ridiculous outfit, the tears building in her eyes, but most of all the way her expression begs me not to give up. "You look scared."

Her eyes travel to the road, watching a car drive down it slowly. In an instant, she grabs me by the arm, pulling me toward the guesthouse. "We can't talk out here. People will gossip and that's the last thing I need right now."

"Oh?" I chuckle. "But my car sitting in this driveway is invisible so long as we're not standing by it?"

She scoffs. "Just get inside before the whole town begins talking."

Her fingers move quickly as she punches in a code on the door, a code that I see and memorize. Once it beeps, she opens the door and we go inside. Without hesitation, she closes and locks it behind us.

She moves to a small window facing the driveway and bends over to look outside. Her hand is shaking and her breathing is rapid, as if we just ran a marathon. "I think we're good. I don't think anyone saw us."

"So what if they did? We're not doing anything wrong. It's not like we're having an affair." I laugh, but the way she straightens her back and her eyes widen leads me to believe that's what she's worried people will think. "Is that what you're worried about? People thinking you and I are sleeping together?"

"No," she stammers. "Not at all. You're my student, Wilder. Why would anyone think that?"

I shrug my shoulders. "Then what's the big deal?"

"This." Her hands glide between us. "Us together. Talking outside of school. It's extremely unprofessional."

"Us?"

She tries to brush off the comment, waving her hand in the air. "You know what I mean."

I step closer to her, watching as her breath hitches. "No, I don't. Care to elaborate?"

"Bad choice of words. I just mean—"

My hand presses to her chest, right over her heart. "You feel it, too, don't you?"

"F-feel what?"

"This thing between us." My forehead drops to hers and I inhale her lavender scent. "The way the world stops spinning when we're in the same room. How our eyes always find their way to one another."

She shakes her head and separates us, averting her gaze. "You're delusional. I-I don't feel any of those things. I'm your teacher. I can't."

"You keep saying that." I take another step toward her so that nothing separates us now. "But why am I here?"

Her shoulders lift, caging in her neck. "You tell me."

"I wanted to see you." I stand tall, my hand falling to her cheek and stroking it gently.

"Well, here I am. You can go now." The way she leans into my touch reminds me of a cat, and it makes me smile. My beautiful CatEyes.

"Is that what you want?" I question after a moment of just touching her. It's the first time she's really allowing it and I want to stay in this moment forever.

There's a beat of silence between us and it's all I need to reaffirm what I believe. She does feel it.

"Of course it is. Troy is going to wonder where I am when he checks the cameras. I need to get home."

"Then go." Another step closer and our chests touch. I look down at her, she's so petite and fragile. The thought of anyone hurting her has my fists clenching.

"I am." But she melts into me more, as if she needs someone gentle to remind her of who she is.

The corner of my mouth lifts. "You're not moving."

"You go first." Her eyes drift shut before she pushes back, creating space between us.

"Fine," I say, before stepping into her and not giving her a choice. I need one more hit of her scent, one more moment where the heat of her imbeds itself in me and brings me to life. I look down at her mouth, temptation eating away at me. I wanna kiss her so fucking bad.

But when I put my hand against the wall behind her, she steps in the opposite direction, away from me.

Her hands fly to her cheeks as she angles her body away from me. It's obvious she's ashamed, or maybe embarrassed about what almost happened. But I'm not, and I don't regret it.

"This can't happen." She covers her face as if she is about to cry. "I'm so sorry, Wilder."

I rush to her side, pulling her hands down and forcing her tearstained eyes to look at me. "Don't be sorry."

"But I'm your teacher…"

"Stop saying that." I pull her into a hug before looking down at her. "Yes, you *are* my teacher, but you're so much more than that."

She shakes her head, likely disappointed in herself, which kills me. "I'm an idiot is what I am."

"Hey." I squeeze her closer, making sure she feels this moment when our hearts beat in sync. "You're not an idiot. You're smart, compassionate, beautiful…" I step back with one of her hands in mine as I look her body up and down, biting my bottom lip. "And sexy as hell."

Her features soften. "That's sweet of you to say, Wilder. But you're forgetting, I'm also a married woman."

I quirk a brow. "Happily married?" I'd bet my life the answer is no, even if she won't admit it to me.

"It's complicated. But I'm married nonetheless."

I pull her hand and spin her body so that her back presses against the wall. The air whooshes out of her, making me smile as my hands move to her waist, and I say, "Then tell me to leave and never come back."

CHAPTER 9
CATHERINE

THE WORDS LINGER on the tip of my tongue. I know exactly what I need to do, but need and want are two different things that come down to self-control.

I've been at war with myself my entire life, making choices that will always please others. For once, I *want* to do something for myself. Something that fills this void in my heart and satisfies the deep hunger for another man's gentle touch—*Wilder's touch.*

I'm drawn to him. I won't deny it—at least, not to myself. I can't explain the emotions I feel when we're together. I have no doubt fate brought us together for more than just a lesson in literature, or help with an essay and an article.

Whatever this is between us is bigger than either of us could have ever imagined. It sounds crazy—hell, it feels crazy—but my gut tells me not to let him go. At least, not yet.

"Don't go," I whisper with bated breath. No regrets, no turning back. I want him to stay. "Just give me a couple minutes. Make yourself comfortable, and I'll be back."

He sucks his bottom lip between his teeth and my stomach does a somersault. "I'll wait as long as you want me to," he says, with a sweep of his fingers across my cheek. "But I need you to know, I didn't come here to make this something more, or less, than what it is. I just want to spend time with you. Even if that means just drinking coffee and talking."

I quirk a brow. "You drink coffee?"

"Of course I drink coffee. Doesn't everyone?" He gives me this stunned look, as if it is normal for a high schooler to require caffeine to wake up in the mornings. A high schooler who has the energy to play a sport that requires you to work out twice a day.

I laugh. "I guess so. But you're only eighteen." I stop myself from saying any more, like how I'd take him to be a hot chocolate kind of person and how I didn't drink coffee until I was in my twenties.

Part of me wants to overthink this again. Wilder is only *eighteen*. He's so mature, though, and thoughtful, and tender. He's more of a man than most men I know. *And* apparently he drinks coffee.

"You're right. I am only eighteen, but I'll be nineteen in July."

"Oh really? My birthday is in July, too. I'll be..." I let my words trail off, not wanting to divulge my age because it makes this situation feel all the more wrong. Once again, I won't go there. I refuse to overthink this. Like Wilder said, this doesn't have to be anything more or less than what it is. We're friends. There is nothing wrong with that.

"You'll be thirty," he finishes for me. "On July third. And I'll be nineteen on July sixth. Age is just a number, Mrs. J. It doesn't have to be complicated."

I'm actually surprised he even knows my birthday. I must have mentioned it in class at one time. It makes my heart beat a little faster knowing he remembered that.

I look down, shaking my head while smiling, before lifting my eyes to his. "Who the hell are you and what planet did you come from?"

He extends his hand and I lay mine in it. "Wilder Christian Cromwell," he says confidently. "I have no idea who I am because I'm still trying to figure that out myself. I'm from Willow Creek, Colorado, and I'll probably live here for the rest of my life. I enjoy the simple things in life and I've found that second-guessing myself is a waste of time."

I bite back a smile. "It's nice to meet you Wilder. I'm Catherine Ann Jenkins, also from Willow Creek, and I have baggage that I'd like to throw in a dumpster and start on fire."

"Catherine," he says softly. "I like it. You look like a Catherine."

I make a gagging sound. "I hate it. I wish my parents would have named me something cool, like Annabelle or Victoria."

"Nah." He shakes his head. "Catherine is perfect."

There's a beat of silence and each passing second has my heart racing more and more, until I finally break it.

I shoot a thumb over my shoulder. "I just need to check in with Troy, then I'll be back."

He nods. "Okay. I'll be here…Catherine."

I instantly feel my cheeks flush with heat at the sound of my name coming off his tongue. But I shake my head because it doesn't sound quite right.

"No?" he says with a smirk. "Okay, how about…" He taps a finger on his chin, looking up as if to think. "Cat."

I swallow hard thinking about my social media name. Does he know? Is that what this is? It can't be. There is no way.

I shrug off the thought and giggle over the nickname I really like. Maybe a little too much. "Catherine is fine."

I move toward the door, pausing to give him one last look before I go out, and he says, "See you soon, Cat."

I push out of the door with a smile on my face and instantly duck my head. The rain has started to come down again, so as soon as I get inside, I go to the bathroom and put a towel over my head. Then I secure a robe around my waist and go to the couch with my phone in hand.

After a quick video call to Troy, I tell him I'm not feeling well and I'm going to lie in bed and read before going to sleep. Fortunately, our bedroom is one of the few places there are no cameras, the bathroom included. He asks about Wilder at the door and I tell him I must have been in the shower when the bell rang.

Thankfully, he seems to buy the story and is actually sweet when we talk. I know it isn't real, that he's just being nice because he's far away and is worried I will run while he is out of town. It's one of the reasons I like his work trips.

I have thought about running when he leaves, but I know there is a tracker on my phone and car, and even if I managed to find and disable both of them, I would not put it past him to have hidden one inside my body or something absurd and obsessive like that.

Once the call is ended, I sneak beneath the cameras and take off my robe and the towel on my head. Leaving my phone on the kitchen counter, I go out the back door with a bag of coffee, creamer, donuts, and a huge-ass smile on my face.

Just friends, I remind myself. There is nothing wrong with spending an evening with a friend. It doesn't matter how old he is, or that he's my student. We're both consenting adults who are just *hanging out.*

I can't deny the excitement rippling through me. It's been a very long time since I've had a relaxed, normal night with another person that wasn't my abusive husband. Hell, no night is relaxed or normal with him.

When I get back to the guesthouse, the scent of coffee floods my senses before I'm even inside. "Wilder," I call out as I close the door behind me. My nostrils flare as I inhale a deep breath. "Did you make coffee?"

His head pokes around the corner from the kitchen, a grin firmly in place. "Sure did."

I like that he's making himself comfortable. It eases the awkward tension in a weird sort of way.

I hold up my hand showing him the creamer I brought. "Great minds think alike, but don't drink that."

"The coffee?"

I nod. "There's no saying how long it's been in there. For your own health and safety, just dump it."

Wilder pulls the carafe out from under the drip spout and holds it up to his nose. "Smells good."

I walk into the kitchen and set everything I brought over onto the counter before taking the carafe from him. "All coffee always smells good, but I can guarantee it's as stale as those open crackers on the counter."

He looks at the crackers before grabbing them. His eyebrows waggle as he pulls a saltine out of the pack. "These crackers?"

"Don't do it," I warn him as he brings it to his mouth, smirking.

Then he pops it in his mouth and his smile immediately shifts to a disgusted look as he chews.

I can't help the laughter that spews out of me as I watch him try and chew, what is probably, a year-old cracker.

"Dump it," he tells me as he swallows down what's in his mouth. "If it tastes anything like this, it will ruin coffee for me for the rest of my life."

"Always a rebel." I sigh jokingly as I pour the coffee down the drain.

It seems he's got his bearings back as he sweeps some crumbs from his lips and picks up the creamer I brought over. "Donuts and French vanilla." He winks. "My kinda girl."

A warm sensation spreads through my body and I literally feel like I could melt into a puddle on this floor.

After giving the carafe a good rinse, I put it back under the spout and pour some grounds over the filter. Moving through the kitchen, I get two coffee mugs out of the cupboard, immediately noticing freshly-stained coffee in the bottom of both of them. It's odd, considering no one has stayed here in a while, but I'm sure it's older than it appears.

I put them in the sink and scrub them vigorously. Suds foam around my hands before I put them under the cold running water because it takes forever to get hot. My nose curls when the musky scent of stale water rises from the drain. It's a reminder that this place has been vacant for quite a while. It's not in bad shape by any means, but it's very outdated and could use a little modern touch, as well as some life inside it.

"Need a hand?" Wilder asks from behind me and I jolt at the sound of his voice. I turn my head slightly to steal a glance and find him looking down into the sink. He's so close I swear I feel his heartbeat against my back. "They look pretty clean to me." Chills run down my body when I feel the warmth of his hot breath roll down my neck.

My shoulders draw back, body tensing as I shake the excess water from the mugs. "Clean enough," I tell him.

I spin around and realize just how close he is when our noses nearly brush. Hands held out with the mugs, I raise my brows. "Shall we?"

He stands there, watching me, and my heart starts racing again as I wonder if he's going to kiss me. I'm not sure why I keep thinking that. He hasn't kissed me yet and he probably has no intentions of kissing me in the future.

God, I wish I would stop thinking like this. Wilder probably has no interest at all in me in that way. Sure, he's flirtatious and he has a way of making me feel special, but I'm old to guys his age. He's probably just being nice.

Eyes on mine, he reaches out and grabs both mugs before lowering them to his side. "Allow me."

Even those two simple words make my insides quiver. It's not just the words, it's his gruff voice and the way he looks at me. No one has ever looked at me the way Wilder does.

I need to get the hell out of my head. This is ridiculous.

I step back and hop onto the counter to sit while I watch him pour two cups of coffee.

"So," I say with a smile. "Are you half coffee and half creamer, or mostly coffee with a little creamer?"

"Let's just say I like coffee *in* my creamer."

My face twists and I stick my tongue out. "Gross."

"Hey now. Don't yuck my yum until you've tried it." He raises a brow but I shake my head at him.

"One teaspoon of creamer for me, please."

"Oh, come on. Just give it a try." He looks back and winks at me, making me bite my lip.

"That's way too much sugar," I practically yell, wanting to cover my eyes at the way he is ruining the precious drink from the gods right before my eyes.

"Ah," he snickers. "So you're a health nut?"

"No. Not really," I tell him truthfully. "I just don't overindulge unless it's a special occasion. Like a wedding with cake, or a walk on the beach with ice cream."

He raises the spoon, putting it in his mouth before licking it slowly. I watch every movement with rapt attention. "Well, since this is our first time having coffee together, it's a special occasion. In that case, I need you to trust me."

I sputter a laugh. "What's trust have to do with coffee?"

His eyes go wide but a smile plays on his lips. "When it comes to the most important meal of the day, everything."

"The most important meal of the day?" I chuckle. "I love coffee, but I wouldn't go that far."

"Well, it taught me how much I can trust you." He points to the very expired coffee he tried to make us before. "Had I drunk the coffee I made, I might be dead right now."

I laugh at the seriousness of his tone. "That's a little dramatic, especially considering you *did* eat that old-ass cracker."

"Mrs. J," he chuckles along with me. "Did you just swear?"

Shit. I did. I just swore in front of a student. I've never done that before. But Wilder doesn't feel like a student right now, and come next week, he won't be anymore.

"What can I say, I'm human." I shrug, trying not to read too much into the situation and end up forcing myself to run out of here.

He glances over his shoulder as he continues mixing our

coffee. "I just never took you as someone who would use curse words. You're so…perfect."

I laugh because it's hilarious that he thinks that. "No one is perfect, Wilder. Especially not me."

He takes a step toward me and taps my nose. "Well, if I had to pick the one person in my life who is closest to perfection, it would be you."

He turns back to the mugs and I let the facade on my face fall for just a moment because it's too hard to smile right now.

Wilder's words should make me feel joy, knowing he thinks so highly of me, but instead, all I feel is immense guilt. I'm not who he thinks I am. It's not even my past that I hate myself for; it's my present. It's what I allow myself to endure without a fight. I could fight Troy. Many times I have thought about shooting him with the gun I bought.

I have it all planned out in my head. I would let him hurt me enough in an area where he has cameras and make sure they were recording, then I would run to our room and just shoot him. I know I would get away with it. With him dead, he couldn't manipulate the system anymore and my secret would stay safe forever.

But I don't. I fall down and let him continue to kick me until he's had enough. I bow, I crawl, and I fucking obey. I am not perfect. Nothing about me is.

Right now, though, I have to put on a front. The same front I put on every day of my fucking life. For some reason, it hurts to do it with Wilder, but I have to. If he knew the truth, he would try to save me and that will only end with him getting hurt.

"You're sweet, Wilder. But don't ever let images fool you. What you see is not always what you get."

Wilder spins around and hands me a cup of coffee before taking a sip of his own. He nods at the coffee in my hand, gesturing for me to take a sip, so I do. It's not terrible, but it's nothing special either. Just a whole lot of creamer in a small amount of coffee. Wilder is pretty proud of what he made me, so I'll play along. Besides, it's caffeine, so I'll take it.

"And for the best part." He reaches into the donut box and pulls out a powdered donut hole before handing it to me.

I snicker as I go to take a bite, but he stops me.

"Whoa, whoa, whoa." He grabs another donut then dunks it right into his coffee. "You're doing it all wrong. You gotta soak the donut *then* eat it."

"Is that so?" I tilt my head to the side, unaware there are rules about how to enjoy a donut and coffee.

"Yup." He says it so matter-of-factly I can't help the grin that spreads across my face. "Go ahead and give it a try."

Watching him, I dip a small part of the donut in my coffee then bring it to my mouth. The sweet sugar coats my lips as I bite off a piece. It falls apart on my tongue like cotton candy, but the bitterness of the coffee is still there. He was right, it *is* good.

Chewing, I nod. "This is amazing."

"Right?" He pops the rest of his donut hole in his mouth. "It's two treats in one."

I bring my cup to my mouth, the savory scent of coffee and vanilla filling my nostrils and immediately offering me a sense of peace. It's strange how smells and sounds can do that. The bittersweet taste hits my lips, spreading warmth through my body. I raise my brows at Wilder, a smile forming on my lips before I take another sip.

"How's the coffee?" he asks.

"Sweet. Very sweet," I say, almost in a whisper. Just like him.

Holding his cup with two hands, he lowers it in front of his chest. "So," he begins. "I have to agree with what you said, what you see is not always what you get, but I want to know what people get with you."

I tilt my head in confusion. "What do you mean?"

"Play a game with me. If you came with a warning label, what would it say?"

"Oh boy." I turn around and set my coffee down before

chewing relentlessly on my bottom lip. "Honestly," I say. "I think it would be read something along the lines of...*run*. Don't look back. Just keep running."

It's painful to admit that, but it's the most honest thing I've said in a very long time. My fingers grip the edge of the counter so tight they are almost numb in just a few seconds. I should come with a warning label. It would help keep everyone at a safe distance.

"Oh, come on, Cat." Wilder puts a hand on my upper arm and I roll my shoulders inward, eyes closing momentarily. I don't dislike the way he calls me Cat. I should, but I like it better than Mrs. Jenkins or Mrs. J. Those titles come with the reminder that I'm an authoritative figure to Wilder, and also that I carry the last name of a monstrous man.

When I don't respond, he begins to rub his thumb in small circles. "You're too hard on yourself. Whatever it is you think people need to run from, might very well be the reason they gravitate toward you."

I look up slowly and his hand gently falls to his side. Taking the focus off myself because it's too uncomfortable, I move it to him. "What would your warning label say?"

"Puts on a good show while hiding his own inner turmoil." He exhales heavily before continuing. "Walks the straight and narrow and pleases everyone else before himself."

"Wilder," I say softly as I rest my hand on his shoulder. I don't know what to say because we share that same toxic trait. We are people pleasers before our own wants and comforts. I can attempt to give him advice, but that would only make me a hypocrite.

Instead, I just ask another question. "What sort of inner turmoil are you talking about? Is everything okay?"

"Yeah," he says with an upbeat tone. "Yeah. I'm okay. It's just tough, I guess. You know how it is. You've been there. Graduating and feeling like you need to have it all figured out."

I nod in response because I remember exactly how that felt.

The thing is, he's wrong and I was too. "I get it. But you don't have to have it all figured out, and those who do probably won't five years from now. All I can say is, follow your heart and it will lead you where you're meant to be."

"Is that what you did?"

I lower my hand, averting my gaze. "No. I'm one of those few who thought they knew what they wanted and years later they are exactly where they never imagined ending up." I swallow the lump forming in my throat as I whisper, "Not in a good way."

"You're unhappy, aren't you?" I can't see his face, but I can feel his eyes boring into my soul. I get this feeling he knows more than he's letting on, and I just don't know what to say anymore. He keeps pushing and pushing and I can only build these walls around me so fast.

I gulp. "I'm…okay, I guess."

He doesn't say anything. Just takes a step back and sips on his coffee. I can still smell him from here. He smells so good. Woodsy—like musk, pine, and earth.

"Enough of this." I raise my voice to a more chipper note as I hop off the counter. "No sulking. Only positivity for the rest of the day."

He holds his mug out. "I'll cheers to that."

I clank mine against his, feeling a little more at ease.

"We can sit in the living room," I tell him, wondering if that sounds too forward or if it's weird to have coffee in the living room with your teacher. "I mean, if you want?"

"Works for me." Without hesitation, he heads there. This is a tiny house so it is only a few steps, but I really enjoy seeing him comfortable enough to move around in this space.

I follow behind him into the small living room, and he takes a seat on one end of the brown floral-printed couch that I'm pretty sure is from the early 90s. I sit on the opposite end, curling my feet into a pretzel as I turn to face him.

Wilder sets his coffee down on the table in front of the couch, then leans back, eyes narrowed at me as he clears his throat. "Can I ask you a question?"

I raise my brows. "Sure. I guess. If I know you like I am beginning to, you're going to ask anyway."

He doesn't miss a beat as he chuckles, then his voice becomes serious. "Why do you always wear turtlenecks?"

I nearly choke on my coffee. I wasn't expecting that. "They're comfortable," I lie, wondering if it would be safe now to wear a normal shirt. The bruises were nearly gone yesterday, but I didn't want to risk anyone seeing the remnants of them.

Wilder nods at my response, but there's something about his demeanor that tells me he isn't buying it. I have no doubt Wilder has grown suspicious of Troy after that evening last year, but he's never expressed any concern other than asking me how I'm doing. In which, I've always told him I'm fine.

I am fine. I'm not dying. I'm healthy. I'm strong. It's not like Troy would ever kill me, or seriously injure me. He just gets angry and I become his punching bag. It'll get better once the election is over.

Changing the subject, I, once again, move the focus to him. "Any new jobs from your dad?"

"Not yet but he mentioned something big next week. Some speech he plans to give at the school board meeting." He shakes his head. "I'm still not sure about this. I don't even know why he asked me to take on a task that's so important."

I sip on my coffee as he talks, and suddenly the mood begins to feel lighter—relaxing, even.

"I am." I shrug my shoulders. "I know you can do this. Your dad asked you because he knows you can too."

"I guess," he says dispassionately. "I mean, it's only a few speeches and some articles. It'll be over after the election."

"You'll do great. I believe in you, Wilder."

His head cranks to the left, facing me. "Thank you for believing in me."

My lips press into a tight smile. "Of course."

Wilder and I spend the next hour talking about life outside of school and politics. Then, when the conversation takes a turn and he asks about my family, my skin gets clammy and my heart starts racing.

"I don't talk to my family anymore," I tell him. "There was no big fall out or anything that could have been done differently, we just live separate lives."

It hurts to say that out loud, but it's true. I don't hate my parents and being an only child, I don't have siblings to rival with. Life just turned us in separate directions and we all kept moving on without looking back. Now, so much time has passed, I don't even know who my parents are anymore and I don't care to know them either.

"I'm sorry to hear that," he says with a look of pity on his face. I don't want that. I don't want his pity or anyone else's. I'm alive and I'm healthy and that's more than I can say for a lot of people who have been through what I've been through.

"Don't be." My voice is tight. "It just is what it is."

"You're right," he says. "The past is what it is, but the future can be something else. Only you have the power to make sure it's more than what it once was."

I think about what he said for a minute, seeing the truth in his words. "So deep," I tell him. "How is it possible that you're only eighteen years old and yet you speak like that?"

He chuckles as he grabs his coffee. "I just think too much. That's what my brother tells me anyway. He's always telling me to get me out of my head. He jokes that I look as if I am trying to solve the world's problems with a simple answer."

That sounds like Rome, always dismissive and never deep. I don't understand how he and Wilder are twins any more than I can comprehend a tomato being a fruit. "So tell me then, when you're not dissecting life, what goes through that head of yours?"

He lifts a brow. "You want the truth?"

"I'd rather hear the truth than a lie. So yeah, tell me."

"All right then." He takes a more serious note. "It's you."

My heart does a little flip-flop. "Me?"

"Yeah," he says. "Lately, you're all I think about."

His words warm my heart in a way I can't explain. I've never experienced a sort of comfort and safety like this with another person. He's saying everything I've always wanted someone to say to me. There's this ache inside me that tells me to quit pushing him away—to stop fighting this. But my brain is at constant war with my heart. I don't want him to get hurt, but I can't seem to let him go either.

"I'm sorry," he says as he gets to his feet. "I shouldn't put you in this position. I know it's uncomfortable for you."

He goes to step forward, but I stop him by grabbing his hand. "Don't go."

Curious eyes look down on me as I hold on to him, reveling in the way his soft hand feels against mine. "I think about you a lot, too."

There. I said it and I can't take it back.

Wilder pulls me up from the couch, my heart literally ready to flee from my body. I exhale rapidly through my nose, anxiously awaiting his response.

A wide grin spreads across his face. "You do?"

I nod, biting back a smile. "More than I probably should."

His arm wraps around me and he touches my forehead to his as he closes his eyes. "You have no idea how happy I am to hear that. I wasn't sure if I was imagining whatever this thing is between us."

It's hard being vulnerable and it's especially difficult putting yourself out there for someone you know is off-limits. But is Wilder really off-limits when no one has to know? I like who I am with him and I can't help the way he makes me feel.

In a moment of honesty, I say, "I thought maybe I was imagining it, too."

There's a small part of me that's wondering if I'm *still* imagining things. He says he thinks about me, but in what way? The same way he thinks about his friends and family, or someone he has a romantic interest in? Do I give him the same giddy feelings that he's been giving me? Or am I totally delusional and Wilder is just a student who is worried about his teacher?

Here I am overthinking again. Like Wilder said, this doesn't have to be complicated. Maybe I need to stop making it complicated and just see what happens next instead of trying to plan fifteen steps ahead like I do with Troy. I don't even know why I try anymore.

Wilder slides down on the couch, pulling me with him and leaving only a scant space between us. "I think we both know this is real," he says, voice gruff and masculine in a way that has a rush of heat shooting through me. In a slow, deliberate movement he puts his hand on my thigh, just above my knee.

I watch his strong grip, one that makes me feel small, as he caresses me with his fingertips. I feel every stroke. Even with the barrier of my sweatpants, his touch is more real than anything I've ever felt.

Not holding back, I give in to the feelings coursing through me and I put my hand over his. "Yeah," I tell him with a slight nod. With that one word, the door to unknown possibilities opens for us. A heavy weight leaves my shoulders, all my fears and anxieties parting ways because it's right now that I realize, I don't want to fight this any longer.

"I like you, Cat," Wilder says with a grin playing on his lips as he averts his gaze. "I like you a lot and I know you're married and I'm your student, but I can't stay away. You're all I think about anymore."

His words are everything I wanted and everything I feared wrapped with a shiny bow. Knowing I'm on someone's mind, keeping them awake and distracting them from other thoughts. I always wanted to be in someone's thoughts and heart at the same time. Not in an obsessive or possessive way like Troy's, but in an endearing and thoughtful way like Wilder's.

"So what now?" I ask him. "I mean, it's not like this can ever go anywhere." It hurts to say that out loud but we both know it's true. And the two of us probably need a healthy dose of reality right now.

His honey brown eyes fix on mine and he reaches out, tucking a stray strand of hair behind my ear. "I think living in the moment is a pretty good start. No plans. No expectations. Just you and me, here and now."

Brushing his fingers against my cheek, he cradles it in his palm and I lean into him, relaxing against his touch.

"Okay," I whisper in agreement. "I like that plan."

More than anything I want to throw myself onto his lap and have him hold me like there is no tomorrow. The desperation to feel his strong arms around me is agonizing.

Then, as if he's read my mind, he wraps an arm around me and pulls me close. My face nuzzles against his chest and I curl my legs up onto his lap. It's safe here. I feel untouchable, unbreakable.

I close my eyes, relishing the warmth running through my body. If I could pick a perfect moment in time, it would be this one.

We sit like this for a few minutes, and small talk turns those minutes into hours. Wilder tells me how he got started on his SnapTok account just over a year ago, and the urge to tell him about my account hangs heavy on my mind. I'll tell him eventually, just not yet.

Our coffees turn cold and the clock keeps ticking, but neither of us get up, we just sit here sharing stories and getting to know one another.

Wilder talks about how he lost his mom his sophomore year of high school, and the pain in his voice when he speaks about it slices through me. I literally feel it for him. I've grieved the loss of my parents, but they're still alive so it's nowhere near the same thing.

The next thing I know, a sliver of daylight is cracking through the blinds. My body jolts upward at the sight, eyes wide. "Oh no!" I clap a hand over my mouth in a panic. "I have to go home."

Wilder moves forward on the couch as I stand up. "Whoa," he says calmly, taking my hand in his. "It's okay. So we're gonna be a little tired today. It was worth it."

He doesn't understand and now is not the time to try and make him understand. "I need to get home right now. I'll see you in class, okay?"

I walk toward the door, leaving everything as it is because if I'm not in that house within the next ten minutes, Troy is going to know something's up, but Wilder stops me. With his hand on my wrist, he pulls me back and spins me around to face him. I look up, finding serenity in his eyes.

"I liked this," he says with a subtle grin that reveals his deep dimples. "We should do it again sometime."

Biting the corner of my lip, I nod in response because I one hundred percent want to do this again, but next time I have to be smarter.

Wilder leans down and my heart jumps into my throat, but just when I think his lips are going to land on mine, they move to my cheek in a chaste kiss. "Have a good morning, Kitty Cat," he mutters, letting his mouth ghost my skin before taking a step back.

"Kitty Cat, huh?" I giggle. "That's new."

His face nuzzles into the crease of my neck and he squeezes my body tightly against his. "Came up with it all on my own," he jokes. "What'd ya think?"

Suppressing a smile, I press my lips together tightly, feeling a swarm of butterflies in my stomach. "At this point, I think you can call me whatever you want and I'll respond."

Straightening his back, he lets his hands linger on my hips. "In that case, let me call you mine."

Jaw meet floor! Did he really just say that? We both know that's not an option, but I'll play along. "You said living in the moment is a good start, right?" He nods and I continue. "So at this moment, sure. Why not?"

A smile spreads across his face. "Until next time, Kitty Cat." His lips press to my forehead, then before I can even catch my breath, he's out the door.

Pressing a hand to the frame, I hold myself up because my knees feel weak and my head feels dizzy. This is absolutely insane, but I've never claimed to be levelheaded. The past ten years of my life are proof of that.

Once Wilder is out of the driveway, I haul ass down the trail to my house, leaving everything in the guesthouse as it is. I have plenty of time to clean up before Troy comes home.

I'm going to be dead-ass tired today, but I'd do it again a thousand times over to feel what I feel right now. Now I need coffee. Lots and lots of coffee. And to put on a show for the cameras so that my husband believes I was in our bed all night and not in the arms of another man.

CHAPTER 10

WILDER

I LOOK up from my phone and watch Cat reach for hers, confirming my suspicion. What surprises me is the smile that instantly grows on her face.

Her head is down, her long sleek hair cascading around her face as she taps into her phone. As always, she looks stunning. She's not wearing a turtleneck today, and I'm positive it's because her jackass husband hasn't been around to beat on her. The last marks he left must've faded and she's able to wear what she wants to wear. Today it's a long black dress that matches the color of her hair. She even wore lipstick today, which is new. Maybe Mayor Jackass doesn't allow her to wear it. Wouldn't surprise me. He's going to rue the day my suspicions are confirmed.

I keep watching her, taking in the most beautiful thing about her—the sheer happiness on her face. She's glowing. If she could just find the courage to leave her husband, I believe she'd have this same zest for life every single day. Yet, for some reason, she stays. I'm just not sure why…yet.

CatEyes: One of the best days I've had in a
very long time.

Her words make me smile and I can't help but wonder if it has anything to do with last night, or this morning.

WildMisfit: It's still so early. What's got you in
such a good mood?

I lift my head again, expecting to find her typing into her phone, but instead, I catch her watching me. Does she know I know? I doubt it, but she will soon.

Her head drops again, her fingers gliding over the screen of her phone before another message comes through.

CatEyes: Have you ever had someone come
into your life and rearrange it in the best way
possible?

She has to be talking about me, about us.

WildMisfit: I have, in fact. Tell me more about
this person.

I might be fishing here. *No…*I'm definitely fishing. This is my chance to find out exactly how she feels about me.

CatEyes: It's someone I shouldn't want to
spend time with, but I find myself looking
forward to the next time I'll see them. They are
just easy to talk to. For the first time in a while, I
was able to let my guard down and be myself.

An instant smile grows on my face because I know exactly what she means—I feel it, too. I love everything I learned about her and how close we got in just one night. It was like our souls were twin flames coming together.

> WildMisfit: Sounds special. I bet this person feels the exact same way. Care to tell me who it is?

> CatEyes: Not a chance.

I see her smirking as she clicks around on her computer now, feeling like she's getting away with playing this little game. I love it, but I also don't want to lie to her. It's taken a while to get to where we are and her trust in me is still growing.

> WildMisfit: Can I guess?

> CatEyes: You're welcome to try. Doesn't mean I'll tell you.

And here it goes. No going back now.

> WildMisfit: Can you see this person right now?

As she lifts her head, our gazes lock and a jolt of recognition passes between us. This time, I don't look away as I type back to her. Flashing her a wink when I lift my phone slightly, I feel a sense of relief flood through me as her secret identity is revealed.

It's out there now. Cat has been caught.

Suddenly, her eyes go wide and a deep blush fills her cheeks. She looks away in an instant and it's the reaction I suspected. In an attempt to ease her humiliation, I send her one more message.

> WildMisfit: Can I see you again tonight?

Her nostrils flare and she tucks her hair behind her ears nervously just before the bell rings. She lurches at the sound, chest rising and falling rapidly. I don't want to make her anxious, but I crave to spend every moment possible with her.

Without even dismissing the class, she stands up, frazzled as her hands smooth down her dress, and she paces small steps in the front of the room.

I don't get up, I just sit here waiting for everyone to exit so we can talk.

Elodie stops in the doorway before leaving, her cautious gaze moving from Mrs. Jenkins to me. Eyes frozen on mine, she shakes her head in a small movement, expressing her disapproval. It sort of pisses me off because I've never once passed judgment on her dating Rome—my twin and her stepbrother. In fact, I helped them work their shit out.

Mrs. Jenkins, noticing her suspicious glances, turns to face the window. I'm certain it's because she can't look Elodie in the eye. But the minute Elodie is out the door, she's walking steadfastly toward it. In a swift motion, she closes it and clicks the lock.

Still facing the door, her chin drops to her chest. "How long have you known?" she says quietly, but loud enough for me to hear.

In two seconds flat, I'm at her side, palm pressed to the door she's still in front of. My body molds with hers as her scent floods my senses. "Does it matter?" I whisper in her ear, letting my breath fan over her neck.

A puff of air escapes her. "Does it matter?" She turns to face me, the look on her face not one I was expecting. This is a good thing. This is a moment of clarity. Why is she pissed?

"Do you know how humiliating this is?" Tears well in her eyes as she throws her arms out wide and I take a step back even though I want more than anything to pull her close and wrap my arms around her. "You should have told me you knew. Instead, you just kept on pretending you had no idea who CatEyes was."

I shake my head, slightly pissed off that she would think I would keep this a secret for long. The only reason I did it in the first place was because I needed to know how she felt in case this scared her off. "I did tell you. Just now."

She looks away again, swallowing hard. "You should have

told me right away, or at the very latest, last night." She wipes at her cheeks then faces me. "So how long have you known?"

"Hardly a full day. It's not a big deal, Cat. You don't have to be embarrassed." I reach for her arm but she steps back, eyes darting around the room nervously.

"No!" she blurts out. "You can't touch me. We can't talk anymore. This has to end." My heart cracks in my chest as confusion fills me. Why is she doing this again?

"This doesn't have to be complicated. I like talking to you and you like talking to me, right?"

"Yes. I mean, no." She pulls at her hair as she begins to pace in front of me. "It doesn't matter what I like. If we keep going like this, we'll hurt not only ourselves but so many other people. I'm doing this for you, Wilder. To protect you."

I scoff. She's doing this because she's scared. "I don't need, nor want, your protection." I chuckle, but there is no humor in the sound. "Besides, we're just talking, Cat."

"Don't call me that," she says softly. "It's Mrs. Jenkins. Not Cat. Not Mrs. J. *Only* Mrs. Jenkins."

I shake my head as pain slices through me. "Why are you doing this?"

She looks into my eyes and for the first time, I literally feel the pain I see. "You don't know what he's capable of."

A single tear trails down her cheek and I reach out to gently brush it away with my thumb, feeling the dampness and warmth of her skin.

Then she breaks down and I throw my arms around her, pulling her body close to mine. "You don't have to face this alone. Let me be there for you."

She takes a deep breath, breathing me in as I remind her that she is safe here. I will keep her safe. "I'm scared. Not just for myself. For you too."

Those words speak volumes. It's the revelation I needed to keep bringing her walls down. I was right all along. Cat's in danger and she needs me just as much as I need her. No matter how much distance she tries to put between us, there's this undeniable pull I can't seem to shake.

"I've got you," I tell her as my fingers run through her hair. "I need to see you again. Assuming you want to see me, too?" It's a question more than a statement because I don't want to pressure her, but every second we're apart feels like too long.

She lifts her head from my shoulder, our eyes beaming into one another's as she nods. "I do."

The corner of my mouth tugs up and I lean down to brush a kiss over her forehead, rewarding her for her honesty. "Name the time and place and I'll be there."

She closes her eyes when I pull back, then looks up at me the same way she did last night. No longer with fear, but that joy I love seeing inside her. "Eight o'clock at the guesthouse. Not a minute sooner."

"You got it." I go to lean in to kiss her cheek, but a sudden pound on the door has her jumping out of my arms. Her fingers swipe frantically under her eyes. "Go sit..." She stops herself. "No. Go to the closet. Dammit," she mutters. "Just act cool."

I can't help but laugh. "It's fine. Just open the door. We're good."

Straightening her back, she clicks the lock and pulls the door open, coming face to face with three students for her next class. She steps aside, allowing them in.

"Looks like you're set," I say to her as I wiggle the door handle. "It was just a sticky lock. You shouldn't have any more problems with it, but if you do, let the office know and they can have maintenance take a look."

A smile creeps on her face. "Thanks, Wilder."

I waggle my brows as I step past her. Once I'm out the door, I spin around and look at her. "See ya later."

Gripping the doorframe, she watches as I walk away. I know because I can't stop turning around to look at her. The smile on my face has never felt more real.

Fuck. I've got it bad.

CHAPTER 11
WILDER

"Where's your brother?" Dad asks as he loosens his tie and takes a seat at the dinner table.

I look around, wondering what brother he's talking about since I've got three, and I notice it's Callan who's missing.

I shrug my shoulders. "Don't know."

This is the fourth time in a week Callan has missed dinner with no explanation other than "I had shit to do." Ever since football season ended, Callan's been a bit of a miscreant. He's running around with some sketchy guys and making some pretty shitty choices. Dad's on high alert with his behavior and I can see the trepidation on his face right now.

"I need you all to rally and spend some more time with Callan," he says sternly. "He's heading down a path he shouldn't be on. He and Brogan are about to finish their junior year and they've got one more to go before they're out in the real world. I don't feel Callan is near enough ready to face what's waiting for him."

I look around at my siblings who are all nodding and offering responses like, *yes, sir,* and *of course.* Then there is Lake, my youngest stepsister who's a sophomore, she's scribbling some sort of art onto her hand and paying no attention to anyone around her.

Being in high school is fucking hard. We're all just trying to find our place and our people while knowing that soon, we'll be thrust into the real world and all the strings we've tied will slowly unravel. Maybe not right away, but eventually, they will. Then we have to start all over and do it again—*find our place, find our people.*

I've got one more week left, and I'm terrified.

I shouldn't be but the unknown is terrifying. Will I make it out there? Will this cruel world change me?

I've got a plan, but there is still so much to figure out. My job is lined up. I'm still making content and growing my following while monetizing off the SnapTok app. And now, I've met someone who makes all that other stuff seem less significant.

Just thinking about Cat has all my worries slipping away. In seven days I will be free to see her whenever I want. I'll no longer be her student and she will no longer be my teacher.

"What are you smiling about?" Rome asks with a nudge to my shoulder.

I look up, feeling a rush of heat in my cheeks. I didn't even realize I was smiling. "Nothing." My eyes wander around the table and I see that everyone is looking at me, even Lake who has paused her Sharpie tattoo to see what's going on.

"I know," Elodie says with a smirk.

I give her a look, practically begging her not to say anything, because I think she really does know.

"Well," Sayer says. "Don't leave us hanging, El. What is it?"

I sweep my hand through the air, blowing out a breath of air. "She doesn't know anything."

"Sure I do," she says confidently as she folds her hands on the table in front of her.

I fix her with a stern stare, moving my head in small, deliberate shakes. *Don't you dare mention Mrs. Jenkins,* I internally beg of her.

Eyes deadlocked on mine, she says, "We're done with high school next week. That's all. Am I right, *Wilder*?"

My body relaxes, shoulders dropping from their tense state. "Yeah, of course. That's exactly it."

Once everyone continues eating, I stab a piece of steak with a fork and glower at Elodie who looks like she's about to burst out in laughter. How is that girl so damn intuitive? She's too smart for her own good. Probably why she got away with fucking her stepbrother and getting our parents' approval. Too bad for her and Rome, they'll be parting ways this fall, but I have no doubt they'll make it work since their schools are sort of close. The love between them is clear as day, you can't help but notice it.

"Sayer," Dad says, clearing his throat. "You and Callan start football day camp in two weeks. I want you two to go there and come home together. That way I know he's actually showing up. If he steps out of line, you let me know, okay?"

Sayer nods, but I call bullshit. He'd never rat on Callan. Those two are as close as Rome and me, and I'd never throw Rome under the bus. They're as opposite as me and Rome, too.

Sayer is a lot like me—eyes on the future, treat others how we want to be treated. Whereas Rome and Callan like to raise hell for fun and have no problem using the backs of others as steppingstones to get what they want.

"Well, for anyone who cares," Brogan says chipperly. "Cheer-leading starts in two weeks as well, but I think I've got this alone. No need for anyone to trail behind me to make sure I get there."

Brogan is on the varsity cheer team, and she lives for that shit. She's already got her future mapped out for herself. After graduation next year she plans to attend the university in our neighboring town while cheering for the Devils' football team.

As for Callan, no one knows what his plans are. Dad will likely bribe him just so he'll attend college for a couple years because there's no way in hell he'll try and bring him into his company. He'd have to be a fool to do that. Callan doesn't have a working bone in his body.

"I don't doubt that," Dad tells Brogan with a smile. "I just wish Callan had that same mindset with sports and school."

"And what mindset is that?" Callan's voice booms through the dining room as he enters, the musky smell of marijuana rolling off his all-black clothing. He pushes his unkempt hair off his forehead, exposing his squinted, bloodshot eyes.

Jerking a chair out from the table, he drops down with his legs spread and his head resting on the tall back cushion. He looks from person to person before saying, "You all talking smack about me behind my back?"

"Glad you could join us, Callan," Dad says as he adjusts the napkin on his lap. "Is there a reason you're late for dinner… again?"

"I was at the library." He smirks and we all know it's a lie. Callan wouldn't be caught dead in a library. Not unless there were chicks there serving up pot and booze.

Dad rolls his eyes. "We'll talk later, son." He takes in a deep breath before moving his attention to me. "Jillian said she's emailed you twice with no response. I need you to get on that. She'd like the draft for the board meeting by tomorrow evening."

"Tomorrow evening?" I gasp. "Dad, I've got finals coming up and I'm behind on batching videos for…" I let my words trail off because that's not a valid excuse for him. When he gives me a stern look, I know I already dug myself into a hole. School can be an excuse, but the thing I am passionate about that is actually making me money is not valid.

"I'll get it done." I stab a piece of meat on my plate a little too hard as my stomach sours.

"I know you will, Wilder. You're doing great. And I have no doubt you'll ace your finals."

"Kiss ass," Callan coughs into his fist before spewing laughter.

"Can we all just have a nice dinner?" Celia asks with a scorned look on her face.

"Shut up," I snap at him, ignoring Celia's plea. "At least I'm doing something productive with my time. We can't all spend our days getting high and chilling." I put air quotes around the word chilling so he knows that I am aware of exactly what he does with his buddies when they get high.

Callan sits up in his chair, scowling. "Of course not. Someone needs to crawl up Dad's ass and remove the stick that's buried up there."

Fuming, I go to stand, but Rome pulls me back down in my chair. My teeth grind as I grit out, "Shut your damn mouth or next time I'll shut it for you."

Unfazed, he just sits there all calm and collected with a shit-eating grin on his face. "Original, Wilder." He braces his elbows on the table, leaning in to tell me a secret that is loud enough for everyone to hear. "I'd like to see you try."

"Enough!" Dad shouts as his chair flies back and he gets to his feet. He stalks toward Callan then grabs him by the collar of his worn black tee shirt, pulling him out of his chair. "Outside! Now!"

"Chill out," Callan scoffs, raising his hands in mock surrender. "I'm just fucking with him."

Dad smacks his palm to the back of Callan's head. "Watch your mouth, young man. My wife and your sisters don't need to hear you speaking like some misfit punk."

"Wow," Brogan draws. "That was intense. What's gotten into him?" She looks from me to Rome.

I exhale a pent-up breath of rage. "No idea but if anyone can put him in his place, it's Dad."

"Everyone, just calm down," Celia, my stepmom, says. "Callan is just going through something. We've all been there. He's just dealing with it in ways we can't understand. Just try to be there for him when you can, okay?"

We all nod in response then finish eating in dead silence.

Lake is the first to stand and she excuses herself to go to play basketball at the park. Looking at the petite girl with purple streaks in her dark hair and art drawn all over herself, you wouldn't think she'd be baller, but she's got mad skills on the court. Lake is a little weird, but at least she has hobbies to occupy her time, unlike Callan. He's got football and that's only five months out of the year. And that's all to say he doesn't royally fuck that up his senior year because all he wants to do is get high.

I thought Rome processed our mother's death in a piss-poor way, but Callan just seemed to shut down. Believe it or not, he and I used to be close. We would practice throwing the ball together in the yard and even attended football camps together. He's always been my little brother, but something has changed this past year and it started the day we buried our mother.

A glance at my watch and I see that it's already quarter to seven, so I scarf down the rest of my steak and mashed potatoes then excuse myself, too.

"I've gotta head out to clear my head so I can work on the speech for my dad," I tell Celia. "I'll be back later."

I pick up my plate and head into the kitchen when I'm joined by Elodie. "So," she begins, "care to tell me the truth about what's got you in such a good mood lately."

I scrape the excess food from my plate into the garbage then set it in the sink. "Do I look like I'm in a good mood?" I look at her glumly.

"Well, not now. But that's because your brother is being a jerk. But before he got here, and every other minute of the day, you're always smiling. I know it's not Sam, so tell me who's really got you so giddy all of a sudden."

I laugh, that girl has been spreading rumors that we are practically getting married. "Definitely not Sam."

"You do realize she's been telling everyone you're going to prom together and just meeting there, right?"

"I heard. She can think what she wants. She knows what I

told her. I don't want a date for prom." I don't buy into girls' drama. Sam can pretend in her head. I won't be dancing with her or even sitting by her. It was her choice to lie and it will be her choice to face the consequences of that lie.

I step aside so Elodie can clear her plate. Once she gets all the food off, she sets it in the sink and turns on the water. "You say you don't want a date, but is there anyone you would absolutely go with if they asked?" She raises her brows, a smile playing on her lips as she awaits my response.

I play it cool because I know where she's going with this. "Nope. Not a single soul."

"Hmm." She taps her chin. "No one at all?"

"I know what you're doing, El." I try not to get angry with her. I love the girl as if she were my blood sister, but I will fight for what I want. And I want—no, need—Elodie to keep her lips sealed.

"Oh yeah? What's that?" She looks so damn smug.

I take a deep breath and shut the water off for her before leaning into the counter. "There's nothing going on, if that's what you're thinking."

"For your sake, I truly hope there isn't. A lot of people would get hurt if there was." Her eyes narrow at me as if she were my mother.

"Look who's talking," I say, stating the obvious. "Did you consider that when you started sleeping with my brother, *your stepbrother*?"

"No one got hurt in that process." She points a finger at me. "Besides, the heart wants what the heart wants."

"But that doesn't fly in my case?"

"It's different." She leans in, dropping her voice to a whisper. "She's married. To the mayor, I might add." Her eyebrows shoot to her forehead. "Your dad's opponent in the election."

"You're telling me everything I already know, El. But…I think she's in trouble."

Fuck. Why did I say that? In the process of trying to defend myself, I shared something I shouldn't have shared. I don't owe Elodie excuses or reasoning for what I do. I should have kept my damn mouth shut.

Her eyes widen. "What kind of trouble?"

"Nothing." My hand sweeps through the air. "Forget about it." I walk toward the doorway to the dining room, but Elodie grabs the back of my arm.

"Wilder. You can't just say something like that then walk away. You can trust me."

"I know I can," I say to her truthfully. Elodie and I have gotten pretty close and I've helped her through some shit so I know she just wants to help me, too. The thing is, I don't need help. It's Cat who needs *my* help.

"So tell me. Maybe there's something I can do. You don't always have to be the hero alone."

Just as I open my mouth to speak, Rome comes into view. He shoots us a look of confusion. "Everything all right?"

"Does he know?" I say quietly to Elodie.

Her head tilts slightly to the left, a look of sorrow on her face. "I tell him everything."

I figured. But it's fine. I know I can trust Rome, too.

"Do I know what?" Rome asks, and his question has me dropping my head back with a sigh.

"I can't do this right now, you guys. I've gotta shower then I have somewhere to be. We'll talk later."

"I'm holding you to it," Elodie says with a stern eye when I glance back. "If something is going on, we want to help."

"Something's going on with who?" Rome asks, stupefied by the conversation he just walked in on.

"Later," I tell them both before walking out of the kitchen. Before they can say anything else, I head up the stairs.

Once I'm in my bathroom, I take a quick shower before throwing on a pair of gym shorts and a Misfits football tee shirt.

With my hair still glistening from the dampness, I head to the Cat's guesthouse. I am careful to pull into the driveway at eight o'clock on the dot. With the car in park, but still running, I send Cat a message on SnapTok.

WildMisfit: I'm here.

She responds right away.

CatEyes: Me, too. You can come in.

With a smile on my face, I kill the engine and get out. I'm halfway to the miniature house when the front door comes open.

Cat steps out, nearly taking my breath away. She's wearing a pair of black shorts that show off her long and impressively toned legs, a white tee shirt that hugs her curves, and her long hair piled in a bun on the top of her head.

Her bottom lip is tucked between her teeth as she gestures for me to hurry up. Her eyes dance around the yard, clearly fearful that someone might see me. I just hope that no one suspects anything or realizes it's my car.

I guess it's more of us being seen together that makes her nervous. Then again, if her husband is as possessive as I think he is, he could have people watching this place. I glance behind me to check just once, but everything seems quiet.

Stepping to the side, Cat gestures for me to come in then closes the door behind me.

"It's good to see you," I tell her. "You look beautiful."

Her nose scrunches as she looks down her body. "I do?"

"You always do." I brush my fingers over her cheek, loving the way she sighs into my touch.

"Thank you. You, umm…look nice too."

I laugh and she does too. "No, I don't. But thanks anyways."

"Look, Wilder," she begins, her voice growing serious as she walks into the small living room. "I told you to come here because I need to tell you this has to be the last time. We can't keep doing this. The more I think about it, the more certain I am that we can't talk like we have been. I know it's my own fault. I started messaging you on that app and it was a mistake."

"Hey." I close the space between us, so sick of this damn conversation. "Don't talk like that. It wasn't a mistake. Those conversations meant a lot to me."

She draws in a deep breath before saying, "They meant a lot to me, too. You have no idea how much." I can hear the tremble in her voice and see as her eyes grow heavy with unshed tears. It makes me want to wrap her in my arms.

But something tells me she won't let me this time. So, I approach her carefully, keeping some space between us, but not much.

"So why throw it all away?'" My voice is gentle, careful. I have no idea what happens when she speaks her mind to her so-called husband, but the way she's already flinching has me moving with caution.

Taking a couple steps back, she sits down on the couch and drops her face in her hands. "You were never supposed to find out it was me. Talking to you was my escape from the life of Catherine Jenkins."

I sit down beside her and on instinct my hand goes to her back, trying to sooth her. "I happen to like Catherine Jenkins. A lot, I might add."

"Well, I don't," she confesses. "In fact, I don't like her at all. She doesn't have a backbone. She never makes decisions for herself—" I cut her off with a finger to her lips and she side-eyes me.

"Then make one," I say, practically begging her with my tone. I drop my hand only for her to reach for it, then she stops herself. It's infuriating to watch this battle in her mind of right and wrong, of what she wants and what she is willing to settle for. So, I try again. "Please. Make this choice for yourself. You said you like me, so stop pushing me away."

Sad eyes land on mine and she gently shakes her head as my heart starts to break in my chest. "I don't want to hurt you, Wilder. One way or another, we're both going to get hurt in the end."

CHAPTER 12
CATHERINE

"Who's going to hurt us?" Wilder questions. I have a feeling he already knows something he wants to hear me admit.

"I just mean figuratively." I try to brush off the comment, but I should have known better.

"Why are you so scared then?"

My body starts to shake as I remember that day, those gunshots. I thought Troy was going to take me away from the pain and the violence. I thought I was going to be saved—that I was one of the lucky ones. "I signed my life over to him," I whisper. "In more ways than one."

I can't look at him, so I keep my head down and be submissive just like Troy taught me. If I stay weak, then it hurts less.

But it's not harsh words that demand the truth, it's Wilder's gentle soul begging to help me. And I want to let him. "What's he got on you, Cat?"

The question crashes into me, making me realize just how much I revealed. "Nothing," I blurt out.

"Oh yeah?" He aggressively sweeps my hair to the side and tilts my head. "Then how the hell do you explain the ghosting of his fucking handprint on your neck? He hurt you, didn't he?"

His voice rises as the reality of what's going on sets in. He knows, and I know it too, even as I shake my head adamantly.

"He beats you mercilessly, without care or regret, doesn't he?"

Tears stream down my face as I choke down the truth. I wish I could tell him everything but that would only put us both at risk. Wilder will never let this go and I need to find a way to make him.

To keep him safe.

"Answer me!" Wilder shouts, rattling my bones. I've never seen him so worked up and angry. If I weren't seeing it with my own eyes, I wouldn't believe he was capable.

I look at him, petrified that he'll see the truth in my eyes, but I can't control the emotions pouring out of me. "Please let this go," I beg, my voice cracking on the last word.

I've already let enough walls down, this one has to stay up. If Wilder knew what happens behind the doors of my house, my whole world would change, and I fear it wouldn't be for the better.

Wilder's features soften and he drops his head, running his fingers through my hair. "I'll fucking kill him," he says, his tone laced with intent. "Just say the word, and he's a dead man." He grabs my face in his hands and looks deep into my eyes. "Just the thought of him laying a finger on you makes me crazy."

I put my hand over his as he palms my cheek, leaning into his touch. "I've got everything under control. I'm okay. I promise."

His dark eyebrows dip and he looks down between us, realization dawning on his face as he senses my trembling. "I'm sorry. I'm so sorry. I didn't mean to yell." He pulls me close, wrapping me in a scent that has the promise of comfort. "You don't have to tell me. I already know. Just understand that I'm here for you and if you want me to intervene, I will."

"I don't want that," I say without a second thought. "I can handle Troy. But this has to stay between us. If it got out..." My words trail off because I can't even fathom what might happen. Troy would likely take me far away from Willow Creek. He'd start a new life somewhere else where he can start with a clean reputation and I'd probably be rat food in a cellar. Or worse, he'd hold true to his promise and feed me to the men he saved me from. Or to the police. Or both.

"All your secrets are safe with me." He tips my chin with the pad of his thumb. "I promise. You can trust me, Cat."

I believe him. I'm not sure why, but I truly feel like my secrets are safe with Wilder, and I feel like my body is safe with him, too. Possibly even my heart. Lord knows Troy doesn't handle it with care. It's high time I give it to someone who will protect it at all costs.

"I know I can," I tell him with a shake in my voice. "And I want you to trust me, too. Which is why there's something I need to tell you."

"Of course." He runs his hand down my arm, resting it on my lap. "You can tell me anything."

Part of me knows this is wrong, going against Troy and sharing one of his sketchy campaign tactics, but I don't want the Cromwells to get hurt in this process. If Troy wins, it should be a fair win.

"Before Troy left, he told me he's digging into what happened a couple years ago with your brother. I'm not even sure what happened, but from what I heard, your stepmom, being the district attorney, helped have the case thrown out and I think Troy plans to create his own narrative of what happened."

Wilder grumbles, "That son of a bitch." His hands run through his hair and his jaw clenches. "Rome was protecting Elodie when that shit went down. In my opinion, and everyone else's, that asshole got what he deserved."

In hopes of getting a better understanding of the situation, so maybe I can help, I ask, "What exactly happened? If you don't mind talking about it."

His hands drop and he locks his fingers in his lap. "Elodie

was visiting town with her mom and her sisters. This was before our parents were married, or even dating. She went to a party, gave Rome some shit, then left. Apparently he caught up with her in Ravencrest Park and she was in the midst of being assaulted by some of that shithole's finest. Rome stepped in and knocked one of the guys in the head with a broken pipe. Apparently he did it as the guy was trying to take Elodie's clothes off."

I gasp, covering my mouth with my hand. "Oh my God. That poor girl."

"Elodie ran off," he continues. "And the guy he hit ended up in critical condition in the hospital. Thing is, he didn't know who Elodie was at the time so there was no way of getting her statement about what happened. So Rome was charged. He lost his scholarship, his acceptance at UCLA, and his offer to play football there."

It's beginning to make sense now, so I take a guess at what happened next. "So once Elodie and her family moved here, Rome realized it was her and she was able to tell the truth—that Rome saved her?"

"Exactly. The charges were dropped, Rome got his acceptance back and they still want him to play ball. In fact, he leaves next month to start preseason practice."

"How does Elodie feel about that?" It's clear as day that Elodie and Rome are inseparable. How will they handle the distance?

"Actually, I think she plans to go out there and stay in an Airbnb for a few weeks before heading to Stanford. One way or another, they'll make it work."

"I'm sure they will," I tell him as I rub my ankle, feeling the swell of it from being on my feet all day, every day.

He looks down as I massage it, his eyebrows raised. "What's wrong?"

"Oh nothing," I tell him, wondering if he thinks this is another injury from Troy. Just in case, I explain, "One of the downfalls of being a teacher."

I'm not sure why I'd care if he did think it was Troy, but there is still a part of me that defends his actions, even when I know I shouldn't.

I feel his firm grip around my calf, and the next thing I know, my leg is lifted onto his lap. I give him a sidelong glance as he carefully removes my sock, exposing the chipped pink nail polish on my toes. I'm a little embarrassed that it's been so long since I've had a pedicure.

"What are you doing?" I grin.

His thumb presses firmly into the arch of my foot, releasing knots and tension that have built up from long days at work. I literally have to hold back a moan. It feels so good.

"You said your ankle hurt." He gives me a grin as he squeezes then goes back to using his thumb in my arch.

It feels good. No. It feels *amazing*.

I can't break the smile on my face even if I tried. "Thank you," I tell him. "No one has ever done anything like this for me before."

"That's a shame," he says with a disappointed tone. "You deserve to be spoiled every single day. In fact, it sort of pisses me off that you aren't."

I know there is so much he'd love to say about Troy. The hate in his eyes is clear. There is so much I'd love to say, too. But Wilder is respectful in that way. He could force me to talk. I am sure all it would take is him asking one more time before that wall I worked so hard to build comes crumbling down. But he doesn't.

We sit in peaceful silence for a few minutes while I embrace someone touching me with care. Every few seconds my mind drifts to what would happen if my husband found us here. My heart rate kicks up and my palms sweat. But then Wilder smiles at me and the sensation ceases.

It doesn't matter. Troy isn't here. He will never know what's been going on while he's gone. Right now, all I care about is this time with Wilder. I know it will be short-lived, and after this weekend we'll have to stop seeing each other, so I plan to enjoy it while I can.

Wilder hits a spot in my calf that has me wincing. The sound grabs his attention and he looks at me with his heavy dark brow raised. "That hurt?"

"Yes, but in all the good ways," I tell him truthfully.

The warmth of his touch travels up my body. It's a new sensation because it's true, no one has ever rubbed my feet before, or pampered me at all for that matter. Unless it was a paid service like a massage or a pedicure.

I lean back on the arm of the couch, sinking into it as my body enters a state of relaxation.

His fingertips trail up my leg, just below my knee, sending shivers across my skin. He moves higher, teasingly slow until he reaches the sensitive flesh of my thigh. Each stroke has my body igniting with tingles of anticipation.

"Next leg," he says, curling his fingers and flashing a devilishly sexy grin.

I watch him intently as he settles my leg onto his lap right beside the other. His lips part slightly and his tongue drags across the curve of his upper lip as he works aimlessly to make me feel good.

I bet he'd be amazing in bed. I'm sure his sole focus would be on the girl he's with as he satisfies all her needs.

I shouldn't be thinking like that, but it's hard not to when his strong hands are caressing my body.

CHAPTER 13

CATHERINE

A FEW MINUTES later and I'm more relaxed than I've been in months, maybe years. Then the next thing I know, Wilder is sliding his body down on the couch beside mine until he's sandwiched between me and the back cushions. I shift slightly, making room for him as he settles in. His arm drapes across my stomach and he pulls my body snug against his.

Warmth spreads through my chest and a ball of nervous excitement forms in my stomach. Everything about this feels so right and I won't dare question it. With each passing second of us lying in here with our breaths as the only sound, I find myself falling more and more for Wilder.

Before I know it, I'm in too deep and I can't get out. I turn to face him, our noses brushing as I inhale his exhale.

Wilder puts a hand on my cheek and guides my mouth slowly to his, but he pauses just before our lips touch.

"Tell me you want this. Tell me you don't want me to stop."

I suck in a breath, no words can escape me. I want this more than I want to breathe. I want him more than I want to do the right thing. I've always done what was expected of me. I always obey. But this time, Wilder is making it my choice.

I know if I told him to stop he would. It would hurt us both, but he would. Which is why I lean in, our foreheads touching as I whisper, "Don't stop."

Our mouths crush together in an instant, the band of tension that had pulled so tightly between us finally snapping. At first, my lips stay sealed because I have never been kissed like this before, then Wilder drags his tongue across my bottom lip and I part them slightly, granting him entry.

His heavy breaths flow into me and I swallow them down. The next thing I know, his hand is on the back of my head, fingers dragging through my hair as he pulls me closer.

No kiss has ever made me feel dizzy with desire. No person has ever made me this terrified and yet safe at the same time. So much so that my body is literally shaking. My heart skips beats. So many beats. *My God, he tastes so damn good.*

I never knew how bad I wanted Wilder until this moment. I've always found him attractive and I've felt this pull toward him since the start of the school year, but anytime I started to think of Wilder as anything but my student, I shut my thoughts down. Except, over this last week, something has blossomed between us. Now, more than ever, I want him. *I want him so fucking bad.*

Wilder begins to explore my body with his free hand and I yearn to do the same. Moving my fingers down his strong arms that make me feel safe, I find his waist. My hand slides slowly up his shirt, fingers trailing over the rigid cords of his abs. At the same time his hand slips under my shirt on my back and he pulls us closer with a firm palm.

Our lips move together in perfect unison, building in intensity with each passing second. A spark ignites in my gut and I tug him closer, feeling the growing bulge in his shorts pressed against my core as I moan into his mouth. The sound stirs something in him, making him near frantic.

I'm starving for the touch of a man whose hands don't hurt me, and Wilder delivers like his life depends on it.

Something comes over me—a rush of adrenaline, a ball of

white-hot fire in the pit of my stomach. Feeling freer than I've ever been, I go for what I want.

And what I want is him.

Sliding my hand down his shorts, I feel his body tremble beneath my touch. As if he wasn't expecting me to be so forward. Tingles shoot through my body when I find his hard cock waiting for me. My fingers wrap around the shallow end and I glide my hand up and down slowly.

Wilder shifts slightly, giving me room to work. Lustful eyes peer down at me and his nostrils flare. "W-we don't have to…"

The fact that he's even saying that speaks volumes to his character. He's one of the good ones. And just for tonight, he's all mine.

I lick my lips, hungry for more of him. "I want to." My words offer reassurance, not only for Wilder, but for myself. And when he gives me that panty-melting smile, I can't help but take it up a notch, twisting my hand slightly as I stroke him. His eyes drift closed in ecstasy and I get to witness this perfect god of a man—that so many women want—give himself over to me.

I want this more than I've ever wanted anything in my life.

I stroke faster, my body aching for his release just as much as it aches for my own.

Wilder's mouth meets mine again, this time with renewed tenacity. We deepen the kiss, our teeth clanking as I slide my hand up and down his smooth, engorged cock, feeling the veins bulge against his soft skin. He's bigger than I imagined—much bigger than Troy or any of the guys I've been with in the past. He's got at least a good two inches on Troy and his girth is double in size.

I've always heard assholes have smaller dicks and they treat people poorly to boost their own self-esteem. It's the nice ones that are supposed to be well-endowed. I've never touched a guy who isn't a total jackass, but I am quickly starting to believe in that theory.

Wilder moans subtly just before his hand trails featherlike

touches down my side. He keeps going until he's at the bottom of my shorts, then balls his hand in a fist to rub his knuckles over my center. I push into it, wanting every bit of what he will give me. When he retreats I gasp with need before he begins to unbutton my shorts. The second he has the zipper down, I part my legs instinctively, already feeling the wetness of my want for him between my thighs.

"Mmm, Mrs. J," he mutters into my mouth as his lips curve into a grin. "You're so wet, baby."

The way he calls me Mrs. J makes my insides stir with excitement. I love it when he calls me Cat—I didn't think I would, but I do—but Mrs. J sounds so sexy rolling off his tongue.

I spread my legs farther, giving him as much room as I can being wedged on this couch. We could move. We *should* move. But I don't want to ruin the moment, and I need him right now.

His long fingers stroke me, going back and forth between circling my entrance and my clit. It drives me wild as I continue to give him everything he's giving me. My mouth waters, wanting to take it further, but knowing there is no room. I want to see his massive cock and lick it until he is panting as hard as I am while he toys with me.

Finally, Wilder gives me what I need, two fingers pressing into me slowly as his tongue dances with mine. It's intimate and sexy and has me soaking his fingers. I can feel him grin against my lips, clearly approving. But I'm not prepared when Wilder curls his fingers at just the right angle while pressing the pad of his thumb against my clit. Bursts of electricity shoot through me as I arch my back and slowly lift my hips up and down, my body begging for more.

I push into him, desperate to feel him deeper. When he goes as far as he can, nearly knuckle deep, I cry out in pleasure as those fingers twist inside me.

"That feel good, baby?" he whispers as he kisses his way down my neck, sucking on the thin skin above my collarbone.

"Mmmhmm." I grumble, releasing an airy moan. I have to

roll my lips together to prevent myself from saying something embarrassing like, "This is the best it has ever felt," or worse, "I want more."

Instead I focus on him, rolling my thumb over the bead of moisture at the tip of his cock before reaching down and grabbing his balls. "Feel good for you?"

"God damn," he hums. "You have no idea."

I smirk as I massage him, then wrap my fingers back around his impressive length. More than anything, I want to feel him inside me. I want our bodies to cement together and never come undone.

I can't even remember the last time Troy put his fingers inside me. For the last few years, it's always been sex with no warm-up and I've always just pinched my eyes shut, praying for it to be fast. And an orgasm for me was out of the question.

But this…I want this to go slow. I want it to last *forever*.

I close my eyes and my body relaxes—every limb except my left hand. My mind clears and I focus solely on everything I'm feeling. Every nerve ending in my body feels like it's being touched as his fingers slide in and out of my sopping cunt.

Another moan slips through my lips and when I open my eyes, I see Wilder watching me. Our gazes lock as we come undone together.

He pants, and I pant. My chest rises and falls, and his mirrors it. His mouth falls open and his beautiful eyes that have given me so much strength the past few days sparkle just for me.

I lick my lips and clench my thighs as I come around his fingers, feeling my arousal drip into his palm as I ride the wave. He doesn't stop moving inside me, prolonging the pleasure even more.

My vision blurs and I gasp and shudder, crying out in ecstasy.

Wilder flinches and holds his breath, not even hesitating as he releases into his shorts. I continue to stroke him until I am sure he has given me every last drop.

We relax into each other, not wanting to break the moment. I don't want to regret anything with him anymore. Wilder looks at me in wonder as we lie there nearly breathless when all we've done is use our hands.

Good God, imagine how much more incredible the sex would be with him.

With a hum of approval, Wilder leans in to place his lips on my forehead, holding them there as he whispers, "We didn't have to—"

"But I wanted to," I tell him as I put my hands on either side of his head, holding him close. I need him to see I don't regret this—him.

He pulls back slightly to look at me. "You didn't let me finish." A smile plays on his lips. "I was going to say, but I'm glad we did."

We laid on the couch silent for a few minutes before we both decided we needed to clean up. Wilder ran out to his car to grab a pair of gym shorts he had in his backpack, and I just removed my panties and threw them in the bathroom trash can. Fortunately, I didn't get much on my shorts, so I'm still comfortable.

When he returns from changing, something inside me settles. His presence is like a wave of peace, and his touch reminds me that I am still alive.

It's selfish to want him like this. To throw him into my world of hiding and fear. But he wouldn't stay away, and now I don't want him to.

It's a Friday night and I'm sure there are much better things he can be doing instead of hanging out with his boring, old teacher. Yet, he stays.

We lie back down on the couch, this time with me wedged between him and the cushions, and I put on a movie—*The Note-*

book. He holds me so close, so tight, and I savor every second of being in his arms.

My eyes are on the movie, but I'm not watching it, when I see Wilder raise his hand with his phone in it.

"What are you doing?" I giggle, moving my head away from the camera's sight.

"I haven't posted in days and I've used up my batched videos. Just a quick one. Don't worry, you won't be in it."

I watch him as he makes a quick video of himself, telling his followers that in one more week, he'll be free from the confines of school. His energy is contagious and his grin is wide. It's obvious how much he loves entertaining and creating content.

Once he stops the recording, he adds a soft background sound and replays it for me, obviously seeking my approval.

You can see a few strands of my hair on his chest, but it's not incriminating. Besides, he looks hot as hell with his disheveled hair, so I give him my blessing and he posts it.

The next twenty minutes are spent talking. Wilder tells me he has another speech to write for his dad so I make a promise to help him with it tomorrow, but in my heart, I don't even want to think about tomorrow. It's the last day Troy will be gone, and I'm not ready for him to return. Ever.

Before I know it, my eyes are closing and I'm lulled to sleep by the sound of Wilder's breaths in my ear.

CHAPTER 14
WILDER

WHEN I WOKE up this morning, the sun had barely broken over the clouds and Cat was still asleep. Last night I watched her sleep peacefully through an entire movie, and another hour after that. I couldn't get enough of the way her nostrils flared slightly with each breath. Or the way her lips moved subtly as if she were speaking in a dream before curving into a smile. I'm pretty sure my eyes were still on her when mine finally shut, too.

With her still on the couch, I went into the bedroom and got a blanket off the bed and covered her up before creeping out quietly to head to get a few things for breakfast. It's hard to leave her, but after the night we had, I think she deserves someone to cook her a nice meal.

I pull up to the mini-mart and glance at the dash in my car to see that it's only eight o'clock. It's a rarity that I'm awake this early on a Saturday, unless it's training season for football. But I couldn't make myself go back to sleep once I saw her beautiful face. All I knew was I wanted to make her smile again, and I have an idea how I can do that.

Getting out of my car, I'm surprised to find that the mini-mart is packed. I guess it's prime shopping time for the older generation.

After grabbing a cart, I hit the produce aisle and get some green peppers and onions before heading down the cold section where I get a few more things.

I've never grocery shopped before and it makes me feel mature in some really messed-up way. I push the cart with confidence, as if I've done this a hundred times.

"Cromwell," I hear my name from behind me in the bread aisle and the hairs on the back of my neck stand at attention. I spin around and see Luke, Aiden, and none other than Rome. If anyone can see when I'm lying, it's my twin brother.

Fuck my life.

I stand there, gripping the handle of the cart while hoping they'll just turn and walk away, but there isn't a chance in hell they'll do that.

"Where the hell were you last night?" Luke howls from the end of the aisle as they make their way to me.

Shit. Luke's party was last night. I've never missed a party with the guys and I need to come up with a damn good excuse before they get on my ass.

"What are you guys doing awake so early on Saturday morning?" Once I'm surrounded by them, I get a strong whiff of alcohol. All three of them look like hell. "Have you guys even slept yet?"

"Nope," Luke says, popping the p while throwing a few chips in his mouth. Pretty sure he's high, too. "Now answer the question."

I scratch the back of my head, averting my gaze. "I, umm… had work to do. For my dad."

Rome glowers at me. "Where at? Callan said you never came home last night." Shit. I knew he would be able to tell it was a lie. Well, it's not really a lie. I did need to work on stuff for Dad, but Cat and I just didn't get to it, yet.

"None of your business," I snap back, hoping if I'm firm he will leave it alone. "Does it really matter?"

Luke tips his chin, while Aiden rummages through the donut

section, pulling out a box of powdered donut holes. "You're holding out on us, man. Who is she?"

"What the fuck are you talking about?" I ask, playing it cool.

"You know exactly what he's talking about," Rome scoffs. "So answer the question. Who is she?"

"Yeah," Aiden cuts in as he opens the box of donuts. "You know what he's talking about. The girl in the video you posted last night." He pops a donut hole in his mouth, waiting for a response as he chews it. Powder covers his lips and his eyebrows rise.

"Just some chick," I tell them, confident that will satisfy their need to get in my business.

"Everyone's talking. Your investigative followers are determined to find out who she is." Rome tsks. "Might as well just give her up because some are even doing image searches of her ear."

"Bullshit," I growl as I reach in my pocket and pull out my phone. I immediately go to the app, then to the video and I gasp when I see that the video has went viral. Like hella viral. 1.6 million views in six hours. "Holy fuck," I mutter under my breath.

I start scrolling through the comments, and it's obvious people have made it their mission to find out who I was with last night. Some girls are even jealous, talking about how they are heartbroken that it's not them. Then there are the ones who seem genuinely happy for me.

I keep scrolling, my eyes skimming for two specific words—Mrs. Jenkins. Fortunately, no one has suspected her, so I breathe a sigh of relief.

Rome throws an arm around my shoulders, walking me away from the guys. "Just tell me, bro. Was it her?"

"Who?" I scoff, playing dumb. We might not be near the guys, but this isn't something I wanna talk about in a packed grocery store. Actually, it's not something I wanna talk about at all. What I have with Cat is fragile. I need to be careful if it's going to last. And fuck, I need it to last.

"You know who I'm talking about." Rome's voice is calm as he pleads with me. My brother and I have always been close, so it is hard not to confide in him. I just don't know if I can trust him yet. "It's me, Wilder. Just fucking tell me the truth."

"Why?" I step out of his hold on me. "So you and Elodie can give me shit? So she can judge me and you can spread rumors like you always do?"

Rome shakes his head, disappointment in his gaze. But what did he expect?

"No, bro. So we can help you."

"Yeah. Okay," I sputter a sarcastic laugh. "Tell me why I'd need your help anyways. If anything, you all need my help."

"What d'ya mean?"

I use this opportunity to tell Rome about Mayor Jenkins digging into their past, hoping to take the attention off of the girl in the video and where I was last night. Besides, he, Celia, and Dad deserve to know. "Troy Jenkins," I spit out. "That's what I mean."

"He's a shady politician. So what about him?"

The mention of the mayor seems to have sparked the interest of Luke and Aiden. Now, both eating the box of donuts, they listen keenly to our conversation.

Ignoring them, I look at Rome, that fury when I heard about what that fucker is doing returns. "He's digging into your criminal record and wants to destroy Celia's reputation for having the charges thrown out."

Rome goes silent, which speaks volumes. His jaw tightens and his fists ball at his sides. "That son of a bitch."

"Damn. Homeboy is ruthless," Aiden squawks with a mouthful of food.

Luke throws in his two cents. "What's the big deal? It's not like she did anything illegal."

Rome scrubs a hand over his face, sobering up really quick.

"Just because she won't be incriminated by law, doesn't mean it won't make her look really fucking bad."

"So what are you gonna do?" Aiden asks him, and I'm curious myself. Whatever his plan is, I'm in. We can dig as far back as the day that asshole mayor was born and find whatever dirt we can on him if necessary.

"I'm gonna tell my dad," Rome says with a snark to his tone. "There's no way in hell he'll lie down while this sneaky fuckwad tries to destroy his family's reputation."

"And if he does?" I ask Rome, knowing that our dad is a pretty stand-up guy who prefers to err on the side of caution. He won't believe us easily, and he definitely won't react quick enough unless there is some solid proof.

Rome lifts a shoulder, a cocky grin on his face. "Then we'll handle it for him."

I hold out a fist and we bump knuckles. "Hell yeah, we will."

I'd love nothing more than to take that abusive prick down, as long as Cat isn't hurt in the process.

Luke looks in my cart, his eyebrow quirked. "Who the hell are you cooking breakfast for?"

"Like I said, it's none of your business." I look from one of them to the other. "I gotta go."

I push the cart down the aisle, feeling three times my age as I walk away from my best friends. They were living it up last night like carefree teenagers while I was curled up on the couch with Cat. And I'd do it again in a heartbeat—every damn day.

"Your secrets aren't safe," I hear Luke call out as I approach the end of the aisle. "One way or another, we'll find out who she is."

Let's hope like hell that doesn't happen.

I get back to the guesthouse and I'm surprised to find that Cat is still sound asleep. She must've really needed a good night's rest. I stop for a moment in the living room and take in her form. She's got the blanket tugged up over her shoulder, sleeping on her side with her knees bent. She's pure beauty and everything I never knew I needed in my life.

When she stirs a little bit, I continue into the kitchen with the bags of groceries and get started on breakfast. I don't want her to wake up before the food is ready.

A few minutes later, the pan is sizzling and the small space fills with the aroma of bacon, eggs, and toast.

I'm cooking away when a shadowy figure to my left catches my eye. I turn my head and see Cat leaning against the door-frame with the blanket wrapped around her and a smile on her lips.

"Hey now," I sing. "You're supposed to be sleeping."

She begins toward me. "How can I when it smells so good in here?"

I stir the fluffy eggs then set the wooden spoon down on a napkin beside the stove. "Come here," I tell Cat and she leans her head against her shoulder, biting her lip. Jesus, this girl is killing me with all her sexiness. When she doesn't move, I curl my fingers at her. "Come here," I say again, my eyes hooded.

She giggles then strides toward me, dragging the blanket on the floor. When she's about a foot away, I grab her by the waist and jerk her body against mine. Her arms surround me along with the blanket, wrapping us in our own little cocoon of warmth.

"Good morning," I kiss her forehead softly.

"It certainly is." She beams up at me, a smile so bright on her face my heart warms. I've never seen her glow the way she is now, and I want to ensure it never ends. "Did you go out and buy all of this?"

"Yep," I say, standing tall and proud. "The fridge was empty, aside from a very suspicious-looking carton of milk."

She chuckles. "You're something else, Wilder Cromwell." Her head nuzzles against my chest and I slide my hands beneath the blanket and wrap my arms around her warm body.

This feels surreal—me and Mrs. Jenkins. It's insane how quickly things have progressed between us, but I can't imagine us not being here together.

Pulling back a tad, I peer down at her. "Why don't you go get comfortable and I'll finish up here? Then we can have breakfast. Together."

Her nose scrunches as she steps out of my hold. "But I wanna help." She heads over to the toaster that is still holding two pieces of toasted bread that I have yet to take out. She pulls them out and sets them down on a paper plate. Turning around, she lifts a brow. "Butter?"

"Shit," I huff. "I knew I was forgetting something."

"No worries," she laughs. "Dry toast works for me. I still can't believe you're doing all this. You're too good to me." She peers around at the spread I have for her, a fog coming over her. I can't imagine Troy does stuff like this for her, and that thought enrages me a bit. Cat is a woman who deserves love and happiness. She doesn't deserve to be afraid. I just need to keep reminding her of that and maybe one day she will trust me enough to tell me the truth.

"Cat." I reach for her cheek, brushing my fingers over it as I peer down at her gorgeous blue eyes. "You deserve this, and more." I flash her a wink before the strong smell of burning eggs fills my nostrils. "Dammit." I spin back around, immediately turning off the stove. My nose scrunches up as I glance over my shoulder. "Burnt eggs work for you too?"

We both burst out in laughter as she says, "I'll eat just about anything with you, Wilder."

A strange sensation runs through me, as my heart squeezes. "Same, Mrs. J."

Once we've both got a plate of food, we decide to sit on the bed because this was supposed to be breakfast in bed, after all.

We're halfway through our meal when I decide to fill Cat in on my run-in with the guys at the grocery store. Not only that, but also the video.

"...so everyone is making assumptions about the video. It now has almost 2 million views since last night."

Her face goes stark white. "Do we need to worry?"

"Nah." I brush my hand through the air. "There's no way anyone can figure out it was you. We're good, baby." At least I hope not. If anyone did say anything, there's no proof anyway.

Finally, some color returns to her skin and she cracks a smile. "I believe you."

I lean over and kiss her cheek. "I never wanna let you down, Cat. I mean it."

We finish eating, then both decide it's a good idea to head to our own homes and clean up for the day while alleviating any suspicion that we were together. The minute I walk out the door, I begin to miss her. The only thing keeping this smile on my face is knowing that in a few short hours, we'll both be back here together.

CHAPTER 15
CATHERINE

I'VE BEEN in a cloud the past two days. All I think about is Wilder. All I want to do is be near him. Even right now as I stand here staring out the window at the guesthouse, waiting for him so we can work on his dad's speech.

In a strange way, I need everything that's happening between me and Wilder just as badly as I want it. The way Wilder's hands roamed my body and the taste of his kiss was healing for me. It's proof that I have a voice and I'm allowed to do what is right for me. Good men still exist, and intimacy doesn't always have to be forced—nor should it be.

I know he's still my student, and that makes this wrong. But I can't help it. Wilder is safe, and I need something safe in my life before I go insane. The amount of times I have prayed for, craved, and searched for something that made me feel whole and not in the thousands of pieces Troy always tries to break me into is infinite.

Wilder is that for me. He is an answered prayer, a wish come true. He lights me up from the inside out and I am terrified this feeling will go away. He makes me want to leave my husband. Not that I haven't thought about it every day for the past eight years. But now, it feels different. I have someone's arms I can run into. I have someone who will protect me.

Just seeing the way Wilder responded when he thought Troy was hurting me was proof enough. And now I plan to stop being the person who puts myself last. I'm putting myself first, and Wilder too.

The minute I see his lights come down the driveway, excitement stirs inside me. My heart races as he comes closer and closer, finally bringing the car to a stop. With the anticipation of seeing him too high, I pull open the door and run outside barefoot to meet him at the driver's side.

Wilder pushes open the door with a huge grin on his face, and before he can even get out, I grab his face in my hands and press my lips to his. "I've missed you."

His hand goes around my lower half, resting on my ass. "Now this is how I like to be greeted." He kisses me again, giving my ass cheek a gentle squeeze that sends my blood rushing through my veins.

Pulling back a tad, I keep my hands on his face and look deep into his eyes so he can see the intensity of what I'm about to say. "I need you," I tell him. "Right now."

All I've been thinking about is the orgasm he gave me last night and the way his cock felt in my hands. For the first time, I felt happy to make another man feel good, and he returned the favor tenfold.

It was amazing, but I want more. I *need* more.

Wilder side-eyes me, brow raised. "I'm gonna need you to be a little more specific."

He wants specific? Specific is what I'll give him. I've never been one to talk dirty, but I read romance novels. I want to make Wilder feel as good as he made me feel. I want to show him I'm not just this scared little creature I've forced myself to become because of Troy.

I want to be *me*.

I lean back down, my mouth ghosting his ear as I whisper, "I want you to fuck me like there is no tomorrow."

Those words hold so much truth. I want him so damn bad, to the point I might literally explode. I also have every intention of spending this day like tomorrow doesn't exist because that's when the beast returns from his work trip.

It's funny how I no longer think of him as my husband. Just the man who ruins me every day. The beast not just in my nightmares, but in real life.

I'm taking away his power over me one step at a time. And this is the first step, taking something I want for myself.

Wilder throws a leg out of the car and gets up, both his hands now firmly gripping my ass as I feel the growing bulge in his shorts. "You sure?"

I love that he's so attentive to my wants and needs; it's new and refreshing. "Surer than I have ever been about anything in my life."

The next thing I know, I'm being hoisted up by his strong arms. My legs wrap around his waist and he kicks his car door closed before carrying me through the threshold of the house.

I grab the door and swing it closed. Leaving all of my reservations outside. I know what I want, and it's clear he wants it too, so I'm going to let us have this even if it might end badly.

My mouth lands on his neck, kissing and sucking as he carries me into the small bedroom off the living room. I want to mark him as mine. I want the world to know that Wilder Cromwell is taken, at least for now.

His hands roam my body in a loving way, making my core heat with love and lust. It's so powerful that I swear Wilder and I were written in the stars. The way my body responds to him is unlike anything I ever knew existed. It's magnetism you only read about in books—something from a fairy tale. It's pure and gentle and just *ours*.

We get to the small back room and Wilder lays me down gently before cloaking his body over mine. He kisses me on the lips then moves to my neck, my collarbone, and down to my stomach. I've never craved a man like this before. The way his mouth causes goosebumps to erupt over my whole body, how his touch sends electricity into my soul.

He lifts up slightly and his fingers grip the hem of my shorts and panties, pulling them down slowly while our lustful gazes cement together.

Biting his lip as he takes me in, I smile at him. He will never understand how much his light has saved me.

Wilder helps me up until I'm sitting and removes my top. I wasn't wearing a bra because I didn't feel like throwing one on after my shower, so the moment the shirt is tossed to the side my breasts are freed. A smirk grows on his face before he leans in.

"Fuck, you're beautiful."

He gently cups one before lowering his head to suckle on my pebbled nipple, causing adrenaline to rush through me. When he moves to the next one, giving it the same attention, I gasp as pleasure builds within me.

I want everything all at once and I want it with him. I think my body must convey that somehow, or Wilder is capable of reading my mind, because in the next second, he stands up at the foot of the bed and tosses his shirt to the side.

I'm completely naked, watching him as he rids himself of his clothes. I blink and suddenly a man stands before me. Wilder is no boy, he is not a student—he is a man in every sense of the word. Tight, rigid abs, toned skin, and muscles for days. He's sculpted to perfection.

My chest rises and falls rapidly as my want for him intensifies. I can literally feel my arousal between my thighs.

"Perfection," I whisper, not even realizing the word came out of my mouth until he chuckles. My cheeks heat in embarrassment, but he steps up to me, pinching my chin when I try to look down.

Nibbling on his bottom lip, his nostrils flare as his eyes skim up and down my body, the heat of his stare turning me on even more. We take our time to drink each other in and I try not to let any of the hateful words Troy has thrown at me ruin this moment. And they can't. Because the way Wilder looks at me leaves no room for doubt in my mind. I am beautiful. I am enough. For myself and for him.

When we finally snap out of our daze, I crook a finger at him. Wilder smiles as he crawls up the mattress on all fours. Using the palms of his hands, he separates my trembling thighs and lowers his face between them.

"Mmm, Mrs. J," he hums. "I can't wait to see how good my teacher tastes." His words light a fire inside me that hasn't burned in years.

The pad of his tongue drags up and down my sex and my legs tremble before I even have a second to enjoy it—before I even have a chance to try and hold back. I don't want this to be over so soon.

Wilder chuckles, his head peeking up at me. "Don't worry, Kitty Cat. I might be younger than you, but I know how to make you come more than once."

A shiver runs down my spine, the best kind. Before I can blink, he is back to work and all too soon I cry out in pleasure.

I grab a fistful of his hair, forcing pressure as I buck my hips upward. I can't even remember the last time a man has made me feel so good. Everything feels extra sensitive, but it's like I need him more than I need air.

Wilder separates my thighs farther, kissing one, then sucking on the other. He pushes two fingers inside me, curling the tips at just the right angle. My mouth falls open just in time for him to look up at me with delight.

He wasn't kidding; he knows exactly what he's doing. And I can already feel myself yearning for more.

Wilder's experience is obvious with the way he moves his mouth and works his fingers, but instead of being jealous of all the girls he's been with in the past, I'm grateful that it's me he's with right now. In a weird way, I feel privileged to have this amazing man all to myself, even if it's only for a little while.

Pushing deeper, he hits a spot that has a moan parting my lips. I lift slightly so I can see him because I'm a visual kind of girl and the sight of him sucking on my clit while electricity courses through my body, drives me absolutely wild.

His fingers move in a fluid motion as he gives attention to every inch of my core. Every nerve ending is hit and my body feels like it's soaring in the clouds.

I grab his head, not knowing anything else at this moment beside my need to come for him.

"Oh God," I cry out, arching my back farther. I'm desperate for more. I crave the moment I'm sent over the edge into ecstasy, but I also don't want this to end.

Wilder makes my body feel so damn good.

Adding another finger, he pumps feverishly and the pleasure is almost more than I can handle. His teeth graze my clit, nibbling on the sensitive nub, and I suck in a shaky breath just before my walls clench around his digits.

I come undone—completely unraveled as my orgasm hits me full force.

"Wilder," I moan, nearly singing his name. "Oh, baby."

I surprise even myself with how vocal I am. I've always been a mouse in bed, but this man does things to me that I can't explain.

The next thing I know, Wilder is sliding up my body. His mouth lands on mine and I taste the bitterness of my arousal on him. "My favorite dessert," he says.

I quirk a brow, unsure what he's talking about.

"You taste like my new favorite dessert."

I feel my cheeks flush with heat and the shade only deepens when he drags his tongue across my bottom lip. "I can't get enough of you, Mrs. J."

I cup his face in my hands and kiss him again. "The feeling is mutual."

His erection presses into my thigh as he slides up and down my body, gyrating against me. "Are you on birth control?" he asks with a raised brow.

"Yes," I tell him. He looks nervous for a second so I pull his face to me. "What is it?"

This time it's his face that turns red. "I wasn't expecting this to happen so I didn't come prepared."

I kiss his cheek, reassuring him. "I'm clean. If you are too, then I trust you."

The next thing I know he's sliding his big cock inside me, filling me to the brim. There's no pain, only pleasure.

My arms wrap around his torso, fingers pressing into the skin of his back.

His movements are slow to start and it's nice, just feeling him inside me while our bodies connect. Every few seconds he kisses my forehead, my cheek, or my neck.

I savor every moment, warmth radiating through my core.

Inch by inch, he picks up his pace, driving faster and faster. I thrust upward, spreading my legs wider as I envelop his cock.

"You feel so good, baby. I never want to leave." His voice is gruff and raspy and it turns me on to the point of no return. I thrust up and down, riding him from beneath while my nails delve into the skin of his back, dragging them downward.

"Fuck yeah, baby. That's it. Mark me."

Sounds of pleasure escape me, my walls gripping him so hard I'm surprised he can even move. I want him buried deep—all the way inside me, forever. This euphoria is unlike anything I have ever known.

Wilder lifts one of my legs, bringing my knee to my chest as he plunges deep inside me.

His head lifts and our lustful gazes meet, staring longingly at each other as we both come undone together.

When he's done, I wrap my arms around him and his body relaxes over mine. Peace settles inside me and for the first time in, what I think, may be forever, I feel content.

We lie there panting as we catch our breaths, the air in the room heavy. Once my head has stopped spinning, I kiss Wilder's shoulder. "That was...something else," I tell him with bated breath.

"Something amazing," he grumbles back, nuzzling into my neck as if it were the only place he would want to be right now. It makes me feel like I bring him some of the comfort he brings me and I love it.

After a few more minutes, Wilder slides out of me, my thighs slick with our arousal. When I stand up, I feel the remnants run down my leg.

I go into the bathroom and clean up, and Wilder joins me. Standing behind me at the sink, he wraps his arms around my body. "You're incredible, Cat. In every sense of the word."

I spin around, engulfing him in my arms. "Not as incredible as you." Pushing myself up on my tiptoes, I kiss his lips then leave the bathroom to get dressed.

As I pass through the living room, I notice my phone. Anxiety washes over me as I grab it off the sofa so I can turn off my location. I can't believe I didn't think to do that sooner.

But before I can, I see that Troy sent me a text message.

> Troy: Surprise. I'm coming home early. I couldn't stand to be away from you an hour longer. My plane lands at seven and my driver should have me home by eight.

Oh no!

I read the next message...

> Troy: Just landed. See you soon, my love. I can't wait to hold you in my arms.

His fake charm does nothing for me. They are empty words and I'm sick to my stomach knowing I'll be seeing him soon.

"Wilder," I shout as I make my way to the bathroom where

he is while glancing at the time—seven forty-two. "Wilder!" I shout again. "We have to go!"

As I turn the handle and push open the bathroom door, I see him standing over the toilet, the steady sound of piss hitting water. His shoulders shake slightly as he relieves himself and he quickly looks over his shoulder. "What's wrong, baby?"

"We have to go now!" I tell him with dire urgency. "Troy is coming home. Write your dad's speech draft and email it to me. I'll do my best to get to it tonight."

"I thought he wasn't coming home until tomorrow?" He reaches out and flushes the toilet then moves to the sink to wash his hands, all too casually.

"His plans changed," I say quickly. "He'll be home in, like, twenty minutes. Maybe sooner."

Patting his wet hands on his shorts, he sulks a bit. "I'm not ready to say goodbye."

Moving things along, I grab him by the arm and pull him out of the bathroom because I don't think he understands the gravity of the situation. Once we're in the living room, I start gathering his things and handing them to him—his shoes, phone, hoodie.

"Baby." He puts two hands on my shoulders, steading me. "Slow down. We've got time."

I stomp my foot to the floor, a desperate beat of fear and urgency. "We don't have time! Wilder, you don't know what he'll do."

I shake my head, fear filling my body until that's all I know. I swear I almost drown in it until soft lips meet mine.

"What will he do, Cat?"

I can see the situation finally settling in for him, but it's like he thinks he can take on the whole world for me, and that's not what I need. I need to keep Troy happy until I can leave. I almost have the right amount of cash saved up and if he can have another work trip soon then maybe I'll be able to disappear.

I shake my head at his question, not ready to give in. He'll try to fight this battle for me and I am so close to escaping on my own. I just need a few more weeks.

But if Troy comes home and sees Wilder's car in this driveway, there is no telling how violent his outburst might be for either of us. We need to get the hell out of here and I have to hope he doesn't come over to this house before I have a chance to clean it up.

Wilder is standing there, a concerned look fixed on his face. I want to be the person he needs right now, but I can't.

"Just slow down, Cat. Please."

"There is no time," I snap at him unintentionally as I pull him toward the front door. I stop us in front of it, the realization of what's happening hitting all at once. Who knows when Wilder and I will have another opportunity to watch movies while snuggled on the couch, make breakfast together with limited ingredients, or dunk powdered donuts in overly-sweetened vanilla coffee. I run my hand down his arm. "This weekend was everything to me, so thank you."

"Hey." He puts a hand on my cheek, thumb stroking my skin. I lean into his touch and close my eyes. "This isn't goodbye, Cat. It's just goodbye for now. We always have CatEyes and WildMisfit. And I'll drop anything, anytime to see you. Just name the place."

He's right. This isn't over. In fact, it's only just begun.

I push myself up on my tiptoes and kiss him goodbye—for now.

CHAPTER 16
CATHERINE

AFTER RIPPING off my clothes frantically and tossing them to the floor, I step into the hot shower. Steam rolls out of the opening and I rest my head back under the cascading water, letting it run over my tense muscles.

Troy will be home any minute. Knowing him, he'll try to sniff out another man on me so I have to wash off Wilder's scent, along with the proof of my orgasm sticking between my thighs.

I'm running a sudsy loofah up and down my body when I hear the bathroom door creak open. My heart jumps into my throat and I brace myself for the moment I've been dreading—the return of my own personal nightmare—my husband.

Long fingers grip the side of the shower curtain and he pokes his head in. "I was wondering where you were hiding. I see you're getting nice and clean for me."

"Mmhmm." I force a smile on my face. "Just for you."

God, he makes me want to vomit. Now, more than ever. I tolerated Troy and his behavior for the longest time, but now that I know what it's like to be treated with respect and adoration, I loathe the sight of him. It only cements my plan in my mind. I *will* leave him.

Troy disappears from my view and I find myself holding my

breath because my gut tells me he didn't leave the bathroom. When the curtain comes back open and his naked body appears, I choke down the bile rising in my throat.

He nudges me to the left, taking the space under the running water, and I flash him a shrewd smile. "I was just finishing up anyways," I tell him as I move to the end of the bathtub to get out. "It's all yours."

Just as I grip the curtain, ready to pull it open, Troy grabs my arm. "Not so fast. I want you to stay with me."

He's always like this after he's been gone. He wants to be sweet and clingy and remind me of the man he used to be. It just makes the moments when he finally hurts me again worse because I fall for it every damn time.

Not this time. Not now that I have Wilder.

I shoot a thumb behind me. "I'm not feeling the best. I think the heat got to me. It's been a busy day."

He looks at me with a fixed gaze. "It's the weekend." His voice rises with each word that comes out of his mouth. "What could have possibly kept you so busy that you need to leave me and go to sleep when I just got home."

I hate that I feel the need to explain myself to him, even if everything I'm about to say is a lie. "I did a lot of gardening today. Went for a jog around the lake. Stuff, Troy." I scoff as I jerk my slippery arm away from him. "I stayed busy."

Before he can stop me, I step out of the bathtub. *I tried.* I really tried to fake my excitement of him coming home, but I'm ready to run like hell from this man. Even if I'm only going as far as our bedroom.

Troy always stays up late watching television in the living room, and more times than not, he falls asleep out there. Once in a while I wake up to him in the bed, or he wakes me because he's horny, but for the most part, he spends his nights away from me.

Thank God for that.

I grab my towel off the hook and wrap it around my body,

tucking the corner so it stays put. Then the water goes off and the shower curtain is tugged open with a force that has it nearly ripping from the hooks.

Taking a step back, I hit the wall, feeling the towel hook gyrate against my spine. One look at his face and I know he's furious. I should have just stayed in there and endured the misery of one quick shower with him. Now, I'm going to have to pay for my mistake with my body.

"I'm sorry," I tell him with an added sweetness to my tone. "It's just been such a long weekend without you, Troy." I walk toward him, hoping to calm the storm before it hits. "I was lonely and I tried to make the house nice for you. I worked so hard and I think the sun might have gotten to me."

He looks me up and down, not fully believing me just yet, so I try to sweeten it a little more and turn the tables on him. "I guess part of me is a little hurt that you left me for so long."

I watch as his features soften in slow motion. That smile that says he is about to get his way stretches over his face, causing me to swallow hard.

"You really missed me?" He brushes his fingers over my face gently, but I still flinch. He doesn't seem to notice. But the only thing I can think about is that Wilder would have noticed. Not only that, he would have helped me through it. But Troy isn't that man.

Of course he completely ignored that part where I said I was hurt that he left me. He wants reassurance for himself; he doesn't dare give it to me.

My hand goes to his head, stroking his fluff of dark hair. "Of course I missed you."

A devious grin washes away the look of sympathy on his face. "Then I think you need to show me how much?"

"I'm so tired," I whisper, hoping he will be somewhat generous tonight and let me just go to bed.

But when he flicks the corner of my towel and it falls to the ground, I'm not the least bit surprised. I should have known better than to think he was capable of anything but self-grati-fying acts.

His hand presses to the top of my head as he lowers me to my knees. My stomach churns with equal parts affliction and dread.

I turn my head as Troy pumps his semi-erect dick. But he doesn't like that my attention isn't on him so he grabs my face, pinching my cheeks as he forces my jaw to unclench.

I wince, suppressing the growl threatening to climb out of my throat.

Instead, I do what I have to do so I can have a decent night without worry of Troy erupting into an unmanageable beast.

I open my mouth and I take him—every inch. And with added emphasis, I cup his balls in my palm while imagining how good it would feel to squeeze them and bring him to his knees in tears.

Ignoring every disgusting word that comes out of his sexist mouth, I pretend this is the last time I ever have to touch this hairy sack or suck this mediocre dick. Because in my mind, I plot his demise.

It would be a slow death—a painful penance for all his sins. A hammer to each kneecap, a snap of each finger, then a thin slice around his neck that has him bleeding out little by little until I jab the knife into his carotid artery. I might get away with it, or I might not, but either way I'd be free of him until he meets me at the gates of hell.

The next thing I know, the salty taste of cum hits my tongue and I take him all the way to my tonsils, letting him finish down my throat. If I don't, I know he will be back for more later.

He steps away and runs his hand over the foggy mirror. "I guess you really did miss me," he says as he admires himself. "By the way…" He flashes a grin over his shoulder. "Once you're done working for the summer, I need you at the office. I'm in need of an assistant. Beth is quitting and moving out of Willow Creek, effective immediately."

I jump to my feet, bringing my towel up with me. "Beth quit? But why?"

"She's pregnant. Or did you already forget because you were too busy being fake with her."

I narrow my eyes at him, but the bastard doesn't even look back at me.

"Women are good for two things, Catherine. Being mothers and keeping houses. Beth was no longer reliable because of the baby, so I made her see that quitting was the best option."

The mother comment hits close to home, but it's moments like these that I am glad I took control of that situation. Troy could never have a baby and I don't want one with him.

"What is she going to do now?" I ask.

He shrugs as he begins to moisturize his face, still staring at himself in the mirror.

"Don't know and don't care. All I know is I need someone, and that someone is going to be you. Count your blessings that I'm going to do what I can without an assistant until the school year ends."

This time his gaze does leave his reflection, but only to give me a warning glare.

I don't know if I am overly confident right now or just plain stupid, but I push because there is no way he is going to do this to me. He forced me to be a teacher and now that I actually enjoy it, he does not get to take that away from me.

"Put out an ad for the job, Troy. I can't be your assistant," I spit out. "I'm a teacher. Besides, I took on a couple weeks of summer school classes, and I have to organize my classroom…"

He pulls up his boxers, snapping the waistband before bopping my nose. "Well, your plans just changed."

As he heads out the open bathroom door, I have to refrain myself from jumping on his back and digging my nails into his face. I can't believe him. He is a top-notch asshole. The worst of the worst.

He's dreaming if he thinks I'm going to work in that office every day, for him. Over my dead fucking body.

Luck was on my side tonight and Troy crashed hard and fast on the living room recliner after his shower. I'm actually surprised he didn't stay up to drill me about what I did all weekend, or if I met up with any "friends." Not that I have any.

I still can't believe he thinks I'm going to work for him this summer. The man has seriously lost his mind. One of our agreements was that he wouldn't interfere with my career, not that he's a man of his word.

With my bedroom door closed and *Friends* playing quietly on the television, I get comfortable in bed with my laptop by my side.

Taking a deep breath, I try to recenter myself. Troy has this way of making my world feel flipped on its axis and I need time to focus on me for a second to get it to recenter.

Picking up my phone, I open the SnapTok app, a smile immediately spreading across my face when I see about a dozen messages from Wilder.

I skim through them, my heart growing in size with each one. He tells me how much he loved spending time with me this weekend and how it ended too soon. He goes on to say how he can't stop thinking about me and how he's already looking forward to seeing me again. He says he emailed the speech and any help would be appreciated. Finally, he asks if I'll sneak out and meet him tonight, which isn't a remote possibility.

I type out a reply...

> CatEyes: This weekend with you was amazing, and you're heavy on my mind, too. I wish I could meet you tonight, but it's not an option.

As if he was holding his phone in his hand when I hit send, a reply comes right back.

> WildMisfit: Did he hurt you tonight?

I didn't expect that question, but it makes me feel good knowing that there is someone out there looking out for me.

> CatEyes: No. He wasn't too bad.

It's the truth. When Troy comes back from a trip, he is either clingy and sweet or mad about everything and just my voice can set him off. I was surprised after the news of Beth quitting that tonight didn't go downhill quickly, but I will take my blessings where I can get them.

I open up my email and download the doc Wilder sent as I wait for a reply. It's not very long, which is not a bad thing, but I'm sure his dad is going to want a little more depth with his speech.

Then, my phone buzzes with a response from Wilder.

> WildMisfit: I'm glad he wasn't too bad. And if you ever need help, or anything at all, please tell me, Cat. You don't have to go through anything alone ever again.

His words hit deep in my soul, so much so that tears form in my eyes. I've been alone my entire life with no one in my corner. At one time, I thought I had Troy, but it turns out, he only pulled me into his corner temporarily before pushing me back into mine all alone. It's a lonely life when you don't have someone to count on, and knowing I have Wilder now makes living so much more bearable.

CatEyes: I still can't figure out what planet you came from, but I'm glad we found each other. You're hands down the most amazing person I've ever met and now that I know you, I can't imagine my life without you in it.

I wait a second before typing the truth. With Wilder, I find that I want to tell him everything on my mind. So instead of hiding my feelings, I just lay it out there.

CatEyes: It kind of terrifies me.

A tear rolls down my cheek as I hit send because the truth hurts. Wilder isn't a permanent fixture in my life. He's a young man who has so much going for him that doesn't involve his almost-thirty-year-old teacher. This is just a phase and he's going to outgrow me before I outgrow him.

WildMisfit: I'm not going anywhere.

For now, is what he means. He's not going anywhere for now. He'll leave eventually but I'd endure the heartbreak of that loss for this limited amount of time with him. I'm falling hard for this guy, even when I know it's going to hurt in the end. I won't press on any of that tonight because we still have right now.

CatEyes: Neither am I.

I finish going over the document and add some fluff and words that I know will grab the attention of Grant's audience. I also fix up some punctuation errors and reword a few sentences that are already there. Then I email it back to Wilder.

When I go back into the app, I see another message from him.

> WildMisfit: Sweet dreams, Kitty Cat. I'll see you soon.

I giggle at the nickname.

> CatEyes: You, too. I emailed the speech back. Good night.

A strange feeling washes over me, as if I'm being watched, and when I look up from my phone, I see a pair of dark eyes glaring at me in the doorway.

"Troy," I gasp as I slam my phone over on the nightstand. "I thought you were asleep."

I have no idea how long he's been standing there but the look on his face tells me he's not happy with what he just witnessed. He steps into the room and closes the door without a word, so I spit out the first excuse I can come up with.

"I was just scrolling through some funny videos before I fell asleep."

A devious grin plays on his lips, one that sends shivers down my spine. "Those videos make you smile like that?"

I gulp, scooting up farther on the bed until my back is straight against the headboard. "One of the videos was sweet and funny so maybe that's why it was a strange smile?" My mouth twists in a grin, but I'm hoping my eyes don't betray me with their wide, panicked stare.

"Is that so?" He tsks, making his way over to the bed. He sits down right beside me, legs dangling off the side as he tips his chin. "Show me."

I put my hand on my phone, my heart ready to flee from my chest. "I already closed out of the app. In fact, I was just about to shut off the light and go to sleep."

Suddenly, Troy snatches my phone before he sends it flying across the room like a Frisbee. I don't even have time to react to his outburst when his hand wraps around my throat. He squeezes so hard I feel the air leaving my lungs, but I'm unable to get any more back in.

"Troy, please," I beg with the little breath I have left.

"Please, what?" His face contorts into a fit of rage. "Believe your lies? Let you go to sleep?" Raising his voice, he jerks my neck upward, until I'm forced to look into his eyes. "How about you tell me the goddamn truth, Catherine!" He squeezes so hard I can't even swallow.

I open my mouth to speak, to convince him I'm not lying, but nothing comes out. White spots dance around my vision, blurring the room around me.

This is it. This is where Troy finally kills me.

My ears feel full as my eyes begin to water. I don't even realize when they close, but soon everything fades to black.

For a second, there is nothing. No fighting, no pain, no worry. I feel weightless—like I'm on a cloud. Maybe this is what it's like to go to heaven?

I try to look around but everything is dark. Where is the white light everyone talks about?

When my body starts to come back to me, I feel faint kisses on my face. I want to smile, but I feel numb and can't quite figure out why.

A smile finally parts my lips because my first thought is Wilder. Then I hear Troy's voice.

"Wake up, Catherine." He kisses my cheek again while shaking my body. "Please. I'm so sorry, honey."

My eyes open fully as I gasp for air, a coughing fit assaulting my lungs as tears fall from my eyes. My ears pop like I was underwater. My head aches and I feel dizzy as my reality slams into me with the force of a freight train.

Troy cries out in relief as he throws his arms around me while I struggle to even move my body. I don't want him touching me.

The second I see his face, all my strength returns. In a swift motion, I shove my hands to his chest, pushing him off me.

I can't contain my rage, the fear clawing inside me so sharply it hurts. I need to get away from this man.

"I hate you!" I scream at the top of my lungs, feeling the words scratch my throat as they come out.

He goes flying to the end of the bed and I use this opportunity to get up. Feeling off-balance, I grab my dresser to steady myself, keeping an eye on Troy.

I see him coming toward me out of the corner of my eye, the waterworks continuing because that's what he does. He tries to play the victim when he almost killed me.

I hold up a hand, still bracing myself on the dresser. "Don't!" I grit out, causing him to freeze because I never stand my ground like this. "Don't you dare come near me."

This was a first. Troy has used my body as his punching bag for years, but he's never knocked me out, or choked me unconscious. He leaves bruises, but never anything like this.

He holds up both of his weaponized hands as if to surrender. "Don't do this, Catherine. It was an accident."

I turn my hung head and look him dead in the eye. "You're telling me not to do this? What the hell did I do, Troy? Please fucking tell me what I have ever done to you!" My words erupt like molten lava, surprising even myself. His eyes go wide, panicked because no one will be able to say I wasn't just choked out based on the bruising on my neck. I can feel it swelling already and I am certain I won't have a voice tomorrow because of it.

I'm done. Completely fucking done. I will no longer cower in fear of his abuse.

"An accident?" I shout as I straighten my back. This time it's me that walks toward him. I keep my chin up and my shoulders taut even though it hurts like hell. "You could have killed me!"

With each passing moment, I feel myself breaking free from this hold he has on me.

"You are evil, Troy Jenkins." I point my finger in his face when I finally get near him. The shock from him is still evident, so I make sure to give him everything I've got. "Pure fucking evil, and I am done!"

The look of empathy on his face twists into one of humor and he sputters a laugh. "Do you know how many times I've heard that?" He waves his arms up and down. "Yet here you are and here you will always be."

My jaw clenches and I shake my head. "This is the last time you'll ever hear it because I mean every goddamn word." My voice is final, making his back straighten.

He steps to the side, out of the path to the door. "Go ahead and leave. But keep in mind, the minute you walk out the door, I will make the call that will seal your fate."

I shrug my shoulders, not giving a fuck. For once, I don't care. Not about his threats, or his power. I just don't care. "You do what you gotta do," I glower as I walk past him toward the open door.

Just as I step out, hopeful he'll let me walk away, I hear him say, "Who were you fucking at the guesthouse this weekend, Catherine?"

His words hit me like a tidal wave. My body goes cold as all the blood drains from my face. I'm forced to put a hand on the doorframe to keep my weak knees from giving out on me.

Maybe I heard him wrong. I did just pass out, after all. "What did you say?" I ask without turning around.

The sound of his heavy footsteps padding across the room has my entire body trembling. Then, I feel his hot breath on my neck as he puts something in front of my face. "You heard me."

I'm forced to lean my head back to get a good look, but once I do, I gasp at the sight. "Those aren't mine," I blurt out the lie.

He shoves them in my face, covering my mouth and nose and I'm forced to breathe them in.

"I know what my wife fucking smells like!" he howls as I try to wriggle myself free. "And I know her fucking panties! But what I want to know is why they were in the goddamn trash can next door!"

I'm pushed forward and flung out of his grip. But this isn't over. I know the look in his eye, and this is only the beginning.

"You think I will ever let you walk away, Catherine? Think again."

The next thing I know I'm being thrown to the floor and kicked repeatedly in the gut, over and over and over. The pain is so intense that eventually, my body goes numb and I feel nothing at all. I just lie here, helplessly.

"The only way you will ever leave me is if you are in a casket, six feet under!"

I want to cry, I want to scream, but instead I do the last thing he would expect. My body is weak, but my mind is stronger than ever as I look up and make eye contact with the beast. "I hate you with every fiber of my being," I choke out. "And your kicks don't even hurt anymore."

Blood spurts from my mouth on a cough and he finally pauses. I chuckle, though, knowing his concern isn't for me, but himself.

"Can't have the great mayor get caught with his beaten-to-death wife. How would that look?"

He scowls down at me, tossing my panties over my face as I lie there, a shell of a human as he walks away in all his glory.

Then, I fall asleep curled in a ball on the floor because I can't bear to move a muscle.

But I do know one thing for sure. Troy knows I was with someone and he knows I want to leave. And those two things might very well cost me my life.

CHAPTER 17
WILDER

For two days, mine and Cat's chat log has been silent—aside from me messaging her about a dozen times. Each time, she doesn't respond. I can't shake this growing unease inside me. I find myself circling in front of her classroom door, waiting for her to show up. I even got here right when the doors to the school unlocked.

I drove by her house twice yesterday and wanted to stop, but the thought of getting her in any trouble with her husband paralyzes me.

The hall is fairly empty, aside from a few students lingering. I put my back to the wall beside the door and kick my foot up as I glance at my phone in my hand. She should be here by now.

Mr. Hargrove, the principal, comes down the hall and I immediately push myself off the wall. "Hey, Mr. Hargrove." I wave as I make my way toward him.

"Good morning, Wilder. You're here early."

I walk by his side down the hall as he sorts through some keys in his hand. "Yeah. I was hoping to get some help from Mrs. Jenkins on something. Have you seen her yet this morning?"

"Actually, I have. I'm headed to unlock her classroom now for the substitute. Mrs. Jenkins is out sick today."

He stops at her door and sticks the key in the hole while I try to rationalize what he just said.

"What kind of sickness?" I ask, speaking manically. "A cold? A stomach bug? The flu? What is it?"

He turns the handle and pushes the door open an inch, only to close it again before putting the keys in his pocket. "I'm not the one who spoke with her. There's no reason to worry, though. I'm sure she'll be back tomorrow." With that said, he walks back the way he came.

My whole world stops, time standing still as I try to think of why she would be out today, but nothing makes sense.

Something's wrong.

I can feel it in my gut. Cat is in trouble.

Without a second thought, I jog down the hall. As soon as I reach the front doors, I shove them open and I take off running to my car.

I should have hurried and helped her clean up the guest-house. She was so scared her husband was coming home and my immature ass just pouted because I wanted more time with her. I should have done so much more to help her.

Students are beginning to arrive and the parking lot is filling fast so I waste no time getting in my car and driving straight to Cat's house.

Repercussions be damned, I pull right up to her front door. With the engine still running, I get out hurriedly, leaving the driver's side door open.

Walking briskly to the front door, I immediately begin knocking on it. "Cat," I holler. "Are you here? I need to know you're okay."

I pound a few more times, the intensity of each one growing louder and louder. "Mrs. Jenkins!" I shout. "Please answer the door."

Taking a step back, I look up at the camera pointed at me, noticing the steady greenlight. "Where is she?" I raise my voice even louder. "I know you did something to her!"

"You have some nerve coming here again, young man." His voice cuts through the speaker, making me grit my teeth. Of course he won't face me like a man. I knew he was watching. He's always watching.

My jaw tics in fury as I scream with balled fists at my sides. "I'm not leaving until I see her with my own eyes!"

The greenlight stays on, but he doesn't say anything else, so I resume beating on the door, hoping she's well enough to get up and answer.

A few minutes later, I lean over with my hands to my knees, unsure what to do next. I could break in, but that'll just get me arrested. Then again, it might be worth it just to know Cat is safe.

Or I could find her beaten to a pulp on the floor and then what? Just give Troy the opportunity to blame me, or worse, hurt her more.

Fuck! There's no right answer here.

The sound of an engine roaring down the driveway at full speed has me shooting up. I see Troy's truck—a black Toyota Tundra.

Fuck.

He pulls up right behind me and the next thing I know, he's rounding the front of the truck, shaking a stern finger at me with his keys clenched in his fist. "Get the hell off my property before I call the cops and have your ass arrested!"

Taking a safe approach, I keep my tone low. "I just need to know she's okay. She was helping me with an assignment and she's been ghosting me. If you think no one pays attention to her then you're wrong. I'm not the only one who's concerned," I bluff, hoping it will at least get him to let me see her.

The space between us is closed in two seconds flat and he's in my face. "I could kill you right now for trespassing and get away with it, you know that, right?" He is furious, like a man I have never seen before. How did he become the mayor with a temper like this?

"Is that what you did to her? Did you kill her, *Troy*?" I put emphasis on his name because I've never called him anything but Mayor, or Mr. Jenkins.

He scoffs, shaking his head as if I were just some child. "Have you lost your damn mind, kid? I love my wife more than anything in this world. Why the hell would I ever do anything to hurt her?"

I shrug condescendingly. "Because I don't believe anything that comes out of your sleazy mouth."

"You're going to regret this, Wilder." He snarls. "Mark my words. Your reputation is about to go up in flames if you don't get the hell away from my house right this damn minute."

I throw my hands up, then let them fall to my sides. I have to refrain from laughing because he could do nothing to my reputation. He might be the mayor but my father has more money and reach than he could ever hope to achieve. I'm not untouchable by any means, but I hold power here and he knows it. "Just let me see her and I'll leave. It's that simple."

Reaching into his pocket, he pulls out his phone, speaking with a smug grin as he taps his index finger to the screen like an old man who just got his first phone. "Don't say I didn't warn you."

"Wait," I blurt out. "I don't want any trouble," I assure him. As much as I want to stay until I see Cat, there are other ways. This will kill my dad if he finds out I came to the mayor's house and raised hell.

He slowly lowers his phone. "Leave," he grits out the word grimly.

With a heavy sigh and no choice in the matter, I walk to my car. He might have defeated me this time, but I won't rest until I know Cat is safe.

I get in, close the door, and pull down the wraparound driveway slowly. Every few seconds, I glance in the rearview mirror and see him standing there with his head down as he taps into his phone.

When I reach the end of the driveway, I look again and see that he's gone, but his truck is unmoved.

I take a sharp turn into the guesthouse driveway and pull all the way to the front so my car is blocked by the trees between the two lots.

Then I get out and take the trail cautiously back to the Jenkinses' main house.

Creeping quietly and carefully, I make my way to the backyard, looking through each window I pass by only to find no sign of Cat or Troy.

It isn't until I'm on the back porch looking through the glass sliding door into the kitchen that I see movement. A shadow flickers past the far room that I take to be the living room.

When it passes by again, I see that it's Troy. The sound of his angered voice pierces my ears and I realize a window is open close by.

I pull out my phone and start recording because I need proof of his abuse—Cat needs proof. Maybe then she'll find the strength and courage to finally leave him.

"Tell me the truth, you fucking bitch!" I hear him shout, and my heart nearly stops.

My entire body shakes with rage when I see Cat come into view. She's curled over as she limps slowly into the kitchen. "I am telling you the truth. I swear to you, Troy…" Her timid voice unnerves me because I know he's beaten her into submission.

Suddenly, Troy appears again and like a movie playing in slow motion, I watch as he clenches his teeth and raises his hand in the air.

He hits her in the back of the head without warning and she drops to her knees.

My heart sinks into my stomach and without hesitation, I grab the handle of the glass door and slide it open with force. I burst into the room, my heart racing with adrenaline just as Troy fists her hair and pulls her head back.

With my phone still recording in my hand, I immediately

look at Cat who is doubled over in agony. Her eyes meet mine with a look of shock and fear. My first instinct is to go to her, but when I hear Troy's voice, I'm reminded there is something I need to do first.

"I thought I told you to leave!" Troy growls with a malicious tone. "You won't get away this time. Now, I am calling the cops, and your dad." His threat hangs heavy in the air, but I leave it there because it means nothing to me. He's not calling anybody.

I walk over to him, feeling the rage inside me grow tenfold. My mind isn't even my own when I cock my fist back and lunge at his face. Except Troy throws his hand in the air, catching my strike.

He squeezes my hand, jaw ticking in fury as he lowers it to my side. "You best leave and pretend you were never here, Cromwell."

With my hand free from him, I shove him hard in the chest, forcing him to stumble back a few steps. "You lay another hand on her and I'll be the one calling the cops."

He chuckles deviously as he regains his footing. "You're delusional. I'd never hurt my wife."

"Oh, give up the act, old man. You're nothing but a wife beater and before long, the whole world will know it." I wave my phone in the air and he seems to just now realize what I was doing with it. He pales, giving me a grim sort of satisfaction.

"Wilder!" Cat shouts from the floor. "Just go. Please." My eyes shoot to hers and I see the look of panic in them as she pleads with me.

I join her side while Troy follows behind me like the possessive son of a bitch he is. "Get away from her!"

Ignoring him, I crouch down on the floor beside Cat, taking in all her injuries. There's a bruised handprint around her throat, and she's got a busted lip that has fresh blood on it. She looks frail and exhausted, nothing like the woman I kissed goodbye just two days ago. "I'm not leaving you like this," I tell her as I attempt to sweep some hair away from her bloody lip.

She swats my hand away, taking me by surprise. "I don't want you here," she whispers, but I see the truth in her eyes. "You have to go, Wilder. You're making everything so much worse."

Those last words are like a dagger straight to the heart. "Okay," I whisper, "I'll go." The last thing I want is to make things worse for her. I've seen her husband's angry side now and I don't want to be the reason he strikes her again. But I've got something to ensure he can't make it any worse.

I stand up, narrow my eyes on Troy, and say, "You lay a finger on her again and I'll make damn sure everyone knows about it."

He steps up to me, nose to nose. "You speak a word of this, and I'll make damn sure every dream you have is a distant memory. As for your dad, I'll bury his ass right along with yours." I chuckle, this time giving him a taste of his own medicine.

"You have no power when it comes to me, Troy. I can see that infuriates you. So let me make one thing clear. Your threats to me are useless, and if anything happens to her, I will bury *you*."

With that, I glance back down at the woman I am falling for. I told her she didn't have to do this alone, and I meant it. I might have to leave right now, but I will be coming back and next time, I'll make damn sure she leaves with me.

CHAPTER 18
CATHERINE

My heart breaks every time I see a message from Wilder. Forced to ignore it, I go on with my day.

After Troy caught me on my phone, I'm careful to avoid it as much as I can while he is home. I downloaded one of those domestic violence apps that help disguise messages as other things so Troy doesn't see anything, but for now I have to ignore it.

When Wilder came into the house and threatened Troy, I messaged him to explain a few things. He deserved to know I was okay and that Troy held my phone hostage all weekend. I can only assume he gave it back to me because of Wilder's threats.

I told Wilder that what we have isn't over, but I need Troy to back off for a little bit so that I can find a way to leave without ending up dead or hurt. Wilder agreed and I've only gotten a few messages here and there.

What I didn't tell him is that Troy knows we slept together. At least, he suspects it. I never came right out and gave him an answer, but I didn't deny it either. He did some digging after that day and found Wilder's account. He saw the video Wilder made at the guesthouse and he recognized the couch.

Every excuse in the world came out of my mouth, but nothing sufficed. His mind was made up. I was belittled and made to feel like a dirty whore. But he didn't lay a finger on me, which surprised me.

After he knocked me out and cleaned my blood off of the carpet, he helped me to bed because I couldn't move. He's been more cautious with me. Not to be mistaken for kind or caring, but he hasn't hit me since Wilder threatened him.

It's been four days since Wilder showed up at my house like a knight in shining armor. There was nothing more painful than telling him to walk away. I didn't do it for myself, but for him. Troy holds true to the threats he makes and he'd do everything in his power to bring down the entire Cromwell family.

So I made a deal with the beast. I told him I'd stay away from Wilder and we could work on our marriage if he takes anger management classes. I'm not staying with him. In fact, I'm already planning my escape, but I need time.

Today, I returned to work. My body is still sore and tired, but my visible wounds have healed. I've been pacing the classroom since I arrived, knowing Wilder will be coming through the door any minute—for the very last time.

The seniors are done with school after today. It literally pains me to know I won't see his smiling face in this room ever again. I'm not even sure *when* I'll see him again.

As soon as the door comes open, I freeze. Eyes watching keenly as the gorgeous soul who stole my heart enters.

I fold my hands in front of my body, rubbing my sweaty thumbs together. "Hi," I say softly.

Wilder forces a smile, but it's cracked and frayed and not the expression I'm used to seeing on his face. *I did this to him. I hurt him.*

He closes the door gently then we meet in the middle of the classroom, silence hanging heavy between us. "I've missed you," he says on a whisper.

I shouldn't admit it because it will only hurt worse when I have to run, but I can't help myself. "I've missed you, too."

A gentle hand reaches out and he strokes my cheek with the back of his fingers. "You look good."

Cracking a smile, I say, "Thank you."

I know what he means. He's saying I look better than the last time I saw him. When I felt like I was on the brink of death.

"Things are better," I tell him, partially believing the words. Strangely, things actually are better. Troy hasn't hurt me since that day. There have even been days where I convinced myself this situation changed Troy. Maybe he realized how close he was to losing me and he's making a conscious effort to be better. Other days, I still see the malice in his eyes and I'm reminded that, like a chameleon, a beast can change his colors, but he's still a beast.

"I'm glad, Cat. I really am." The pain in Wilder's eyes cuts through me. Tears prick the corners of my eyes and he takes notice. "Hey," he says in a hushed tone. "Don't cry, Kitty Cat. Everything's gonna be just fine."

I can't help myself. I break down in tears and the next thing I know, I'm in the safety net of Wilder's arms.

The door to the classroom comes open and I immediately jump back. It was short-lived but that hug was the reminder I needed to break away from the chains Troy has me in.

I hastily wipe my face to greet my students, but when I see it's Rome and Elodie, I immediately turn away. For some reason, Elodie is glaring daggers at me. I'm not sure what she knows, but she knows something and she doesn't seem to approve.

"We'll talk later," I whisper as I step past him. Other students will be arriving soon.

Moving to my desk, I listen to their hushed voices as they drill Wilder. I'm pretty sure Rome demanded the truth, whatever that means. Followed by Elodie saying, "People are talking, so you need to come up with something quick."

"Talking about what?" I blurt out as I pivot to face them.

We're alone in here so I feel like we can have an honest conversation without this whispering that spikes my anxiety.

All eyes land on me, but it's Wilder who speaks up. "It's okay," he says in a reassuring tone. "Everything is fine."

My eyebrows shoot to my forehead. "What is fine?" I ask authoritatively. "Someone tell me what's going on."

Wilder looks from Rome to Elodie then to me as he scratches the back of his head. "It's a video I posted. Students are beginning to speculate..."

Oh, dear God. I sure as hell hope they don't think, or know, it was me. If the staff here caught wind, I could lose my job. "What are they speculating, Wilder?"

He doesn't say anything and his lack of response speaks volumes. I saw the video. I read the comments. Wilder's entire female following have become detectives ever since that video was posted.

"Dammit," I spit out. "Someone tell me what is going on right now!" I lower my voice to a near whisper. "Please."

Elodie steps forward, a look of remorse on her face. "One person made a joke about it being you in the video, and Wilder's followers ran with it. Some even went as far as doing reverse image searches of the side of your head...err, the girl in the video's head."

My face drops into my hands and I massage my temples. I can't believe this is happening. Just when I thought things might settle down enough for me to have a few minutes alone with Wilder so I could tell him how much I still care about him and how badly I've missed him—now I have to stay away from him more than ever.

Soft hands land on my shoulders and when I look up, I see the brown eyes I always get lost in. "There's no proof," Wilder says confidently. "We're good."

I look past him at Elodie and Rome, curious of what they're thinking. They must know something is going on with us because they aren't fazed in the slightest right now. "Do they know?" I ask Wilder because I have to know how many mouths can speak on this.

Wilder lifts his shoulders, caging in his neck. "They just figured it out and Rome read right through my excuses."

"We won't tell," Elodie says. "Your secret is safe with us. We just want you and Wilder to be safe from…" Her words trail off but I know what she was going to say. This means Wilder told her about Troy.

My expression drops, right along with my heart. "You told them?"

"I was so fucking scared, Cat. I didn't know what to do and I had to talk to someone."

That makes sense. The scene he walked in on with Troy and me had to be traumatizing. I just don't want everyone to know about it. My reputation is at stake here, too.

"Who else?" I stammer.

"No one. I swear." His eyes lock with mine.

I believe him. His eyes don't lie to me, not that I think he would. Wilder has never given me any reason not to trust what he says.

"No one else can know." I look from him to Elodie, who is already nodding her head in agreement. "You need to delete that video and stop this chain reaction."

He shifts on his feet a bit and pops the tip of his thumb between his teeth, chewing on his nail as he glances at his brother.

"Oh my God," I hiss. "Is this about your view count and your followers?"

"No!" His cheeks flush red. "Not at all. I'll delete the video. No problem. I'm just worried about you. What happens when this gets back to your husband?"

More students begin to enter the room so I end the conversation with, "I can handle my husband."

At least, I hope I can.

All throughout class there are whispers circulating. I pay

them no attention and when the bell rings, I dismiss everyone while wishing the seniors well.

Wilder hangs back, and we say goodbye with a hug. His mouth ghosts my ear and his warm breath sends a shiver down my spine. "Check your SnapTok."

He isn't even completely out the door when I open the app on my phone.

> WildMisfit: We always have CatEyes and WildMisfit, right? Please just talk to me on here.

I want to smile, I really do, but how can I when my heart is so broken? Rome and Elodie know we slept together, that I am cheating on my husband with my student. And what's worse? They know my husband physically abuses me.

I type out a response, but it's not what I want to say, nor what Wilder will want to hear.

> CatEyes: We need to give it time. It's too soon. Once things cool down and we're not the topic of everyone's conversations, we can talk.

I hit send and I can't help but feel like this is the beginning of the end for us.

CHAPTER 19
WILDER

As much as I wanted to respond to Cat's last message, I'm giving her the space and time she needs, at least, for now.

She's still on my mind all day. I can still smell her sweet lavender scent on the clothes I wore the night we slept together, and sometimes I swear I can hear her voice. After school yesterday I was walking through the parking lot and saw a brunette standing by my car. For a split second I thought it was her, until the person turned around and I realized it was Sam.

For some fucked-up reason that girl can't get it through her head that I'm not going to prom with her. She's told everyone in school that we're going together, but meeting there. When I approached her in the parking lot, she told me her dress color is burnt orange, as if she actually thinks I'm going to match my suit to her and get her a corsage.

In the end, I just nodded and let her think what she wants. Prom is the last thing on my mind, but nonetheless, here I am getting help from my dad with my tie—baby blue, *not* burnt orange.

I stare in the mirror as I watch him tie it for the third time. I know he wants to say something but he is holding back for some reason.

Did I fuck up his speech? I felt like I was able to put something decent together, and Cat definitely improved it.

"Lots of rumors going around," Dad says as he cinches the knot around my neck for what I hope is the final time. "I just hope none of them are true."

I purposely look away, unable to meet his eyes. I'm not sure what he's heard, but I hope like hell it has to do with Callan and not me.

"Rumors have a way of doing that," I quip, keeping my eyes on my reflection. "Good thing we don't believe everything we hear."

"Let's hope you're right. The last thing our family needs is another fuckup from one of its members."

It's not often my dad swears so I know he's pissed. "What did Callan do this time?" But when I look at him, I know it's not my brother he's talking about.

"Not Callan," he deadpans as he jerks my neck forward. "You."

"Me?" I look at him with wide eyes, as if I can't believe I could have done anything to piss him off. "I haven't given anyone anything to talk about so it has to be a matter of miscommunication."

"Is that so?" he seethes as he drops his hands, still glaring at me like I'm an enemy and not his son. He pats a firm hand to my shoulder, holding it there. "Look at me," he demands.

My eyes hesitantly lift to meet his and I see the fury behind them. "He's the wrong man to mess with, Wilder. So if you've been sneaking into his guesthouse with your dipshit friends and using it as your own personal hotel, it ends now."

I exhale a sigh of relief and I almost want to laugh. Is this the rumor Troy is spreading to try and threaten me? Does he think my father will actually turn against me? Dad definitely heard something, but he heard it all wrong—thank fuck.

"It was one time," I tell him, going along with the rumor for now. If Troy thinks he's winning, then he will be more likely to fuck up. "He was out of town, and—"

"I don't care," he stammers. "Don't do it again. I'm running in an election against this man, do not give him ammunition— because he will use it. And certainly do not get yourself arrested in the process. Do I make myself clear?"

"Yes, sir," I say respectfully.

Dad's face softens. He isn't normally hard on us so I know this is weird for him. Especially with me. He looks up at me, a plea and something like concern mixed together in his gaze. "You're on the right path, Wilder. I'd hate to see all your hard work be for nothing."

I nod in response, desperate for this conversation to end. I swear my dad, like Rome, has the ability to sniff lies out of me.

"Watch yourself tonight." He pats my shoulder and smiles. "Make good choices, son. We're almost to the finish line."

He has to mean graduation because the election is still months away. Regardless, I say, "Will do."

The sound of someone laying heavy on a car horn rings in our ears and Dad grumbles as he heads toward my bedroom door. "The dumbasses have arrived."

Dad's never been a fan of Luke's. Aiden he tolerates, but much like ninety percent of the population, he thinks Luke is disrespectful and immature. When I was about thirteen, my father went as far as to try and bribe me with five hundred bucks to drop him as a friend. We laughed it off, but I'm certain he was dead serious. Now, I could probably get five thousand.

Luke's friendship is priceless, though. He's one of those guys who will treat everyone else like trash but he'd defend the ones he loves to no end. And he happens to love me like a brother.

I give myself one last look in the mirror, taking in my light gray suit, blue tie, and matching Oxford shoes. Not gonna lie, I look pretty fucking good in a suit.

The sound of the horn rings again and when I jog down the

stairs, I see Dad rip the front door open, almost taking it off the hinges. "He's coming!" he screams into the dim night air.

I walk past him, patting him on the shoulder as I leave. "Later, Dad."

Luke comes out of the driver's side window, his hands on the roof. "Hurry your ass up, Cromwell. There's a gym full of hot chicks waiting for us to check them out."

I shake my head at his class act as I move faster to the car.

Swinging open the back door, I drop down inside beside Brady. Luke sinks back down in his seat as Aiden passes Brady a bottle of tequila.

Brady takes a swig then holds it out to me but I shake my head. I don't drink too often, and when I do, it's usually because I'm pissed off. The last time I drank was at the end of the football season when Rome took his position back from me as QB and I returned to my spot on the team as running back.

It's not that I didn't like my position, I did. It's what I've done on the field my entire high school career. And Rome was made to be quarterback. It's just, when it was me, I felt like the star of the show. I was the important Cromwell on the field and for a brief time, I wasn't living in Rome's shadow.

Anyway, I got shit-faced that night and when I woke up, I swore to myself I'd never drink to drown my sorrows again. And I haven't since.

Luke, being the hotshot he thinks he is, pulls his car right up onto the sidewalk in front of the high school. Left tires on the pavement, right tires on the walkway. "Dude," I huff. "Can't you park like a normal person?"

He kills the engine and doesn't hesitate to jump out of the car through the window. "Where's the fun in that?"

"You're gonna get towed," Brady warns him.

Luke snickers. "In that case, who's driving me to the impound tomorrow?" He laughs as we all make our way to the front doors.

The minute we step in, my breath catches in my throat.

Standing three feet away, talking to Mr. Hargrove, is Cat. She's dressed in a dark purple satin dress that runs down to the floor, hugging every curve of her body. Her dark hair is piled in a bun on the top of her head with tiny tendrils of curls framing her face.

"Come on, man," Aiden scoffs. "What are you waiting for?"

I snap out of the trance I fell in and keep walking, but I'm unable to take my eyes off her. When she drops her head back laughing, I take notice of a tiny bruise on her collarbone. I'm not sure if it's new, or old, but the rest of her body looks unharmed and I'm thankful for that.

Maybe staying away is beneficial for her, after all. Even if it kills me inside.

As I walk past her, our eyes connect and her surprise is apparent. She draws in a deep breath and I watch as she swallows hard before pretending not to notice me at all. It hurts, but it's necessary. Especially with half the student body thinking we slept together. Not that they're wrong. We just can't allow those rumors to get out because she'd lose her job, or worse.

Both gym doors are open and blue balloons run down the length of them. Two chaperones stand on either side, greeting us as we walk in. Disco lights circulate in the dark room and the theme for the event is apparent when everything looks like it's been covered in blue ice. There's even an ice sculpture of a snowflake in the middle of the dance floor.

"There you are." Sam's voice hits my ears before I even see her. She comes up behind me, putting a hand on my shoulder as she joins my side. "I was wondering when you'd get here."

"Here I am," I sing as I keep my eyes straight ahead. If I give her too much attention, she'll want more.

"Let's dance." She tugs my arm with a pout. My eyes slide to hers, but I don't move. "Oh come on, Wilder. It's just a dance."

I watch as Luke and Aiden join a group of girls on the dance floor and figure, what the hell. It is just a dance. Maybe this will satisfy her hunger for a while and she'll leave me the hell alone.

Maybe it'll also stop people from thinking I slept with my teacher. She does have the same color hair as Cat. This could help get people off my back.

"Fine," I quip. "But just one."

She squeals in excitement. "Of course. Just one."

We walk out to the dance floor together and I make it a point to join the group so it doesn't look like Sam and I are here together. It's not that I care what any student here thinks, but I do care what Cat thinks. I don't want her thinking I've moved on or that I no longer care. Truth is, I'm only here because I knew she was chaperoning and it was a way to be able to see her, even if we can't talk.

Sam uses every opportunity to grind against me to the beat of "Hide" by Creed. My body moves, and my eyes do the same as I scour the room in search of Cat. She was standing outside the gym when I first saw her, but she could be in here by now. I wonder if she's got someone to talk to. I'd hate for her to be standing all alone.

The song ends and I'm about to walk off the dance floor without a word to Sam when she grabs my arm. "One more?" she begs. "It's a slow one and I *love* this song."

Exhaling profoundly, I turn back around and put an arm around her waist, keeping an inch of space between us while "Hanging by a Moment" by Lifehouse plays. Little good that space does because Sam just eats it right up with her body.

If any guy did this shit to a girl, he would get so much hate, but no one says anything to Sam as she keeps trying to take advantage and sell the lies she's been spewing.

With one hand on my side and the other hanging loosely around her, I move in slow circles. When we've done a complete one-eighty, my eyes find Cat as if they knew exactly where to look. Unconsciously aware that I do it, I stop guiding the movements of the dance and follow Sam's lead.

Cat looks lost as she stands there with her hands folded in front of her, eyes moving unhurriedly around the room. Then, she sees me. Our eyes meet and I watch her body tense, literally crushing my soul. I miss the smile I'd get when we'd catch each other's gazes in a crowded room. Her head tilts slightly to the left, her chest rising as she draws in a deep breath. She gives me a hint of a fractured smile, but I see behind the facade of what it's supposed to be.

I want to go to her. Take her hand and pull her away from the noise. Not just here, but everywhere. It's all static and nonsense. This world is full of dream crushers and nonbelievers of things like love and heartbreak.

As people bustle around us, my eyes lock onto hers and everything else fades away—she's all I see. All I want to see. The lyrics of the song speak to us because I'm literally falling even more in love with her as each second passes by.

It will always be her.

I go to pull away from Sam because I'm done fighting this. I surrender to the universe. They can speak what they want; I can't go another minute without her.

But, I'm pulled back in and the next thing I know, Sam is crushing her mouth against mine. I try to break free from her hold but the girl is relentless as she tries to probe my mouth with her tongue. I'm forced to put my hands between us, literally peeling her off me.

"What the fuck, Sam!" I snap as I shake my head and walk off the dance floor.

I don't even give the girl a second look because my focus is on Cat, who is no longer standing where my eyes left her. I have no idea how Sam, or my friends, respond. All I know is that I can't be here for a second longer. This was a horrible idea.

I move frantically through crowded bodies trying to find her, but she's nowhere to be found. I feel like I'm suffocating beneath water and when I step out of the gym, I suck a deep breath of air in my lungs. My eyes move up and down the hall, and I spot her purple dress turning the corner at the end toward the lockers.

Walking steadfastly, I go after her. Once I turn into the hall, I see her go around another corner. "Cat," I call out faintly. I move faster, finally gaining on her. "Hey," I holler again, and this time she stops.

Spinning around, she faces me and I see her tear-soaked eyes. "Just go back to the dance, Wilder."

"No," I tell her point-blankly as I close the space between us. "I wanna be with you."

"You think that's what you want, and maybe you do right now." Tears fall down her cheeks even as she swipes at them angrily. It breaks my heart to see her like this. I never wanted to be the one to cause her pain. "But what about tomorrow, or next week, or next year, Wilder?"

I shake my head, adamant with my words because she has no idea what she does to me. "I'll still want to be with you, Cat. That's all I'll ever want."

She shakes her head, tears continuing to roll down her soft cheeks, bringing streaks of black mascara with them. "Go back to Sam. You deserve to enjoy your senior prom."

"Fuck Sam," I spit out. "I don't care about her. I care about you." My hands go toward her and this time, she doesn't push away.

"This is so hard," she cries as I wrap my arms around her. "I don't know what to do."

"Then do nothing, baby." I stroke her hair, trying to push all of the comfort I can into her body because I need her to know I'm here to stay. "Stop overthinking everything so much. I'm not going to let anything happen to you."

"You don't understand. No one does."

I pull back just enough to see her eyes. "Then make me understand. Tell me what it is that I don't know so I can help you. *Let* me help you."

She draws in a shaky breath. "He'll never let me leave." The terror in her eyes is soul-crushing.

"Why?" I ask. That one word holds so much weight.

"Something happened in my past that involved some very

bad people. Troy saved me from them, but he's made it a point to hand me over the minute I step out of line or try to leave him."

The fear that begins to overtake her tells me this is serious. It isn't something small. But what's worse is it's clear she has wanted to leave for a while now. After what I saw the other day, I know there is more to this than what I can comprehend, but she needs to feel safe and secure to tell me so I can actually help her.

A thought crosses my mind. An irrational one, but a thought, nonetheless. "Run away with me."

She cracks a smile, one I didn't realize how badly I needed to see until now. "You're insane."

"Insane and serious." Taking her hands in mine, I squeeze gently. "I mean it, Cat. We can leave Willow Creek together. Go somewhere where no one will ever find us."

"*He* would find us." Her hands tremble beneath mine. "Besides, I would never allow you to do that for me."

"I'm not asking your permission. I'm telling you that I want to run away with you, Cat. I'd risk everything for you. Don't you know that by now?"

I will throw her over my shoulder right now and take her to the next state over if I have to. This time, I'm not taking no for an answer.

"Okay," she spits out, taking me by surprise.

"Okay?"

"Graduate high school and give me a couple weeks while I try to come up with a more realistic plan, and if it doesn't pan out, I'll run away with you."

All I heard was her agreeing to run away with me and that is enough to have me scooping her up in my arms while spinning her around.

She giggles and it's a beautiful sound. One I want to hear every day for the rest of my life.

I put her back on her feet and she stretches up to kiss my lips. "I have to get back to the dance and chaperone. We have to keep things on the down-low for a while. That's the only way any of this is going to work."

"Of course," I tell her. "But please don't ghost me again. It scares the shit of me when you do that."

She cracks a smile. "I'll try to contact you when I can."

I kiss her again before I watch her walk away. I hate not knowing when I'll see her again, but at least now I know I will.

This isn't the end, it's only the beginning.

CHAPTER 20
WILDER

"LET'S welcome the Willow Creek High class of two thousand and twenty-four graduates." Principal Hargrove's voice booms over the loudspeaker, signaling the start of the ceremony. The sound of clapping and cheering echoes through the stadium as we begin our walk down the red carpet on the football field. It was always assumed that Rome and I would walk together when we graduate, but I gave him the thumbs-up to walk with Elodie and I have no regrets. Except one—I'm stuck with Sam. It's only a short walk and a few pictures, though, so I'm sucking it up while she's eating it up.

The stands are filled with proud guests and their excitement for us is obvious in their loud chants. I look around, searching for one attendee in particular. Mayor Jenkins is here to give a small speech so I can only guess Cat is here, too. Yet, I don't see her with him.

Sam and I take our seats and when the last pair are seated, Brady Newtown is called to the stage as this year's valedictorian.

"Welcome, community members, friends and family, and most importantly, my fellow graduates. We fricken did it, guys!"

"Yes!" I beam with my hands in the air, along with my classmates.

He continues his speech and there are a few laughs, even a few tears. Then, my teeth grit when Mayor Jenkins is called to the stage.

Everyone claps for him, but I roll my eyes and look down, not willing to give him an ounce of my attention. That scumbag doesn't even deserve to be alive, let alone the mayor of this town.

"Good evening, my beloved community, and congratulations to our graduates. During my years in office, it's been an honor to be part of these ceremonies. I remember my high school graduation on this very stage many, many years ago." Everyone laughs but I just scoff. "It's my hope that every one of you will follow your dreams, reach your goals, and remember where you came from…"

I shut out everything else he says because it's all hypocritical nonsense as far as I'm concerned. Reaching beneath my graduation gown, I pull my phone out of my pocket, hiding it beneath the long teal fabric as I type Cat a message on SnapTok.

WildMisfit: Are you here?

As I wait for a response, I flip my phone upside down underneath my gown.

Mayor Jenkins finally wraps up his speech, after reminding everyone to vote for him in the election, of course.

He's a real class act. I shouldn't be surprised that he'd use our ceremony to try and get votes.

Next, our names are called one by one.

After Rome is called to the stage to collect his diploma, it's my turn. Once I'm up there, facing the crowd, I find Cat standing at the end of the bleachers by the fence, alone. I freeze momentarily in front of everyone as our eyes lock. She waves her hand at me, smiling, and I suddenly remember what I'm supposed to be doing.

Shit. I walk across the stage and shake Principal Hargrove's hand before accepting my diploma from Brady.

More than anything, I want to go to her instead of sitting back down and listening impatiently for everyone else's names to be called. Fortunately, our class isn't too large so it goes by quickly.

The past week had been a blur without Cat by my side. I dropped into her classroom during her lunch break on Wednesday, just to see her for a few minutes. We've been chatting on the app every day, but it's not enough. I've been missing her like crazy.

The minute we flip our tassels and toss our caps in the air, I haul ass in her direction, leaving my cap on the ground on the field.

I push through the swarm of families greeting their graduates, and my eyes find hers again, never leaving them until I'm in front of her at the fence. "You came," I say with the little breath I have left in me.

"I wouldn't miss it for the world." She lifts a smile before it quickly drops. "I can't stay, though. Troy doesn't know I'm here and if he…" Her words trail off and I turn my head to follow her gaze and realize why she suddenly looks so pale. "Oh no," she says timidly.

"It's okay," I tell her. "We're in a public place. You'll be fine."

Coming in our direction is Troy. His face is red, his hands clenched while storming toward us with the anger of a pissed-off bull. He wouldn't dare make a scene here with all these voters watching, though. There's not a chance in hell. But that doesn't mean Cat won't reap the consequences later.

Behind Troy, I notice my parents, Rome, and Elodie coming toward us, nothing but smiles.

This can't end well.

"Shouldn't you be home in bed, darling?" Troy says sternly to Cat. "You're sick, after all."

Cat rolls her lips together nervously before nodding. "I was feeling better and thought I'd come watch my students graduate." Her voice cracks and breaks and I fucking hate that he does this to her.

"Congratulations, son," Dad says as he joins us, his hard gaze landing on Troy. "Everything okay here?"

"No," Troy responds harshly. "I don't think everything is okay. Is it, Wilder?"

"Look," Dad begins. "If this is about Wilder and his friends crashing at your guesthouse, I've dealt with it like I said I would."

I look at Cat and I can see she's surprised by the lie Troy told. What I don't understand is why he told the lie in the first place. I can only assume he's embarrassed that his wife is sneaking around with her student and wouldn't dare let it get out to the public.

"It doesn't look like you're handling it at all," Troy hisses. "Everywhere my wife goes lately, your son is there." He steps up to my dad, raising his voice while people begin gathering around us. "If you know what's good for you, Cromwell, you'll keep your damn son away from my wife. I'd hate for us to have to file for a protection order."

"A protection order?" Dad laughs. "Why would she possibly need protection from Wilder? He's just her student."

Dad looks at me and I'm certain he can see right through me. Despite my attempt to hide the truth, I feel like it's written all over my face.

"Is there something you need to tell me, Wilder?" Dad asks skeptically.

"Tell him, Wilder," Troy cuts in. "Tell him the truth. That you're obsessed with my wife and now you're practically stalking her."

Cat opens her mouth to speak, to defend me, but I speak first because I'd rather Troy's anger be directed at me. "That's not true," I blurt out. "She's been helping me with your campaign speeches."

Oh fuck. I can't believe I just said that.

I try to recant what I said. "I mean, with an assignment in a finance class I'm taking online."

All the blood drains from my face when I watch Troy move closer to Cat. Fortunately, there is a fence between her and us. But still, this will not end well for her. She can't be alone with him tonight, or ever.

"No, no." Troy shakes his head. "You said speeches. Is that true, Catherine?" He looks at her with a clenched jaw. "Have you been helping this boy write his dad's campaign speeches?"

"Tell me this isn't true, Wilder," Dad says, disappointment in his tone. "Mrs. Jenkins is the current mayor's wife." He's telling me something I already know, but still, I listen because I'm in deep shit as it is. "Why would you even put her in that position? It's completely unorthodox. I gave you this job because I trusted you were the right person for it. And all this time..." He shakes his head.

"It's not true," I tell him.

Rome steps up, positioning himself between me and Troy. "Don't listen to a word this flake is saying, Dad. Mayor Jenkins is probably just making shit up to save his own ass."

"Watch your mouth," Dad snaps at Rome.

Troy steps up to Rome. "Listen to your father, kid," he grits out with a curled lip. "Watch your mouth."

Rome snickers. "I'll watch my mouth if you wash yours. Your breath smells rancid." He fans the air in front of him with a shit-eating grin on his face.

The next thing I know, Troy lets out a heady growl and lunges at Rome. Dad grabs him by the shirt and pulls him back just before he makes any physical contact with my brother.

"That's enough," Dad shouts as more people gather around us. He points a stern finger at Rome then looks at me. "I raised you better than this." Then he looks at Troy. "And you're a grown man who should know better. These are my sons! And I promise you one thing, you will *not* lay a finger on either of them!"

It's not often I see my dad this fired up, and I'm sort of digging it. Even if much of his anger is directed at me. Aside from Cat being caught in the crossfire, I'm sort of glad this all happened. Now, all these people watching get a taste of who Troy Jenkins really is. A few even snap pictures, likely ready to hand them over to reporters.

"Watch your backs, boys." Troy bares his teeth. "I plan to bury all of you."

"You do what you have to do," Dad tells him, keeping his composure. "And I'll do what I have to do."

Troy walks over to Cat and I listen as he says, "Get in your car and go straight home. Now! We need to have a little talk."

Cat gulps and I can see the terror in her eyes. "Don't," I blurt out, unsure what to follow it up with.

Troy's gaze snaps to me. "Mind your business and let me handle mine." With that, he walks down the fence line toward the gate while Cat walks unhurriedly away. She glances back at me and I shake my head, terrified of what's next for her.

"I have to go," I tell my dad—as well as Celia and Elodie, who look to be in a state of shock right now.

I go to walk away so I can catch up to Cat, but Dad grabs me by the back of the arm. "You're not going anywhere except home so we can talk about all of this."

"It's not what you think, Dad. Cat...err, Mrs. Jenkins is in trouble."

"That's not your business," he stammers.

"But it is my business. Mayor Jenkins is not a good man. He's...he's digging into Rome's past and how Celia dropped those charges last year. He plans to use it against you by putting his own twist on the truth."

Dad shrugs, but I can see the fury in his eyes. "Let him. There's nothing to find. Everything was handled legally. If needed, I'll just come forward with the true story of those events.

You can write the speech, *without* Mrs. Jenkins's help." He rolls his eyes, displaying his disapproval of what I did. "I have nothing to hide, Wilder. Can you say the same?"

"He…he hurts her," I blurt out, ignoring everything else he just said. There, I said it. The truth is out. Cat might be angry at me for it, but it had to be said. I'd rather her live her life hating me than not living it at all because her husband killed her.

Dad's eyebrows cave. "What do you mean, he hurts her?"

I swallow hard, ready to lay it all out there. Reaching into my pocket, I pull out my phone and open up the video I took last week at their house. I tap play, then hand it to my dad. As he's watching, I explain, "He hits her, Dad. Hard. She's practically a prisoner in her home, only allowed to leave for work. She had to sneak here tonight and now she's been caught and there's no telling what he might do."

I turn my head momentarily, catching a glimpse of Cat's car. Beside it is a very pissed-off Troy and who I think is the love of my life. He grabs her arm and she shrinks into herself. Before I can do anything, he rips open her car door and shoves her in so hard I see her head hit before she has the chance to duck.

I can't take this. She can't go home to him. His reddened face turns toward me and we lock eyes. He glances at the phone in my father's hand and I smile. He pales slightly before walking over to his truck and getting in. I think I actually watch him debate on running his vehicle through the crowd just to hit me.

But all too soon, his tires screech and people watch as he disappears down the road.

I warned him if he touched her again what I would do. Now let's just hope I can save Cat before he has a chance to do anything worse.

Without a word to my dad—leaving my phone with him—I haul ass and jump the fence, running toward them.

CHAPTER 21
WILDER

I'VE BEEN DRIVING AROUND for almost an hour trying to find her. I don't have my phone, and I know if I go home to get it from my dad, he'll force me to stay and talk. I can't give him the answers he wants, and worse, I know I've disappointed him. But he won't understand. He doesn't get me or the things that I like. Every part of me wanted to tell him about the cash I made from the video that went viral, but I knew in the end he still wouldn't take it seriously, so I kept it to myself.

This is my fifth time driving by her house and her vehicle isn't in the open garage, but Troy's truck is parked outside it.

It doesn't make any sense. Where would she have gone? With any luck, she's hiding somewhere. I just wish I knew where so I could be with her. Maybe she's trying to call me now—but my dad has my phone.

My knuckles tap out a nervous rhythm on the steering wheel as I circle through town one more time.

I drive down every street, scanning parking lots and sidewalks for any sign of her vehicle. Panic rises in my chest as I pull into the school parking lot and see nothing but empty spaces.

My forehead breaks out in a sweat as I come to terms with what I have to do. The one thing I haven't tried—I have to talk to

Troy. But I can't do it alone. I need backup because there is no saying how this might go down.

Knowing Rome is at Big John's having pizza with, probably the entire graduating class, I make a sharp turn into the parking lot. I don't want to go in and talk to anyone. People will ask questions I don't have any intention of answering.

Instead, I stand outside and catch my brother's attention. He sees me almost instantly. I think it's a twin thing. Rome comes jogging out of the restaurant, genuine concern on his face.

"Bro, you've gotta tell me what's going on."

A few minutes later, after explaining the situation, I've got my brother in the passenger seat of my car and we're headed to the Jenkinses' house for answers.

Rome tells me that our dad is pissed, and I'm not surprised by that. He also tells me he's got my phone and he's contemplating what to do with the video I showed him. But he assured Rome he's not making any decisions until he speaks to me.

This is all a fucking mess and I have no idea how to clean it up.

We pull into their driveway and I'm hopeful to see her car in the garage, but all that hope diminishes when I see she's still not here. It's possible she ditched her car somewhere and Troy made her get in his truck.

I guess we're about to find out.

"You ready for this?" Rome asks, gripping the passenger door handle.

"Ready or not," I tell him as I swing open my door and get out.

We opt to leave the car running, just in case we need to make a run for it. My brother and I aren't pussies by any means, but we're not total idiots either. Mr. Jenkins is dangerous and we have no idea how he's going to react to our unexpected arrival at his house.

An eerie feeling washes over me as we approach the front door. Wind whistles in the background, almost in warning.

"We'll just pretend we're here to apologize," I whisper to Rome as we go up the concrete steps. "Then ask if we can apologize to her, too. Once we see she's safe, we can go."

I don't tell him I have no plans of leaving here without Cat. He would turn around and tell me to come up with a new plan. But it's been too long since I've had my eyes on her, and I won't risk Troy hurting her ever again. I have proof and we will find a way to get her out of here. *Tonight*.

"Let's hope it's that easy." Rome raises his balled fist to the door, but on the first knock, the door creaks open.

We exchange confused glances.

"That's weird," I tell him quietly as I lean close to the door to try and get a look inside.

Troy is the most meticulous man about his house. It is under lock and key like no one I have ever seen before. The cameras, the two deadbolts—one that requires a key from the inside and outside. Yet, his door just opened for us.

I panic a little thinking this is a trick. Is he trying to get us to come into his house so he can shoot us and say we were breaking in?

Rome, being the straightforward guy he is, pushes the door open farther and pops his head in the house. "Hello?"

"Dude." I punch his shoulder. "Could you be a little more obvious?"

He lifts a shoulder. "Do we want to talk to them or not?"

He's got a good point. At some point we have to make our presence known. I'm just afraid of what will happen when we do.

"Anyone here?" Rome hollers as he steps farther into the house. "Mayor Jenkins? Mrs. Jenkins?" Rome raises his brows. "Maybe they're both in her car."

I quickly go back down the steps to look at the camera, immediately seeing that the green light isn't on. Every time I've come to this door, Troy has watched me through that camera. He should have gotten a notification that we were here and the only way he wouldn't check is if he was otherwise occupied. I go back up the steps and put one foot in the door while Rome has fully emerged himself in the house.

"Something's not right," I tell him with a hushed tone.

Hanging back by the door, I let Rome inspect, but when he steps around the wall, and into the living room, I watch as his eyes go wide, his hand flying to his mouth.

My heart jumps into my throat and my first thought is Cat, so I go to Rome's side to see what he's found.

And that's when I see it.

Crimson blood is pooled around a body on the floor. So much blood that I nearly slip in it as I round the corner, but Rome's arm stops me from going any closer. My heart constricts, my breaths come in short gasps, and I choke on a cry of pure and utter relief that it's Troy and not Cat lying there. *Dead.*

"Jesus Christ," I gasp as I grip the sides of my head. "This can't be happening."

"What do you mean this can't be happening?" Rome asks, an unnerving casualness to his tone. "This is the best-case scenario. The wicked beast is dead. Mrs. Jenkins is free, and Dad's the new mayor."

My head jerks back as I glare at him. "Are you fucking kidding me right now? He's dead, and someone did this to him." I gesture to the very real crime scene right in front of us. He has a gun in his hand, but I can't tell where he bled out from. He's face down, his head turned to the side, enough for me to see who it is, but that's all I can really see.

"Do you think…"

He doesn't have to finish that sentence because I know what he's asking. "No way in hell. She's too good to do this."

At least, I think she is. Then again, Troy has been beating on her for God knows how long. A person can only take so much before they snap. The more I think about it, the more sense it makes. "We have to help her."

Rome chuckles sarcastically as he eyeballs the corpse on the floor. "Doesn't look like she needs help anymore. He's certainly not touching her again."

"That's not what I mean." I punch him in the arm. Leave it to Rome to never take anything seriously. "If she did this, her fingerprints are probably on that gun."

Rome shrugs. "Unless she's smart and wore gloves."

"We can't risk it." I nod toward the weapon. "We need to get rid of it."

"I'm not touching that thing," Rome scoffs. "You do it."

Dammit. My eyes search the room frantically, looking for something I can pick it up with. They land on a round doily beneath a vase of fake flowers. I walk toward it, but just as I go to pick up the vase, a shadow in the doorway catches my eye. When I look, I see that it's Cat.

"What are you doing here?" she whispers so low I can barely hear her. "He's going to kill you if he finds you here!" *Is she for real right now?* Curling her fingers, she calls me over. "Come on. We can get out of here before he sees either of us."

Rome pops out from around the corner, his eyes dancing from me to her. "Yeah, I don't think we have to worry about that."

Cat grimaces as she points to Rome. "What's he doing here? What's going on?" Wide panicked eyes meet mine. Is she having a bout of amnesia or something?

She begins walking farther into the house, but I put my hand on her arm, stopping her. "Are you saying you have no idea what's going on?"

"You're really starting to freak me out, Wilder. I sent you, like, five messages saying where I was. Where have you been?"

I'm really freaked the fuck out right now. A man we all just had a public yelling match with is lying dead in the room next to us and I have no idea who did it.

I can't tell if she's being serious, or if this is an act. I would hope she knows by now that she can trust me, but maybe it's Rome she's not sure about. Of course she wouldn't want to confess to killing her husband, but why come back to the scene of the crime once the job is done.

I'm lost in my thoughts when Cat makes it past me, and when I look at her, I see her standing beside Rome, pale as a ghost. Both hands fly to her mouth and she gasps audibly.

Her legs wobble and she staggers to the left, putting a hand on the wall to steady herself. I come up quickly behind her, grabbing her by the waist. "Are you okay?" I ask her, immediately regretting the question. Of course she's not okay. She either just killed her husband, or she just found out someone else did. Either way, we have to get the hell out of here.

"We gotta go," I tell Rome. "Grab something and get the gun and I'll help her out of here."

Cat is in a state of shock as I lead her to the door. "Looks like we're running away sooner than planned, Kitty Cat." Her mouth stays agape, eyes wide and not blinking as I lead her toward the door.

The fresh air hits us, right along with the reality of this situation. I don't know what we're going to do, but I need to come up with a plan really fucking soon.

"Go," Rome instructs me as he comes to the door with his phone pressed to his ear. "Get her out of here. Elodie's on her way. She's gonna park next door and I'll ride home with her. She thinks she knows a way to cover this up and erase evidence of us being here. You need to get your car out of the driveway right fucking now."

"You sure?" I ask him, unsure if I feel safe leaving him here alone.

"Yes!" he says urgently. "Go!"

I give Rome one last look and say, "Thank you."

He nods, then closes the door with us outside. Hopefully Cat can wait a few minutes before she has a solid freak out.

What if someone comes and Rome gets blamed while I'm looking out for her? So many people witnessed my family's argument with Troy tonight. We'll probably be prime suspects.

My thoughts immediately go to my dad. What if it wasn't Cat? What if it was him?

There are so many people who would probably love to put a bullet in that guy. It could be anyone.

Doesn't matter. Cat is safe now and until this is all settled, we're going somewhere I can ensure she remains safe.

I get her in my car, then I drive away, and I don't stop.

CHAPTER 22
CATHERINE

WE'VE BEEN on the road for hours. Wilder stopped at a rest area at some point in the night and we were able to get a couple hours of broken sleep, but as soon as the sun rose, we started down the road again.

I haven't talked much, and neither has Wilder. I think we're both still in a state of shock after everything we've been through in the last twenty-four hours.

I'm not even sure I've grasped the reality of what's happened. I'm not even sure it did happen. Maybe this is all a dream. *That has to be it.*

When I left the graduation ceremony yesterday, Troy told me to go straight home, but I did the complete opposite. I was livid with that man, much like I always am. Part of me was ready to never return. Then the sun started to set and I realized I had no money and no place to go, so I went home.

He must have knocked me unconscious the second I walked through the door, making all this just a dream. In which case, I don't want to wake up. For once I'm not held down by someone else, my heart and my soul feel free.

I'm not sad that he's dead. That bastard has been ruining me for years. I just wish I knew what happened. Yet, I'm not able to ask Wilder about it yet. I don't know who killed Troy, but I do know it couldn't have been Wilder. He's too gentle, too loving, too…perfect.

"He's really dead?" I ask again, still unable to wrap my head around all of this. "It doesn't feel real."

Wilder reaches over from the driver's seat and strokes the back of my head. I find reassurance in his touch. I can't imagine doing this without him. "It's over. You're safe now."

Once the gravity of the situation sets in, I might go through the different stages of grief, but it won't be for the loss of my husband. It will be for the years I lost as his wife. All of the time spent under his thumb when I could have been finding my own version of happiness.

I look out at the open road, our path lit by the bright headlights. It's been a while since I've seen another car and I can only assume we're somewhere desolate.

"Where are we going?" I ask Wilder, hoping it's somewhere we'll be able to have a fresh start. There is nothing left for me in Willow Creek. Everything I want is here in this car with me.

Wilder shrugs. "No idea. Somewhere far away from here until I get word back home that it's safe to return."

My eyebrows shoot to my forehead as panic claws at my heart. "We're going back?"

He looks at me, a glint of uncertainty in his eyes. "Eventually we have to, right?"

He's right. We do have to go back at some point. Wilder has a life in Willow Creek. I can't take him away from that, even if I know he'd give it all up for me. I won't allow it, so I nod. "Yeah, we do."

I can't even think about what comes next right now. *Troy is dead.*

I'm not sure how, why, or who, but he's dead.

"I'm free," I blurt out, tone stoic. "I'm finally free."

For the first time tonight, Wilder cracks a smile. "Yes, you are, baby. He can never touch you again."

I roll down the window, feeling manic as I throw my hands out and scream, "Rot in hell, Troy Jenkins!"

I sink back in my seat, my adrenaline pumping. "So," I quip. "Who do you think did it?"

Wilder lifts his brows with quick glances from the road to me. "You mean it wasn't…?"

"Wasn't who?"

"Nothing," he deadpans.

"Wait a minute." I shift in my seat, turning my body to face him. "Do you think it was me?" I bring my hands to my chest. When he looks at me, I get my answer. "I didn't do it, Wilder. I swear. I'd tell you if I did."

I'm actually surprised he thought I was capable of killing someone. I've definitely thought about it on more occasions than one. I've even gone as far as plotting the act in my head. But I don't think I could ever bring myself to kill another human, no matter how much I thought they deserved it. Besides, if I did kill Troy, I wouldn't have let him off so easily with a gunshot. There would have been many other wounds inflicted first.

"I believe you," he says softly, but the look on his face says otherwise.

"Do you? Because I feel like you don't." I can see it in the way he holds himself. He isn't looking me in the eye, not even really glancing my way. His grip around the wheel has tightened as if he doesn't want to admit it out loud.

"I don't know what to think right now. Everything happened so quickly and part of me wonders if maybe you're just suppressing—"

"I didn't do it!" I shout. "Nothing is suppressed. It wasn't me." I think back just to make sure. After graduation I went to a park outside of town to clear my head. I was not about to walk into a beating from Troy. He needed time to cool down, and I needed time to reset. I was planning on going home and grabbing the money I stashed in order to leave him. I was going to pack my bags and walk out, consequences be damned.

I stayed at the park, watching the minutes tick by and the sun begin to set. I even sent Wilder messages to tell him I was okay and where I was at. I know I didn't go home and shoot Troy. I didn't have time.

Wilder looks at me, his grip on the steering wheel loosening. "It had to be suicide then."

"No." I shake my head. "Not a chance in hell. Troy would never take his own life. He loves himself too much to do that. Someone killed him, but that someone wasn't me." I need Wilder to believe me.

"Okay." He nods. "I'm sorry, baby. My head is just spinning with so many different scenarios and none of them make sense to me." He shakes his head, eyes still on the empty road ahead.

I don't ask if it was him—or Rome—because I trust Wilder. I know he would have told me by now if he had anything to do with it. And I'm not angry that he asked if I did it because I definitely had the motive and means. Nonetheless, someone got to him before I had.

I stretch my hand over and put it on his lap, and he covers it with his. "We're going to figure this all out. Neither of us did anything wrong. In fact, we can probably go back and just tell our sides of the story so we don't even have to run." I try to calm him and give him the chance to go home. I can't tell if he is sad to leave or not.

"Not yet," he says. "We're both going to be suspects in this and I'd prefer the police figure it all out before we're cuffed and thrown in a cell."

He's got a point. We're both probably suspects right now, along with his dad.

A thought crosses my mind, but I quickly squash it. Grant Cromwell would never. *Would he?*

I lay my head back, willing it to stop thinking so much. The winding road we're on seems to stretch for miles. A couple hours later, a small town comes into view. There are only a handful of buildings, one being a run-down gas station.

"Are you hungry?" Wilder asks, and I immediately nod. "Let's stop here." He nods toward the gas station. "I need to gas up anyway. Hopefully we'll find a city soon because I need to buy a prepaid cell phone. I'm itching to know what's going on back home."

"Maybe we could ask the gas station attendant. I'm sure they could point us in the right direction." Whatever the right direction might be.

Wilder pulls up to the pump and shuts off the car. We go inside together, and Wilder withdraws cash from the ATM. He says we need to keep driving because if the cops really want to find him, they can track his card usage. The attendant tells us there is a city about an hour north, so after we get gas, snacks, and drinks, we head in that direction.

"Got it," Wilder says as he sinks into the driver's seat. He closes the door and hands me a cellphone. "Got it all activated inside. Even sent Rome a text already."

I open up the message log and read what he sent, but it's just the word "update" with a question mark.

"How will he know it's you?" I ask him.

Wilder shifts into reverse and pulls out of the parking space. "He'll know."

A few minutes down the road, a message comes through.

Rome: El worked her magic, given her education in pre-law, and did everything she could to make it look like it was intentional, but I'm not sure anyone is buying it. People are losing their minds here. Read this...

"There's an article," I tell Wilder as I click the link.

And when I see the heading, I gasp.

"What's it say?" he asks as he makes a sharp turn into another parking lot, bringing the car to a stop.

I read it, then pass the phone to Wilder with a shaky hand.

Breaking News: Willow Creek's Mayor Jenkins Dead at Age 39.

Troy Jenkins, mayor of Willow Creek, was found deceased late last night from an apparent gunshot wound. Police crews were called to his home on Merry Lane at 10:13 p.m., after an anonymous call tipped off law enforcement. Investigators are working to determine if foul play is a factor in the mayor's death.

This news comes as a shock, not only to the residents he served, but also to those who worked closely with him.

"Willow Creek will not be the same without him," says life-long resident, Bob Denver.

Mayor Jenkins's former assistant, Beth Hill, also expressed her disbelief. "I have no words. It's such a shock," she told reporters. "Mayor Jenkins was such a generous and kind man. He'll be deeply missed."

Jenkins is one of two mayoral candidates in the 2024 election, set to be held November 8th. His opponent, Grant Cromwell, was not available for comment at this time; however, his campaign manager, Jillian Hancock, has informed reporters that he is prepared to step in as mayor of this beloved town.

Details to follow as they become available.

"Who made the call?" I ask Wilder as I pick apart this article.

"No idea." He shrugs. "It has to be either Elodie or Rome. No one else knew."

"Unless it was the killer." I read it again, and again, angered over how people speak so highly of the beast that broke me in every way he could. I get it, he's dead and we shouldn't disrespect the deceased, but these comments are complete lies. Beth called him a kind man and said he'd be missed. *Bullshit.* Troy was far from kind. And why is Beth even commenting at all? I thought she moved because of the baby. Maybe that was another lie Troy told just so he could get me to work for him and be under his thumb twenty-four hours a day.

I don't know what to believe anymore. In just a few short hours my life feels like it was flipped upside down. I'm happy my husband is gone, but I'm terrified to find out who the killer is because nothing makes sense.

Nausea hits me so hard I start to panic; the day catches up with me and Wilder strokes my hair as I try to just breathe.

"Take a breath, Cat. We will figure this out." He's not wrong. With him by my side, I know I can do this. I have to do this. Closing my eyes, I tell myself that maybe if I can just fall asleep the nightmare will be over.

Maybe it's all just a dream, after all.

The next thing I know, we're pulling into a hotel surrounded by restaurants. I roll down the window to look around and my stomach growls when I inhale the smell of grilled steak.

"We'll stay here tonight and if there are no signs of anyone on our trail, we'll stay longer." Wilder pulls us into a spot and puts his hand over mine. I squeeze his, reassuring him as much as myself. Running might look bad, but staying could have looked a whole lot worse.

I'm just thankful we get to sleep in a bed tonight. All I want is to lie down with Wilder's arms wrapped around me. Just for tonight, maybe we can pretend the outside world doesn't exist.

Once we're settled into a king-size suite, Wilder and I walk next door to the steakhouse and I order practically everything on the menu.

"Good?" Wilder asks with a chuckle as I stuff a big piece of medium-rare steak into my mouth and moan.

I chew it up, savoring every bite of it. "So good." He looks down and pokes at his baked potato with his fork. "Hey," I say softly. "Everything is going to work out," I try to reassure him the same way he did me.

"I know. I just hate the unknown, ya know?"

And I hate that I dragged him into this. I don't know the moment when it became him and me running away versus just me, but if I had to guess, I would say prom night was probably the key for us.

I nod because I know that feeling all too well. Every day was unknown to me. I never knew what kind of mood Troy was going to be in. I walked on eggshells for years, but for the first time in a very long time, I can finally move at my own pace.

Sadness of Troy's passing hasn't hit and at this point, I don't think it will. If anything, I want to thank the person who took his life so I didn't have to do it. Wilder has asked a couple times if I think Troy committed suicide, but I don't think that for a second.

No. Someone murdered Troy. Someone hated him as much as I did and finally had enough of his shit. Maybe one day I'll meet that person—maybe I already have. Or it's possible, I'll never see them at all.

We finish eating, pay our bill in cash, then walk hand in hand back to the hotel. "This is nice," I tell him, knowing he's still pretty down about everything that's happened. I'm hoping I can lift his spirits. "It's only temporary so let's enjoy this time we have together, okay?"

Instead of grief, I feel filled with this crazy amount of energy. I never knew what life would be like after I left Troy, but I didn't expect this sort of happiness to fill my core. It could be because I'm here with Wilder, or just because I know I won't have to sleep in the back of the closet or on the floor ever again.

"Yeah." He nods. "You're right. Tomorrow doesn't matter when we've still got today." Finally, he smiles and I feel that warmth of it radiate into my soul. Wilder is healing. He is like the wind beneath my wings. I know his care for me will likely fade, the age difference being so much, but I want to enjoy what we have now.

I'm so done wasting precious time. I want to finally have something in my life that I love. And I think I just might be starting to love Wilder Cromwell.

The minute we get back into our room, I push Wilder against the wall and crush his mouth with mine.

CHAPTER 23
WILDER

THE TASTE of Cat on my tongue gives me amnesia. I forget about it all—the mayor's death, our road trip out of state, getting this hotel room under a fake name while lying about losing my ID. Still not sure how I pulled that one off.

I kiss her until nothing makes sense but her. I'd do it all again in a heartbeat to get to where we are. I'd hide away forever with her if it meant spending forever by her side.

In one fluid motion, I grip the hem of her shirt and lift it up, revealing the milky white skin of her stomach. I reach behind her, pinching the clasp of her bra, and she lets the straps fall down her arms. It hits the floor at our feet.

Cat returns the favor and removes my shirt before snapping the button of my pants.

I kiss her neck, sucking on her delicate flesh. My hands move up from her waist, fingers trailing against her sides before reaching her breasts. I cup them both in my hands, squeezing with gentle pressure.

"Wilder," she sings as I drop to my knees, bringing her pants and panties down with me. She lifts one foot, then the other, and I discard her clothes somewhere behind me.

My fingers trail featherlike up one of her trembling legs until

I reach the crease behind her knee. Then I lift it up and bring her foot to my shoulder.

When I look at her face, I see her wondrous eyes staring down at me. I can feel the joy radiating from her. My girl is finally free. She's safe. And I think she is finally starting to feel happy.

My cock twitches when I drag two fingers through her sex, feeling her want for me. I slip them inside her tight pussy, reveling in the way her walls envelop me.

The scent of her arousal floods my senses and my body responds with a racing heart. I can't wait to make her come all over my face.

Cat puts a hand on my head, gently guiding my face to her heat. A soft moan escapes her lips as I run my tongue along her slick folds, savoring her taste. My mouth latches onto her clit and I suck it between my teeth, making her shiver.

This girl is like a drug—I'm addicted and I know now I will never quit her.

Pumping my middle and index fingers in and out of her while stroking that sensitive spot inside, I suck feverishly on her swollen nub. She guides my movements with her hand on my head, fingers weaved in my hair.

"Oh God, Wilder," she cries out. The sound of my name rolling off her tongue has me aching for her orgasm.

I wanna make my girl feel good every day. She deserves all the praise and pleasure that I plan to give her.

When she drops her head back, resting it against the wall, I pull my face back, working only my fingers. I add another, watching as they slide in and out of her slippery cunt. Then, when she whimpers in delight, I curl the tips and pulse them against her G-spot, my knuckles gyrating against her core.

"Wilder," she cries out again, just before she clenches her muscles, squeezing my fingers inside her. Proof of her orgasm drips from her core, soaking my palm. I keep going, knowing she's capable of giving me more.

And, she does, this time her sounds of pleasure echoing in the small room. She reaches behind her, digging her nails into the wall, dragging fragments of wallpaper. I feel the moment she lets it all go, and it's so different from before. This time she uses her voice and there is no hesitation as she calls out my name.

When her body settles, I pull my fingers out, spread her wider, and suck on her clit until she's screaming. Her shaky thighs cage me in, and this time, she clenches my shoulders.

Suddenly, she puts a hand on my head, pushing me back, her body too sensitive for my touch.

I stand up, putting my hands to the wall on either side of her as I kiss her delicious mouth. "How'd that feel?"

She staggers to the left a bit, unsteady on her feet. "Incredible." Heat floods to my cheeks and my cock. I love making my girl come.

"Good," I tell her before kissing her again. Then I scoop her in my arms and carry her over to the bed, laying her down on her stomach as I stand at the end and strip off my too tight pants.

My erection springs free as I look down at her. I know she is ready for me when she shakes her ass, needing more.

In a swift motion, I grab her hips and jerk them upward. She gasps as I enter her slowly, inch by inch, until I'm submerged in her warmth.

Feelings of contentment overwhelm me as our bodies connect. It's as if her pussy was molded just for me. I may not have been her first, but I sure as hell plan to be her last.

Holding her hips, I thrust deeper, picking up my pace. Each pump inside her sends a rush of electricity through me stronger than the last.

Moving one hand, I reach for her hair, giving it a gentle tug as I pull her head back. "Look at me, baby. Let me see those pretty eyes when I come inside you."

Her head turns slightly, her lustful gaze locked on mine. "That's a good girl."

I fuck her harder and faster, driving into her with a frenzied pace. Her tits jiggle against the bed in sync with her movements. Fuck, she has nice tits. Big and firm with pink pebbled nipples. They're as nice as this ass. I stretch a hand out, slapping my palm to her cheek and squeeze, her meaty flesh splaying between my fingers.

She moans, pushing back into me like she can't get enough. I wish I had more hands so I could massage her tits while holding her hair and her ass as I fuck her.

"Harder," Cat whimpers, taking me by surprise. I give her what she wants, pushing in as far as I can go. Sliding half my cock out, I fill her back up, over and over until she's crying out my name.

My body fills with a dire need to combust, tingles shooting through my veins. I push in one more time, pulsating the tip deep in her core as she milks my cock. I freeze, letting this moment linger for a bit as I give her every last drop.

A second later, Cat collapses on the bed and I drop down gently on top of her. Sweeping her hair to one side, I kiss her cheek. "I never wanna get up."

"Then don't," she says back. "We have nowhere else to be."

I roll over to my side and she curls into me, evidence of our orgasms sticking between us. But I don't care, and she doesn't seem to either because the next thing I know, we're falling fast asleep.

CHAPTER 24

WILDER

We've been at the hotel for two nights now and there haven't been any updates from Rome—until now.

I read the article again, hesitant to show Catherine because she's been in such good spirits. She had to have known people would be looking for her. The police will want to question her. But for the police to put us together is a surprise to me as much as it will be to her.

Cat's hand comes in front of me, holding a cup of coffee. "For you, my love. Half coffee, half vanilla creamer."

"Thanks, baby." I take the coffee and put that and my burner phone on the small round table in front of our hotel window and turn around. My arms go around her waist and I pull her close. Kissing her temple, I let myself breathe her in. "Have I told you lately how beautiful you are?"

She laughs. "Many times and I still don't believe you. I've been living in the same clothes for the last two days."

I quirk a brow. "Maybe it's time we do something about that."

"As much as I would love to go shopping, we need to save the cash you withdrew. Besides..." She turns in my hold and grins up at me. "It gives us a reason to lie naked in bed while our clothes are washing in the laundry room down the hall."

"Mmm," I hum into the crease of her neck as I kiss her. "I love the way you think."

"So." She steps around me, eyeing the phone. "What were you reading there? Any news from back home?"

"Umm. Yeah." I scratch the back of my head as I reach past her and pick it up. There are many people I don't mind lying to if necessary, but Cat isn't one of them. I want her to trust me, and I want to be worthy of her trust.

I read the article again, then before I can change my mind, I pass the phone to her so she can see for herself.

A Wicked Scandal: Deceased Mayor's Wife, Catherine Jenkins, and Former Student, Wilder Cromwell, Missing.

It's been three days since Mayor Troy Jenkins was found deceased in his home from a single gunshot wound to the head. Investigators suspect foul play was involved and are urging anyone with information to come forward.

Throughout the investigation of the mayor's death, police have been unable to locate Catherine Jenkins, former Mayor Jenkins's wife. Her cellphone and purse were found inside their home on Merry Lane, but there have been no signs of Catherine.

A missing person report has also been filed for Wilder Cromwell by his father, Grant Cromwell. Given the situation, Grant Cromwell is now serving as acting mayor and running unopposed in the mayoral election this year.

At this time, Catherine Jenkins, nor Wilder Cromwell, are suspects in the death of the mayor. However, investigators believe the two could be together after a public argument at the Willow Creek High gradua-tion ceremony.

We are urging the community to be mindful when they are out. If you see anything suspicious, please call the Willow Creek police depart-ment immediately.

More details to follow as they become available.

I watch her intently as she reads, her features tightening with each passing second. Her mouth drops open and her chest rises and falls rapidly.

"We're missing?" she spits out as she hands back the phone. "I mean, I should have known I would be, but why are they involving you in an article that has to do with me and Troy?"

I shrug. "Someone must've told the police we've gotten closer. Students have been talking about that video. One, or all of them, probably spilled everything."

"You don't think it was Elodie and Rome, do you?"

I shake my head adamantly. "God, no. Elodie and Rome want to help us. They'd never turn their backs on us like that."

"I'm so sorry you've been dragged into this," she says, and I can tell her heart is heavy right now.

"Baby," I say as I pull her close. "Why are you apologizing? I'm here because there is nowhere else I'd rather be right now." I kiss her head, hoping she believes it. "People are going to talk, but we know the truth. Before long, it'll be revealed."

CHAPTER 25
CATHERINE

A BLINDING realization smashes into me like a wrecking ball. "We have to go back," I blurt out. "We have to go, right now."

I can't believe I didn't think about this sooner.

"Why? What's wrong?" Wilder grabs me by both arms, looking into my eyes.

"You might want to sit down," I say remorsefully. "There's something I need to tell you."

Wilder pulls out a chair and sits down, but he pulls me onto his lap. "This sounds serious."

"It is. There are some things you don't know, but I feel like you need to know. I don't want secrets between us."

Sensing my unease, he rubs my leg. "You can tell me anything. I've got you…always."

"It has to stay between us because if it ever got out to the wrong person, my life would be over."

I never thought I'd share this with another person, but I trust Wilder and he deserves the full story. He deserves to know why I stayed even when my heart called out to his.

"Of course," he says with a tone that is far too casual. I know he's downplaying this for my sake, and I'm grateful for that.

I take a deep breath, doing my best to keep my voice strong. It's been a long time since I've talked about that day.

"You know about the abuse, but what you don't know is why I stayed. I couldn't leave because Troy threatened to hand over my identity to some very dangerous men. At the time, I had no idea he once worked for these men."

"Okay." He nods slowly. "And why would some dangerous men want anything from you?"

For the longest time I'd wished I could go back and change ever meeting Troy. But then, I would have never come to Willow Creek and I never would have met Wilder.

Eleven years ago

I'm sitting at a bar when a handsome man approaches me. He's in a nice suit and his hair is done up in a messy way, but you can tell he tried to style it.

Tonight I ran away from my boyfriend after I found out he's been dealing drugs for a gang in the area. I knew us living out of a car for the past few months had been rough on him, but gangs are not something I ever wanted to get involved in.

When the gentleman sits down, he smiles at me. It's warm and inviting, unlike anything I'm used to. Usually men like this want one thing, but this man looks at me like maybe I could be his one thing.

Troy. He told me his name was Troy.

I expect him to get up and leave, to realize that I'm the piece of shit my boyfriend calls me. Even when I'm the only one that makes us any money. I usually work at this bar, but it's my night off and I needed a drink.

But Troy doesn't just walk away, instead he hands me a card with his phone number and tells me that if I ever need anything to call him.

When I get to the car I'm living out of, I pull open the passenger side door and something—no, someone—falls out.

In a state of shock, I look down at my boyfriend; there are bullet holes in his head and chest.

Before I know it, three gunshots go off across the street, aiming right for me. What I don't expect is crossfire, so when someone steps out of the alleyway beside me and begins shooting back, I duck and plug my ears.

I have no idea how long it goes on for, but when it finally stops, no one is left standing. I try to get up from my spot but it's like I can't move. I'm frozen.

Apparently I do move, though, because I have the card out and my phone to my ear in the next minute.

"That was faster than I thought." The voice chuckles on the other end of the phone, and I begin to cry.

"Catherine, what is it? Are you hurt?"

I have to take a second and figure out if I am. I don't think anything hit me, but I also can't think.

"I-I don't know."

"I'm on my way, sweetheart. Just tell me where you are and I'll make it better."

"There were guns... There are dead bodies all around me. Oh God, Troy. What should I do?"

I'm the only one left alive from a gang shoot-out; there is no way anyone will believe I just got lucky.

"It's okay, Catherine. I have friends in high places. You don't have to worry. I'm pulling up now."

As soon as he steps out of his car, I run to him, breaking down instantly. He holds me and soothes the ache while making phone calls. I don't question anything because I don't want to. I just want to be safe. For so long, that's all I ever really wanted.

Stepping out of the memory, I tell Wilder that Troy kept a recording of that call and threatened to send it to one of the gang leaders he still was in contact with if I ever tried to leave. I tell him my theory that the shoot-out was all a facade for me to call Troy and be in his debt, and Wilder agrees with me.

Sobs rack my whole body by the time I'm done. I tell him about how the beatings started. It was all so slow that at first, I didn't realize it for what it was. Then I go into way too much detail about the first time I tried to leave.

How Troy played the recording for me and threatened to give

it over to the gang members so they could eliminate the only witness from that night. Then, he forced me to unpack my bag while he watched and mocked me for every little item I tried to take with me.

It's all so much. Years of hurt and anger and God only knows what else. The trauma will be a lot to work through, but I plan to do it in spite of Troy. I will never let him win. I can't.

But right now, I break as I let it all out and hope that Wilder doesn't see me the same way I saw myself as I was huddled on the ground on that cold night.

In the end, Wilder just holds me close as I break down in his arms. He whispers promises into my ear about how he is here to keep me safe and that I will never be put in that situation ever again.

"I'm so proud of you, baby. You're so strong," he whispers in my hair as I continue to cry. "You're going to get through this, I promise you."

And I believe him. After a while the room grows silent and I let the heat of Wilder's body pressed against mine calm my racing heart.

"You're right," he whispers in my hair. "We need to go back and get that evidence. But first, we need to come up with a plan. The police are going to want to speak to us both. They're going to want to know where we've been and why we ran."

So next, we devise a plan. A pretty solid one at that.

CHAPTER 26
CATHERINE

As we drive past the sign that reads *Welcome to Willow Creek*, my heart rate kicks into high gear. I straighten up in the seat and glance at Wilder. "Are you sure you want to do this?"

Part of me wants him to say no, to turn the car around and take us back to our happy place at the hotel in Wyoming. It was beautiful there. We could have a happy life.

Then there's the other part of me who knows this is the right thing to do. Eventually the law would catch up to us and staying away makes it look like we have something to hide. When, in reality, we're not hiding anything other than finding a dead body and not telling anyone about it.

I understand why Wilder took me away so quickly now. He thought it was me. Wilder was protecting me like he promised he would. He hasn't let me down yet, and I don't expect him to anytime soon.

"I'm sure," he says with a nod. "My dad will be on our side. He's seen the video of what Troy did to you and he's going to understand. Just let me do the talking and we'll be off that suspect list by nightfall."

I chew nervously on my nail as we draw closer to Wilder's house. Coming out that we're in a relationship creates its own anxiety, but explaining all of this is a whole new level of panic. Especially to his family.

Fortunately, we went over what we're going to say a hundred times on this long drive, and our plan is foolproof. Hopefully.

Wilder brings his car to a stop in front of the house and shifts into park. His hands reach across the center console and he grabs mine, weaving our fingers together. "I've got you, Cat. I promise."

I force a smile on my face. "I know you do."

Sensing my unease, he tips my chin. "Hey," he whispers before leaning over and kissing my lips. "I love you."

My eyes pop wide open at his admission. I wasn't expecting, nor did I know Wilder was in love with me. I mean, I've felt it for a while now, but I was afraid to say anything out of fear of pushing him away. Or worse, making him feel like he had to stay.

I grab his face and look deep into his eyes, this smile real and genuine. "I love you, too."

He kisses me again before saying, "Let's get this over with so we can book a motel in town and forget about it all."

I told Wilder I didn't want to stay at my house anymore. I hate that house and the memories inside it. If I'm going to have a new start, it begins with me leaving everything Troy touched behind, including the pain he caused me inside those four walls.

For now, I'm going to stay at the small motel here in Willow Creek. Over the next couple days, once things settle down a bit, I plan to meet with a realtor, sell the house, and buy something smaller.

But before I can even think about any of that, we have to face the music. The music being Wilder's family, the police, and the fact that my husband was murdered.

Wilder opens his door and I do the same. The first foot on the driveway feels like the ground is going to give out beneath me. The second feels like it's going to just swallow me whole.

Then Wilder comes to my side, takes my hand, and I no

longer feel like I'm sinking. I look at him, a feeling of comfort settling over me.

The minute we walk through the door, we're ambushed. There is shouting, crying, and a few dry humor jokes from Wilder's brother, Callan.

Grant doesn't even say anything; he just nods his head sternly to the left and Wilder leads me to where we have to go.

We step into a room that I take to be Grant's office, and Wilder closes the door behind us, still holding my hand.

"You two have some serious explaining to do," Grant says with a bite of indignation in his tone. "Where in God's name have you two been?"

"I took her away, Dad," Wilder begins, telling the story we came up with. "After graduation, I knew Troy was going to hurt her again, so I went to her house and picked her up in the driveway before her husband got home."

"We're so sorry," I add, playing the part. "We had no idea what was going on until we saw a news article, then we came straight home. I know disappearing like that had to have scared you and I told Wilder to reach out because we knew we had to come back."

"I see," Grant says as he strokes his mouth with his thumb and index finger. "So you're aware of what happened?"

I nod. "I am now. And I can't say I'm surprised. Troy told me if I ever left him he would take his own life. I just never thought he'd actually do it. I had to get away. You don't understand how horrible he was to me." My voice shakes, in no way am I acting when it comes to this. Troy was a man born of the most wicked of nightmares.

When we planned to come back, Wilder called Rome and he and Elodie told us they did everything they could to make the crime scene look like a suicide. The only thing they forgot was my purse, but that lines up with Wilder coming to pick me up before Troy got home. I left my stuff and everything behind because I didn't want to be tracked by my abusive husband.

"What you've had to endure is tragic, Catherine." Grant looks at me with sympathy, and I'm slightly taken aback by the fact that he isn't calling me out on anything. But I guess he feels bad enough for me that he's willing not to hate me for loving his kid, even though the whole situation is unconventional.

Grant walks around his desk, taking a softer approach. I can see how tired he is, the worry is clear as day and I am so thankful Wilder has someone in his life to worry about him, care for him, the way his family does.

"No one should have to go through such abuse. I'm just glad you two are safe now." Grant looks down at our clenched hands. "Care to explain what this is all about?"

I told Wilder I wanted to answer this, and if his family has a problem, we can take things slow. But I want the sneaking around to stop. "I know it's unorthodox given I was Wilder's teacher, but your son saved me in more ways than one and in the process, I fell for him." I look up at Wilder, cracking a smile. "And I think he fell for me, too."

"I did," Wilder confirms. Then he looks at his father with a serious expression. "And I won't be letting her go anytime soon. Doesn't matter what you think or say."

I squeeze his hand because that was not part of the plan, but his thumb just strokes the back of mine. Oddly, it makes me smile.

Grant sighs heavily as he presses his palm to his desk and looks down toward a stack of papers. "We'll discuss all of that later. Right now, we need to contact Officer Benton who has been assigned to this case." He shakes his head, pinching the bridge of his nose. "I have one son screwing his stepsister and the other is dating his teacher. What's next? Is Callan gonna start stalking the preacher's daughter?"

I can't tell if he's joking or serious, but I'd vote for the latter. I know this is a lot for Grant so I'm not taking any of this personally. He's probably been worried sick about his son.

Grant requests a word with Wilder alone, so I leave the room and stand in the hallway to wait for him.

I'm chewing nervously on my nail again when Elodie appears. "Hey," she says as she wraps her arms around me. I'm taken aback at her kindness, but grateful for it nonetheless. "How are you?"

I gulp. "Doing okay, given the circumstances. Look," I begin. "I want to thank you and Rome for all your help. It really means a lot."

"Of course. Wilder is my brother and I can see how much he means to you." She sighs as she takes a step back. "I have to admit, at first I was skeptical. I was scared he'd get hurt, but I know now that you feel the same way about him." She beams at me and I can see her acceptance of us written in every feature.

"I do," I tell her truthfully. "He's incredible and sweet. I could go on for days, but…" I look over her shoulder and see an officer coming toward us. "It looks like it'll have to wait until later."

I knock on the door to Grant's office and once I'm given permission to come in, I push it open. Officer Benton follows behind me. Once we're settled, I give him the same statement we just gave Grant, but with proof. Now that Wilder has his phone back, he pulls up the video he took and hits play for the officer. I go on to tell him that I'd bet my life Troy took his own life, and in the end, he seems satisfied.

"We were leaning toward self-inflicted," Officer Benton says. "And the autopsy revealed that it was highly likely, but we needed to speak to you two first since you both went missing around the time of the mayor's death." He looks at me and I swallow hard, feeling the pressure of his stare. "I'm sorry for your loss, Mrs. Jenkins, but more importantly, I'm sorry for what you've had to endure. We're going to need statements from people you encountered during your trip to Wyoming, as well as those medical records that document the abuse."

I make a promise to go to the police station first thing in the morning, and Officer Benton says he'll put out a press release on the new evidence that's come to light. Thankfully, he said the abuse and video will not be shared with the public, but he told us not to be surprised if word gets out. Even if it does, I'm ready. At least once everyone knows, they won't go on thinking Troy was this amazing man. The truth coming out will only set me free. *Finally.*

CHAPTER 27

CATHERINE

It's been three days since we've returned to Willow Creek. Things are starting to settle down a bit, but everyone has been asking about Troy's memorial service. It's up to me whether I want to have one, and I've made the decision not to. If he has other family members or friends that want to step up and take on that role, more power to them. As for me, I want nothing to do with it. Some may think I'm cold and callous, but that's because they don't know the hell I went through.

Rumors have begun to circulate about his abuse and the way he treated me. Some even say I'm making it all up. But I'm keeping a tight lip and letting everyone think what they want.

It's also no surprise that I was let go from my position at Willow Creek High. I'm not sad in the least because there are better opportunities for me elsewhere.

I pick up my phone and read the latest article from the *Willow Creek Gazette* as Wilder and I walk up to the motel I've been staying in.

Breaking News: Willow Creek's Mayor Jenkins Death Ruled Suicide.

The case in the death of Mayor Troy Jenkins has been closed as new evidence was brought to light. Mr. Jenkins's wife, Catherine, returned to Willow Creek and gave a statement regarding the threats her husband made in the days leading to his death.

Autopsy results have revealed Troy Jenkins lost his life to a self-inflicted gunshot wound to the head.

Since that time, Grant Cromwell is still serving as acting mayor until he's sworn in after the election this November.

"Did you see this?" I pass the phone to Wilder as we step through the door.

His eyes skim over the article quickly and he hands my phone back to me. "Good. I'm glad this shit is finally over."

"Yes," I exhale a sigh of relief. "It is *finally* over."

We approach my room on the first and only floor of the small motel. It's a cute place with only a dozen rooms, but it's well-kept and there's a beautiful garden with benches out back. Wilder and I spent last night out there watching the sunset and a sense of peace washed over me. He's been staying with me every night since I checked in and I'm hoping once I sell the house and buy a new one, he might want to stay with me permanently. I know this thing between us is moving fast, but when you know…you know.

As we draw closer to the room, my nose scrunches as I try to make out what's hanging on the door.

Wilder notices and moves faster, snatching the note and something else that's taped there. A feeling of dread settles into my stomach, one that feels all too familiar.

"What is it?" I ask him. When his eyes go wide, I get the feeling this isn't really over.

He hands it to me, and I read the words that are put together by letters cut from a newspaper.

I know the truth. It wasn't suicide. Bring $20,000

> *cash to the power lines at ten p.m. or the entire
> world will know the truth.*

Then, he passes me a picture. I blink a few times, praying my eyes are deceiving me as I stare at a print of me and Wilder walking out of my house after we found Troy dead. There's a time stamp on the photo, proving we were there.

"No!" I gasp as my hand flies to my mouth. "We thought this was over but we forgot one very important detail." I look at Wilder and as if he's reading my mind, he finishes my train of thought.

"Someone actually did kill him, and that person is still out there."

I wave the note in the air, panic all over my face. "It has to be this person. How would they know it wasn't suicide? They're going to pin it on us, Wilder."

He shakes his head, his features pinching with confusion. "I don't get it. The death was ruled a suicide, thanks to us. They got away with it. Why do this?" Wilder points to the photo, his jaw tensing as if he wants to hit something.

It was supposed to be over…

My head feels like it's spinning and I'm not even sure if I'm making the right decision, but I think we both know what we have to do. "We have to go there and give this person the money. If we don't, we could be in serious trouble."

Wilder rubs his temples before stroking his chin as if he's deep in thought. A minute passes before he finally says, "I have a plan."

I really do love it when he says that because he hasn't steered us in the wrong direction yet. Wilder opens the motel room door and as soon as we get inside, he starts vomiting words on how this is going to go down.

He's waving his arms and begins to send text messages to those we trust. My chest aches with the idea of this not being over, but more so because of the unknown.

Who hated my husband enough to kill him? Who hated him more than me?

In the end, I'm satisfied with the plan because we have no other choice. He made a good point—if we pay this person off, who's to say they won't come back for more? Troy has a hefty amount of savings that is now mine, but I'm going to need that money since I'm between jobs. And Wilder is only eighteen years old; he can't afford to pay thousands of dollars to a stranger to keep them quiet.

There is just enough cash in Troy's safe to bring to the meetup tonight, but with any luck, we won't be handing over a dime.

This is the only way and I hope like hell it works because if it doesn't, we're screwed.

I hug the backpack of money to my chest. Just before coming here, Wilder went into my house and got the cash from the safe. I still couldn't bring myself to go inside. I'm not sure I'll ever be ready.

We arrived twenty minutes early to make sure the details of our plan are in place and as far as we can tell, no one else is around.

We don't intend to hand over any of this money, but just in case it becomes necessary and we don't get the confession, we may have to.

Wilder takes the backpack from me and flings it over his shoulder before taking my hand in his. "You okay?"

I nod, but I'm not really okay. This is all so much and I hate that I've put Wilder in this position. He doesn't deserve any of this; yet, he's going through it with me. "I'm sorry," I tell him, not knowing what else to say about everything.

He spins me to face him, but I duck my head. It's a bad habit that I need to get rid of, but I can't help it. I don't like feeling vulnerable.

"Kitty Cat." Wilder presses up on my chin with a finger. When my eyes meet his, I want to cry. Wilder looks at me with so much love that I don't know if I deserve it. "Don't apologize. We are a team, and teams figure things out together." A soft kiss brushes my forehead and I relax a little bit.

He's right, we are a team. I am not a disappointment to Wilder. Leaning into his touch, I let him ground me. He is everything I never knew I needed; yet, someone I now know I'll never be able to live without.

"We've got a plan in place and if it comes to it, I'll do what I have to do."

"Which is?" I need to know what he was about to say because the look on his face tells me it wasn't good. "What would you have to do, Wilder?"

He reaches into his pocket and pulls out a switchblade and I gasp. "It better not get to that. We're not killers, Wilder."

"It won't," he says, but there's a bit of skepticism in his tone. "Everything's gonna be fine, but you can never be too safe. We're meeting a potential murderer in the dark, after all, and I never plan to take chances when it comes to your safety ever again."

My heart rate excels until I can literally feel it rattling against my rib cage. "I'm scared," I whisper under my breath.

Wilder squeezes my hand. "Don't worry, baby. Just let me do all the talking. Soon this will all be over and we can finally start the next chapter in our lives, *together*."

Suddenly, headlights come toward us down the trail, making my breath halt in my lungs. Panic sets in and I begin second-guessing everything. "M-maybe we should leave and find another way."

"This is the only way," Wilder whispers back. "I've got you, baby."

I have no choice but to trust him. He's got me. He's got *us*.

The car comes to a stop a good ten yards away and when

they kill the lights, we're unable to see anything at all. Wilder points his flashlight in their direction, but it does little good to reveal their identity. The sound of a car door creaking open has my palms sweating. This is it. I still have no idea who this could be. Troy knew a lot of people—everyone in this town for that matter. Now I'm running through all of the faces of who this might be.

It could be the chief of police who Troy had in his pocket for years. I wonder what it was that Troy held over his head for so long to make him so loyal. Or he could just be a corrupt cop who helped willingly.

I wonder if it was Principal Hargrove. I know Troy would have him spy on me and report to him under the guise of making sure I was safe. He could have blackmailed him.

My thoughts begin to morph the shadow in front of us into so many different men that when they get closer, I don't fully believe what I'm seeing. It isn't until Wilder's flashlight shines on their silhouette that we are able to see it's not a man at all.

I heave, barely able to catch my breath as my vision fogs. *It can't be.*

"No." My voice shakes as the last person I could have expected approaches us.

Standing before me is a very pregnant woman wearing all black with the hood on her sweatshirt flipped over her head. But it's not just any woman—I know this one quite well.

"Beth," I choke out. "Wha…what are you doing here?"

"Surprise," she sings as she comes closer and closer until we're face to face. But the look on her face isn't a pleasant one. She looks livid.

"What are you doing here?" I ask, still unsure if this is just a coincidence or if she's the one who left the note.

"I had you come here, Catherine." She glances from me to Wilder. "Both of you."

"You left the note?" I have to ask, even if it is blatantly obvious. It doesn't make sense.

Wilder nudges me, not taking his eyes off Beth. "Who the hell is this?"

Beth smirks devilishly, rubbing her pregnant belly. "I'm the woman carrying Catherine's husband's baby."

My heart drops into my stomach, my ears ringing. "What did you just say?"

Wilder, noticing the way my body is shaking, wraps his arm around my waist and pulls me tightly to his side for comfort.

"That's right." Beth glowers. "Your son-of-a-bitch husband knocked me up. Then he tried to send me away and told me he wanted nothing to do with me or the baby. When I wouldn't go, he fucking strangled me until I agreed." She spits the words out like venom, as if it's my fault she slept with a married man and got pregnant.

"We're having a baby," is what she said when she told me she was pregnant. I now realize she was trying to tell me something more. Her crying makes sense now. She wasn't hormonal; she was heartbroken.

I still can't believe what I'm hearing, but I'm not angry. In fact, I feel bad for Beth. This poor girl. She's a victim, too.

"Beth," I say softly as I step toward her, hoping she'll allow me to help her. "Troy was a terrible man who did awful things. Consider it a blessing that he's gone and not part of your innocent baby's life."

"Oh, I know it's a blessing." She grits her teeth, clearly trying to hold back so many emotions. "And I made sure he wouldn't be a part of my baby's life."

"Beth," I say again, taking another step toward her, and Wilder moves along with me. "Did you shoot Troy?"

"I did what I had to do." Her voice shakes as a tidal wave of fear and sorrow hits her so hard it's like I can physically see it. "H-he turned into a man I didn't recognize. After a year of pretending to love me, he pushed me aside when I needed him the most. The hands that used to hold me began hurting me."

Tears roll down her cheeks and she sniffles, then begins

wiping at her face. "I didn't want to leave," she sobs. "But he told me if I didn't, he would kill me and our baby."

"Oh, Beth," I say somberly. She nearly folds in half and I worry about the baby if she falls. "He can't hurt you anymore. You're safe now."

Those are the same words Wilder said to me, and I can't imagine getting through these last couple weeks without him. Beth needs someone to assure her she's okay now, too.

"What do you want from us?" Wilder spits out angrily.

"I need money," she cries, gesturing to the bag in my arms. "I don't have a job anymore. I don't even have a place to live. I...I have nothing." Her hands wrap around her stomach protectively and I understand. She has nothing but this sweet innocent baby, and she needs to protect him.

"So you're blackmailing us?" Wilder scoffs. "You killed that bastard but you want us to take the fall if we don't pay you."

"Wilder," I stammer. "She's hurting."

"We're all hurting. That man deserved what he got, but it shouldn't be at our expense." He looks down at me, pleading with his eyes. "Don't let her manipulate you, baby. You don't owe her a thing."

I shake my head as I gently put a hand on his arm and step out of his hold. Wilder doesn't understand this pain, even if he understands me. He will never know what it's like to look at the person who holds your fate in their hands as they hurt you. He will never understand how they manipulate and isolate you until you can't see anyone or anything but them. And I'm glad he will never understand—but I do, and so does Beth.

"It's not about what I do or do not owe her. It's about what he did to us both." I take another step toward Beth and reach for her hands. Surprisingly, she lets me take them. "I feel your pain. You might not realize it, but I've been in your shoes. I've lived in hell for far too long because of Troy. Let us help you."

In the blink of an eye, Beth breaks down in full-blown hysterics, falling into my arms. She's not dangerous; she's scared. "I didn't know what to do," she cries out. "He backed me into a corner and I felt like I had no choice."

"I understand," I tell her. "I promise you, Beth. It's going to be okay." I turn around to face Wilder and I hold out my hand. "We have to give it to her."

He cranes his neck, stunned at my statement. "Seriously?"

"Yes. Seriously. I want to help her. You don't get it, and I don't expect you to either. But she doesn't have a Wilder on her side. I want to do this for her."

It takes Wilder a minute before his features soften and he realizes what I said. Beth is fighting this alone, but we can help. Finally, he hands me the bag of cash. I turn back to Beth and extend it to her. "There's twenty thousand dollars in here." She goes to reach for it, but I pull it back to my chest. "This is not a form of payment to silence you. It's not negotiable, and there will not be more. This is a gift from one victim of domestic abuse to another. I said I know your pain, Beth, and I meant it. You don't have to do this alone."

"Why are you being so nice to me after everything I've done?" Her voice cracks and shakes, her chest rising and falling rapidly.

"Because I know how charming that asshole can be. And I know what happens when you're no longer a shiny new toy, but a *thing* he owns."

The next thing I know, Rome and Elodie come out of the woods. Rome holds his phone in the air. "Got it. You're going down, bitch."

Wilder shakes his head at Rome, shutting him down. "Change of plans, bro."

"But I got it all here," he says as he and Elodie join the circle we're all standing in. He looks at Beth. "I've got proof you killed the mayor."

He seems proud of himself, and under any other circumstance, I'd be proud of him too. They did exactly what we asked them to do. Everything has changed, though.

Beth looks at Rome with panic in her eyes. "I wasn't really going to show the pictures I got. I swear. I just need the money until I'm back on my feet."

"It's okay, Beth." I put a comforting hand on her shoulder as I look at Elodie who seems to get it much faster than these boys do. "You're going to destroy those pictures you have and we're going to delete this video. Deal?"

"Of course." She nods frantically. "Like I said, I wasn't going to share them anyways. I was…desperate."

I look at Wilder, forcing a smile on my lips. "Do you mind if Beth and I talk alone for a few minutes?"

"Baby," he says reluctantly. "She killed a man and lured us out here. I understand your desire to help her, but this woman is not your friend."

I tilt my head slightly to the left. "Maybe she can be. She and I could both use a friend right about now."

He scratches the back of his head, a reaction I've noticed he does often when he's thinking. "Okay," he finally says. "But we'll be right over here if you need us."

I nod before kissing his lips. Then I go back to a tearful Beth and lead her to a bench with the flashlight I have. "I meant it when I said you don't have to go through this alone. It would take an entire lifetime for me to tell you all the horrible things Troy has done to me. I get it."

"I know," she mutters. "I saw the way he treated you, Catherine. You didn't deserve that. And you certainly don't deserve what I've put you through tonight. You're a good person."

"So are you," I tell her truthfully. "That's why I want you to take the money so you and your baby can have the fresh start you deserve. I could even have Wilder talk to his dad. He might be in need of an assistant now that he's acting as mayor."

Her eyes go wide. "You'd do that for me?"

"Of course I would. Listen," I begin, "between us, if you hadn't ended him, it would have probably been me that did it and I'd want someone in my corner, too."

Beth throws her arms around me, her round belly pressing into mine. I swear for a moment I feel her baby boy kick. It's strange, but I feel a connection to Beth. We might have been in different paths of the storm, but it was the same storm nonetheless.

"I'm going to pay you back for this," Beth cries into my shoulder. "Every penny."

"Don't worry about it. Just take care of yourself, and your baby, too."

"I didn't want to sleep with him if that makes you feel any better," she says quietly. "I told him no so many times. It wasn't until he said he was planning to leave you that I gave in. But then I saw the bruise on your neck when you left one day and I heard him yelling at you. The day the bookshelf fell over was the day I found out I was pregnant and it felt too late."

That day had been one of the worst. Troy ripped my shirt and told Beth that I tripped getting up and fell into the bookcase. I remember pleading with her to see the truth, and it turns out she did. She was just trapped by him too.

"He said he wanted a baby and I foolishly thought that maybe if I had one, his anger would stop, so I kept it."

I squeeze her hand, understanding. Sometimes those that are being hurt will try anything to get away. They are isolated and afraid and every rational thought goes out the window, all that matters is pleasing your abuser.

"It's okay, Beth." I wrap my arms around her again. "He's rotting in hell, right where he deserves to be."

She nods and I sit there, just holding her trembling body against mine. I can't imagine what her baby feels, but in some way I want to reassure them both. Troy might have brought them harm, but I will be their safe space just like Wilder is mine.

After Beth and I exchange numbers, she leaves and we make a plan to check in with one another. It really won't be too hard since she's decided to get a room at the same motel I'm in. With any luck, we'll both be out of that place soon.

I watch as she pulls away, her taillights fading in the distance. Last time I thought this was over, I didn't fully feel at peace. I think it's because part of me knew the killer was still out there. But now, everything feels right.

Wilder wraps his arms around me from behind and kisses the top of my head. "I'm proud of you, baby."

I close my eyes, savoring this moment. "It's finally over."

"Yes," he sighs heavily. "This time, it's finally over."

CHAPTER 28
WILDER

Three Months Later

"He's beautiful," I tell Beth as Catherine scoops Liam from her arms. I watch my girl cradling this perfect baby, and my heart swells. One day Cat is going to make an amazing mother.

"Thank you," Beth smiles. "I still can't believe he's mine." A tear rolls down her cheek and she sweeps it away. "Catherine was an amazing coach through my labor. I'm not sure I could have done it without her."

"Nonsense," Cat snickers as she stares down at Liam. "It was all you. You did incredible." Swaying the baby in her arms, she looks at me and I know that look. "I want one," she pouts.

I put an arm around her shoulders and peer down at Liam. "I know you do and one day we're going to have one or two…"

"Or three. Maybe four."

"Whoa now." I chuckle, my finger wrapping around Liam's tiny hand. "We're getting a little carried away here. Let's start with one."

She pushes herself up on her tiptoes and kisses me. "Deal."

"How is the new girl doing?" Beth asks Wilder with a raised

brow. She's referring to Grant's assistant that's filling in for her while she's on maternity leave.

He clicks his tongue on the roof of his mouth. "Eh. She's trying her best. But you know how my dad is. He's a stickler for timeliness and organization."

"She'll get the hang of it," Beth says with a chuckle. "And by the time she does, I'll be back to work."

I'm glad my father was on board with Beth working for him. He didn't hesitate and agreed to give it a try. She's been working for him ever since. Well, until now that is. After Cat explained how important it was to her that we help Beth, I started to share that same mentality. She's a good person and she deserves good things in life.

"Your turn," Cat says as she turns toward me and presses Liam against my chest.

My hands go out instinctively, but my apprehension is apparent. "Umm. I don't know what to do."

I've never held a baby before. At least, not that I can remember.

"There really isn't much to it." Cat chuckles. "You just don't drop him. Pretend he's a football signed by your favorite NFL player."

Beth and I laugh. But when Cat steps away, I realize I'm holding him all on my own. "Hey, little man," I say softly. "We're good. I've got you."

I look at Cat, noticing the twinkle in her eyes as she says, "You look hot holding a baby. Not going to lie. I can't wait to make you the father of my children."

I waggle my brows at her, curious if she thinks we need to go home and practice, because that's exactly what I'm thinking right now.

Holding little Liam against my chest, I walk slowly over to Beth and lay him down in her arms.

"We should get going," Cat says. "But please call if you need anything. Otherwise, I'll be back tomorrow afternoon to drive you two home."

Cat and I say our goodbyes and as we're walking through the parking lot, I put a hand on the small of her back, my fingers trailing over her ass. "I know you're not ready yet, but it's never too soon to start practicing."

Wondrous eyes peer up at me. "Get out of my head."

I chuckle. "You thinking what I'm thinking?"

"Why do you think I wanted to leave? The minute I saw you hold that baby, I was ready to climb on you." Cat reaches around and squeezes my ass, making me groan.

"In that case, why are we walking so slow?"

Before I know it, we're sprinting toward my car like kids chasing an ice cream truck, laughter trailing behind us.

We reach my car in a matter of seconds, both breathless from what I think turned into a race that Cat won. She pulls open the passenger door before I can get to it and open it for her, so I hurry to get in the driver's seat.

Flooring the gas, I peel out of the hospital parking lot and speed toward Cat's new house that I practically live in.

As soon as we pull in the driveway, I'm unbuckling my seat belt, my cock twitching in my pants.

Cat takes her time, so being the gentleman I am, I pull open her door, scoop her into my arms, and throw her over my shoulder with a smack to her ass.

"You're insane." She laughs.

"Insanely in love with you. And horny as fuck," I add as I jog up the stairs to the front door. "Get used to it, baby," I say as I turn the handle and kick it open. She slams it closed behind us.

I flip her right side up and her hooded blue eyes look into mine. "Your body is too damn good not to be touched and pleasured every single day."

Cat puts a hand on my cheek, turning my face to hers as I lift her into my arms and carry her into her bedroom. "Is that a promise?"

I lay her down on the bed, immediately ridding her of her clothes. "It's a double promise."

Once she's completely naked, I stand back and admire her perfect form. She literally makes my mouth water. "Damn," I growl as I take off my clothes, tossing them wherever they land. "You are too sexy for your own good, baby."

I pounce on top of her, rattling the headboard against the wall. Then I devour every inch of her skin—kissing her mouth, her neck, her perfect breasts, and smooth stomach.

But when I go to put my mouth on her cunt, Cat puts a hand on my arm. "Not yet. Let me on top."

I quirk a brow. If any man ever says no to that then they are insane. "Yes, please."

A soft giggle escapes her lips as I roll off her, making space between us. She shifts onto all fours, her movements slow and deliberate, then she arches her back and backs her ass up to my face, surprising me.

I run my fingers up her legs until I reach the wetness of her folds. "Fuck, baby. I'm loving this view."

Her skin glistens under the dim light, and she inches closer until her hips are just inches from my face. I reach out, my fingers sinking into the softness of her flesh as I grab her thighs and pull her back until she's ghosting my face.

As her head lowers, her fingers curl around my shaft, sliding up and down with a deliberate rhythm that literally has my toes curling. Her tongue traces circles on the sensitive tip of my head before she envelops my length with her hot mouth.

"God damn, baby." I close my eyes momentarily, willing myself not to come right now because it feels so fucking good.

Grabbing her hips, I drag the pad of my tongue up and down her pussy, savoring her sweet arousal. She whimpers in delight when I push a couple fingers inside her, while my mouth latches onto her clit.

Her delicate fingers stroke my thickness, her head bobbing

up and down as she sucks me off like I'm her favorite lollipop. I swear this woman and her mouth will be the death of me.

Rolling her hips, she rides my face as I bring her to the brink of an orgasm. I pump my fingers faster, deeper, making sure to hit every spot I know she loves.

Circling her clit with the tip of my tongue, I then suck it between my teeth and she howls in pleasure. Her back arches and I can feel her breaths quicken.

Using my other hand, I press my thumb on her back hole, adding a little pressure. Her movements freeze, but she grips my cock tightly, pumping her hand slowly as she comes on my face. I lick her from ass to clit, cleaning her up like the gentleman I am.

Then, she turns around, wide-eyed and euphoric as she sits down on my cock. Reaching back, she puts her hands on my knees, her back bent and her tits mine for the taking. I sit up, taking the bud of her nipple in my mouth and sucking with tenacity. A soft moan slips through her parted lips as she bounces up and down.

"That's right, baby. Ride my cock like you own it."

Her head drops back, eyes closed and mouth agape as she rolls her hips, gyrating her sex against me. "I do own it."

I chuckle as I bite down lightly on her nipple, making her gasp. "Damn straight you do."

Surges of electricity shoot through me and I grab her hips, bucking upward and driving farther into her. I know she can come again, and this time I want her to milk my cock for all it's worth.

I thrust repeatedly, feeding her wet cunt all of my length.

She cries out as I pant and groan. Her hands move to my shoulders, giving her a deeper angle as I fuck her silly. Her nails dig into my skin, and I live for it.

"Mark me, baby. Show the world who owns me."

She bites her lip as she meets me thrust for thrust.

"Fuck, baby. I'm gonna come." Just as she says it, I can feel her walls begin to tighten, bringing me to the edge with her. I reach between us, my thumb stroking her swollen clit. It doesn't take long for her to let go and I follow her like I vowed I always would.

The sounds slipping out of her mouth are proof that she's coming right along with me.

My movements still after I release and our foreheads fall together.

Once we're both finished, I put my hands on her waist and guide her body down on mine until she is covering me like the best damn blanket in the world. We lie there breathless, hearts racing against each other's. I hold her for what feels like minutes until she slides off me, dropping to my side.

Rolling to face her, I admire her beauty while stroking my fingers down her cheek, then the rest of her body. "I don't wanna get up. Let's just stay here forever."

"Deal," she quips.

Moments like this make me feel so close to my girl. I seriously feel like my heart is going to burst because it's so full. Cat has never once doubted me. She's trusted me every step of the way and I want to continue to keep her trust while making her the happiest woman alive.

I push myself up on my elbow and lean down to kiss her forehead. "Thank you for trusting me like you do."

She flashes a warm, genuine smile and I literally feel her happiness in my soul. "Thank you for loving me like you do."

I kiss her again. "Always and forever, Kitty Cat."

EPILOGUE
CATHERINE

Nine Months Later

"Have a seat." Grant slides down on the bleachers, making room for me and Wilder.

"Sorry we're late," I tell him as we sit down. "I had to finish editing the piece about your plans to renovate the town park."

Shortly after I sold my house and bought a small two-bedroom place on the creek, I was able to secure a job I love as editor of the *Willow Creek Gazette*. It's crazy busy because it seems like there is new news every day in this town, but I couldn't imagine doing anything else.

"You're not late," Celia says as she reaches across her husband and pats my leg. "You're just on time."

Celia and I have actually grown very close over the past year. And Grant has come around, too. Everyone is rooting for Wilder and me and I know it's because they can see how much we love one another.

As for Elodie, we've become close friends and talked often while she was away at college. Fortunately, she and Rome are both home for the summer. The two of them had a great first year away at school and said the miles between them wasn't a strain on their relationship at all. I didn't think it would be. Everyone can see how in love these two are.

The traditional graduation song booms through the speakers and the class of two thousand and twenty-five walks out.

"Seems like an eternity ago that we were here for your graduation." I squeeze Wilder's hand. "It's crazy how much can change in one year."

"It sure is." He looks down at my hand, eyeing the promise ring he gave me last week. Wilder moved in with me a couple months ago, but we decided to wait a little longer before a proposal because once we do make that commitment to one another, we're going to have a short engagement and try for a baby right away.

Even though Wilder and I are both financially stable, he's still young and I don't want him to feel like there is any reason to rush into things. Besides, I want it to be a surprise when it happens, and of course I'll say yes.

Wilder pulls out his phone, holding it in the air as he records the ceremony. A lot has changed, but so much has stayed exactly the same. Aside from working as a financial writer at Cromwell Banks, Wilder has become a SnapTok sensation. He's even got a publicist now. I love that he's still doing it because I can see the passion in his eyes—the money is just a bonus. And of course, the occasional travel I get to do with him.

Brogan and her best friend, Avery, come walking down the field and Grant blows out a piercing whistle. My ears ring as I chant and clap for Wilder's sister. It won't be long and she'll be leaving to live in her dorm at Rosewood University, where she'll be cheering for their football team, the Devils.

A few minutes later, it's Callan's turn. He drags his feet, unimpressed with the ceremony, and I'm pretty sure he's high right now. According to Wilder, Callan is also going to Rosewood University, but he's not thrilled about it. He made an arrangement with his dad and if he attends for at least two years, he'll offer him a position at his company. From what I heard, there were a lot of words shared, considering Wilder went to work for his dad straightaway, but Callan doesn't have the grades and experience Wilder does.

Either way, they both made it to this point and it's a huge accomplishment. Before long, Grant and Celia's nest will be empty. Well, for a little while anyway. Wilder and I have every intention of giving them grandchildren to spoil in the not-so-distant future.

When the ceremony ends, we rush to the front to see the newest graduates of the Cromwell family.

Weaving through the crowd of proud parents and friends, we spot them instantly and hug Brogan and Callan as we congratulate them.

Wilder tugs my hand gently, gesturing to the left. "Come here. I wanna show you something."

I squint at him, curious to know what he's up to. "Whaaat?" I drag out the word.

"You'll see." He winks.

This guy is full of surprises. Wilder has held true to his promise to always be there for me, and I've made it a point to prove I'll always be there for him too. What we have might be frowned upon by some given our age difference, but this love we share is unfazed by the judgment of others.

I lean into him as we walk, warmth spreading through my chest thinking about how far we have come in the past year. "I love you so much," I whisper as I try to hold back the emotions threatening to overtake me.

He looks down at me, biting the corner of his lip. "I love you, too, baby."

As we walk farther and farther away, I shoot a glance over my shoulder. "Shouldn't we tell your parents we're leaving?"

"We'll see them at Big John's for dinner. There's something more important we have to do first."

My forehead creases as I look up at him. "What are you up to, Wilder Cromwell?"

"Like I said, you'll see." His brows waggle and it's so damn sexy.

I'm still not sure what's going on, but when we approach a side door at the school, I ask, "Are we supposed to be going in there?"

He winks. "I made a call. We're good." Then he pulls the door open and gestures for me to go first.

The minute I step foot through the doors, the scent brings back a rush of memories. Good ones, though. I don't dwell on the bad anymore. Sometimes I miss it here. I feel like I grew here right along with my students. Other times, I'm reminded that in the process of growing, I outgrew this place.

I never wanted to be a teacher, but I'm glad I was. It taught me so much and gave me an outlet when I needed to get away. But now, I'm finally doing what I love. I'm writing and it feels so good to have chosen it for myself.

Wilder keeps walking, acting really strange. I can tell he's up to something, but I'm not sure what. His palm is sweating against mine and he keeps cracking these mischievous smiles that have me curious as hell.

Then, we turn the hall to my old classroom, but we don't stop. We go straight to the door.

I'm surprised to see that it's open and the light is on—must have something to do with the *call* he made.

Wilder leads me inside and I can't take it anymore. "What are we doing here?" I giggle as I look around the room, taking in the changes the new teacher has made. It's different, but still the same in a strange way.

We go to the front of the room and Wilder reaches into his pocket. My heart immediately stills. I put a hand over my mouth, completely shocked because I think I know what's about to happen.

"Catherine Henderson," he says, using my maiden name that I've taken back. "You complete me. You came into my life unexpectedly and left an imprint on my heart that will never fade. I know you wanted to wait because you think I'm too young. You want me to enjoy all the little things in life and live the experiences people my age need to live. But the thing is, I want to live them all with you. Every second of every minute of every day, I choose you. And what better place than where it all began." He drops to his knee and opens his palm, revealing a beautiful diamond ring. "Will you make me the happiest man in the world and be my wife?"

"Yes," I squeal with no hesitation. What is there to think about? I want this man for an eternity. "Yes," I say again. "I will be your wife."

He slides the ring on my finger that happens to twist perfectly with the promise ring he gave me when I told him we needed to wait a bit longer. Before he can stand, I drop to my knees in front of him, taking his face in my hands. "You complete me, too, Wilder. I can't wait to be your wife."

"Good." He grins with his lips against mine. "Now let's get married and have babies. Lots and lots of babies."

I chuckle as I kiss him. "Deal. I love you."

"I love you more."

Want more of the Cromwell and Astor family?
I think you're going to love who's story comes next! Preorder
Beautiful Devil, releasing the end of 2024.
http://mybook.to/beautifuldevil

ALSO BY RACHEL LEIGH

Bastards of Boulder Cove

Book One: <u>Savage Games</u>

Book Two: <u>Vicious Lies</u>

Book Three: <u>Twisted Secrets</u>

Wicked Boys of BCU (Coming March 2023)

Book One: <u>We Will Reign</u>

Book Two: <u>You Will Bow</u>

Book Three: <u>They Will Fall</u>

Misfits

Heartless Monster

Wicked Scandal

Beautiful Devil

Redwood Rebels Series

Book One: <u>Striker</u>

Book Two: <u>Heathen</u>

Book Three: <u>Vandal</u>

Book Four: <u>Reaper</u>

Redwood High Series

Book One: <u>Like Gravity</u>

Book Two: <u>Like You</u>

Book Three: <u>Like Hate</u>

Fallen Kingdom Duet

<u>His Hollow Heart</u> & <u>Her Broken Pieces</u>

Black Heart Duet

<u>Four</u> & <u>Five</u>

Standalones

<u>Forget Me Not</u>

<u>Ruthless Rookie</u>

<u>Devil Heir</u>

<u>All The Little Things</u>

<u>Claim your FREE copy of Her Undoing!</u>

ACKNOWLEDGMENTS

Thank you so much for reading Wicked Scandal. I hope you enjoyed it!

A special thanks to my wonderful team for all the hard work you put into helping me create this book: My dedicated PA, Carolina Leon. All my girls for your support, friendship, and advice. My Street Team, the Rebel Readers for your help in getting the word out.

A an extra special thanks to…

My amazing alpha reader, Taylor for all your help and patience along the way! You helped shape this story into exactly what it was meant to be. Thank you to Amanda for beta reading! Your help means the world to me.

Lori Jackson for the stunning cover!

Fairest Reviews Editing Service for the beautiful edit!

Rumi Khan for proofreading and being so flexible!.

Valentine PR for spectacular PR Services.

XOXO Rachel

ABOUT THE AUTHOR

Rachel Leigh is a USA Today and International bestselling author of new adult and contemporary romances. She loves to write—and read—flawed bad-boys and strong heroines. You can expect dark elements, a dash of suspense, and a lot of steam.

Her goal is to take readers on an adventure with her words, while showing them that even on the darkest days, love conquers all.

Rachel lives in Michigan with her husband, three little monsters (who aren't so little anymore) and a couple fur babies. When she's not writing or reading, she's likely lounging in leggings, with coffee in her hand, while binge watching her favorite reality tv shows.

Join My Reader's Group: Rachel's Ramblers

facebook.com/rachelleighauthor

instagram.com/rachelleighauthor

bookbub.com/profile/rachel-leigh

goodreads.com/rachelleigh

amazon.com/author/rachelleighauthor

pinterest.com/rachelleighauthor